A
COMPENDIUM
OF
ALCHEMICAL
PROCESSES

Extracted from the writings of:
Glauber,
Basil Valentine,
and Other Adepts

ISBN 1-56459-344-4

CONTENTS.

PAGE.

PREFATORY NOTE.

THIS unpretentious selection from the experiments of the old chemists will, it is thought, fulfil another purpose besides affording to the practical student of Hermetic Physics an insight into the processes by which the great secrets of alchemy were claimed to be achieved in the past. For more than forty years a certain school of interpretation has discerned in the literature of alchemy far other objects than the transmutation of the so-called base metals into gold, or the application of metallic elixirs to the cure of human diseases, and the prolongation of human life. This school recognizes under the veil of these physical designs a deeper end in view—the investigations of spiritual potencies, the development and conversion of the soul, the laws which govern the influxes of eternal life, and so forward through the whole gamut of transcendental possibilities. In a word, the true alchemists were not chemists, and Thomas Vaughan was right when he protested against the application of that narrow name " to a science both ancient and infinite." The hypothesis was large and suggestive; it appealed to the imagination; it possessed all the romance which attaches to the vague and indefinite; and as few persons knew anything at that period of the literature which it pretended to explain, so it obtained a certain favour and credence amidst that large class of persons who are interested in Hermetic subjects without being sufficiently in earnest to have recourse to the fountain-head.

In this respect a great change is in progress, the old books are being rapidly re-published, and are making clear, at least up to a certain point, what was thought and meant and done by their writers. But at the same time the mystery affected by the alchemists, on the one hand, and the mystical philosophy which was combined with their physics, on the other, seem to lend themselves to every species of commentary with such equal readiness, that it will be to many persons a source of altogether new light to see for the first time the processes of alchemy without the speculative setting in which they are commonly imbedded. So, then, as they may be read over, even by a person who is little acquainted with experimental chemistry, it will be as obvious that they belong to the sphere of physics, and thereto only, as it is that the latest metallurgical text books are not manuals in secret concerning the life of the world to come.

When this fact is once recognized there will be no longer any room for the misplaced spirit of imagination which has hitherto shaped so many matters connected with alchemical problems to a wholly false issue ; but at the same time it is another question whether the masters of transmutatory secrets may not have possessed an insight into other arcana than those of a physical kind. The Hermetic philosophy covers all issues of life, and has its highest interests in eternity, but its applications on the material plane should not be confused with its more exalted departments.

A Method for the Potable Gold.

(Glauber, part II., p. 2 1 2, a.)

TAKE of the filings of gold, or thin beaten gold, one ounce : put it into a small but strong glass ; pour upon it two or three ounces of our best Alkahest ; fit to the vessel an air-tight head, and to this apply a large recipient, carefully luted, for, when the spirit comes over, it passes with great violence, and searches everywhere for vent, being the most fiery of spirits, and very subtle withal. Wherefore take care that your lute be good, or else you will never be able to retain this corrosive, fiery spirit. The vessel must stand in sand, and a very gentle fire must be administered at first, so that our secret spirit may by degrees grow warm in the glass, and not be too suddenly heated, for in that case it would fly away without its prey. But if you proceed as directed, then our moist fire will lay hold of the gold, and carry it over in the form of a spirit, but leisurely, and by degrees, at first only of a yellow colour, which then becomes higher and higher. Towards the end the fire must be increased, till the bottom of the glass be red-hot, at which time the heavy spirits will come over, bringing the heavy corporeal gold over with them, a red fixed salt remaining behind, which is of great use in physic and alchemy, as we shall see hereafter.

The yellow spirit, as well as the red salt, may, without further preparation, be used outwardly as well as inwardly, and will perform all that can be expected of a true " potable gold."

THE SAME PROCESS MODIFIED.

(GLAUBER, part II., p. 212, a.)

Take of gold one part, and of the martial regulus of antimony two parts. Melt them together, pour them forth, and the gold will be white and brittle. Pulverise the mass, put it into a glass, pour upon it three times as much of our fiery Alkahest, and by degrees abstract the same, when you will have a higher and better tincture than from the gold alone. For antimony is the " Aries " of chemists, wherein Sol has its exaltation. This red oil of gold and antimony may readily be changed into an universal medicine or tincture, by means of our " catholic coagulator " (lead).

THE PREPARATION OF MARTIAL REGULUS OF ANTIMONY.

(See process above.)

Regulus Martis is prepared by submitting two parts of antimony and one part of iron to a red or white heat, in a strong crucible, in a wind furnace, and separating the reguline product.

A GREAT MEDICINE OF GOLD.

(GLAUBER, part I., p. 265, a.)

Take three or four parts of sal mirabile, and one part of gold (rightly prepared for this operation) : Mix them, and put the mixture into a strong glass or hardware retort, well luted, which place in an open fire, increasing the heat by degrees, until the retort be red-hot. Urge the fire and continue it stronger for an hour. Then cease, and let all cool. Take out the retort, and free it from the lute, that it may not be mixed with the matter contained in the retort, which must remain pure, and must afterwards be accurately separated from the retort, and, together with what is sublimed in the neck of the retort, put into a clean glass, which matter will look of a greenish colour. To this matter put some distilled water, that it may be dissolved at a moderate heat, and that the salt, with part of the gold, may be mixed with the water. Filter this grass-green solution, and draw off some part of the water by distillation, that the green liquor may remain, not corroding nor tasting sharp, nor yet too urinous, but fit to be drunk in all vehicles. The portion of gold not dissolved by the sal enixum can be used again for a fresh experiment, while the green liquor may be put to advantageous use in medicine as well as in alchemy.

By evaporation of this liquid a green salt is obtained, which may be digested with strong alkalizate spirit of wine, and will then acquire a ruby-red colouration

By a repetition of the process upon the pure green mass, Aurum Potabile, or a great Medicine of Gold, results.

How to Prove a True Aurum Potabile.

(Glauber, part I., p. 245, a.)

Rub some mercury upon a small silver plate ; whatever is superfluous and does not adhere, wipe off with a linen cloth, after the manner of goldsmiths (or gilders), who gild with the amalgam of gold and quicksilver. Digest the silver plate in my aurum potabile for the space of half-an-hour, or one hour. Then take it out, and you shall see with how fair a golden colour it will be gilt. For in this digestion the mercury is not so heated

that it can vanish in vapour; it therefore
adheres to the silver plate, and is tinged
by the aurum potabile into the best gold.

———

A Most Excellent Medicine out of the Carbuncle of Gold.

(Glauber, part II., p. 51, b.)

This carbuncle is to be beaten to
powder, and the best spirit of wine is to
be poured thereon, so as to extract the
tincture.

This tinged liquor is to be drawn
off into another glass, and more fresh
spirit is to be again poured upon the
matter, that, in the heat, it may extract
yet more tincture. The like labour is to
be repeated so often until all the tincture
be extracted, and the spirit be no longer
coloured. Then the spirit, being drawn
off by distillation per balneum, leaves
behind a most red tincture at the
bottom, in form of a liquor named c o s—
for here are present colour, odour, and
taste: the colour and odour from the
gold and sulphur, the savour from the
salt. The residue which remains after

the extraction of the tincture is to be converted with new or fresh sal mirabilis and coals made of vine (or other) wood into a red stone, by fusion, and to be so long extracted till all the gold be converted, with the vegetable sulphur or carbon, into a medicine. For one only labour serves to extract the whole gold by the spirit of wine, but repeated labours attain to the end proposed.

Thus hast thou, friendly reader, a medicine of great moment and great efficacy, in which the most pure parts of the gold and of the vine are conjoined ; nor can this be other than a most profitable medicament for men and metals.

A good Sol of sal mirabilis may safely be made of equal parts of salt (common) and oil of vitriol (both as strong and pure as possible).

THE GOLDEN CARBUNCLE OF THE ANCIENTS, ETC.

(GLAUBER, part II., p. 51, b.)

Take one quinta, or small weight of gold (more or less) ; reduce it into thin leaves or plates ; bow them in the fashion of a cylinder, and add thereto six, eight, or ten parts of sal mirabilis, which mixture must be melted in a crucible, with an accurate and strong fusion. When they flow, throw some pieces of coals (carbon) into the salt and gold, as they are melting in the pot, so that the sal mirabilis may dissolve the gold and coals in the melt, which is usually done in half an hour, or thereabout.

The matter, being poured out, will show whether or not the work has proceeded well, for all the gold, as likewise the sal and coals (carbon), will be dissolved and changed into a red stone, that bites the tongue like an alkali (when so applied).

This fiery, red stone is the golden carbuncle of the ancients, " for it shines in the dark like a burning coal," and produces such wonderful effects in medicine and alchemy as we have no mind at present to reveal.

For this gold, being thus conjoined—contrary to its nature—with salt and sulphur, is by that means unlocked, opened, and prepared, so that it may, by easy labour, be made spiritual, and that divers ways by divers menstruums, either acid or urinous, and may be distilled over the helm, the pure separated from the impure, and things will be thus brought to a most happy and wished-for end.

————

THE TRUE TINCTURE OF GOLD.
(Aurum Potabile.)
(GLAUBER, Part I., p. 97, b.)

Take of living gold one part, and three parts of quick mercury (not the vulgar, but the philosophical, everywhere to be found without expense); of living silver, one part may be added with advantage; then put the mixture into a philosophical vessel to dissolve. In the space of one-quarer of an hour these mixed metals will be radically dissolved by the mercury, and will give a purple colour. Afterwards increase the heat gradually, and then the colour changes to a very fine green. Hereon, when taken out, pour the "water of dew," to dissolve (which may be done in half-an-hour). Filter the solution, and abstract the water through a glass alembic in balneo, which pour out again fresh, and abstract; repeat this three times. In the meanwhile, that greenness will be turned to blackness, like ink, stinking like a carcass, and therefore odious. It behoves sometimes to take away the water, re-affused and digested when the said black colour and stench will depart in the space of forty hours, and will give place to a pure and milky whiteness, which appearing, remove the water by evaporation to dryness. Divers colours now appear, and the remaining white mass is to be affused with highly rectified spirit of wine, when the dissolved green gold will impart to it a quintessence as red as blood or ruby.

Dose : from two or three to ten or twelve drops, or more.

The Manner of Testing Aurum Potabile.

(Glauber, Part I., p. 211, b.)

Take of my potable gold one ounce, and one scruple (or half-drachm) of common quicksilver. Put them in a strong glass, and so small that it may be half full with the mixture. The said glass must have a round bottom, whether it be a piece of some small bolt-head, or a small phial, that so the mercury may gather itself into one ball in the bottom. Now place the glass with the potable gold and mercury in sand, to the height of the liquor, then heat it, and leave it for about one hour in a sufficient temperature, so that the moisture being exhaled, the potable gold may stay behind in the form of a white salt. This done, pour again upon that salt so much pure water as is evaporated in the boiling, that so lying awhile upon the said salt, it may dissolve it, which is hereby again turned into the same potable gold, having the same colour and taste, and the same virtues that it had before. The mercury, being freed from the said potable gold, which is to be poured off, is found to be hard, and fixed in the bottom like the best gold. It is also of the same size or quantity as when first put into the glass. If, by some error committed, the quicksilver be not tinged enough, nor yet brought to a due degree, but shall have contracted some blackness, it is to be taken out of the glass, and put into a small crucible, where it must be heated to redness, so that it may receive its due golden colour; which colour it will get, and it will then resemble the best ducat gold, and will abide good and firm in all trials. The aurum potabile used for the coagulation of the mercury may be employed again and again, but less mercury must be used each time.

THE TESTING OF POTABLE GOLD.

(GLAUBER, Part I., p. 212, b.)

Take of my potable gold, or lac virginis, one ounce, and put it in a glazed dish ; which done, and the dish being placed in sand, evaporate all the humidity until there remain about half an ounce of white salt. Put this salt in a crucible with one scruple (or half a drachm) of the plates of silver, or copper, or iron (tin and lead need not be laminated). Place the crucible, together with the salt and metals, over a gas burner, and the salt will presently melt, like wax ; it will penetrate the whole metal, and will transmute it into gold. This operation is effected in one-quarter of an hour, or half an hour at the utmost. The molten salt, being poured forth out of the crucible, the plate of metal remains that was first put in, but now thoroughly transmuted into pure, good gold.

POTABLE GOLD.

Aurum potabile, when brought to a due perfection, has the appearance of a bright, clear water ; it is of a burning, hot, and fiery taste, and it gives out a sulphurous, but yet pleasant odour.

Potable gold being coagulated by means of fire, and reduced to a stability therein, is converted into a stone of a blood-red colour, and yields not in melting any corporeal gold unless a metallic body be adjoined to it, into which the spiritual and philosophical gold betakes itself, that, so clothing itself with a body, it may become corporeal.

How to .Extract a Tincture from Gold by the aid of Liquor of Flints or Sand.

(Glauber, Part I., p. 47, b.)

Take of that gold calx which is precipitated by the oil of sand, one part, and three or four parts of the liquor of crystal or flints. Mix the gold calx in a sound crucible with the liquor, and expose this mixture to a gentle heat, so that the moisture may evaporate from the oil of sand (which is not readily done), the mixture rising like alum or borax when heated, for which reason the crucible must not be more than half filled. Now increase the heat till the pot be red-hot. The mixture standing fast, put a close fitting cover to the crucible, and heat it so strongly in a wind-furnace that the liquor, together with the gold, may melt like water. Keep it fused so long until the liquor and gold together be like a transparent ruby, which will take about an hour's time. After this, it is to be poured forth into a clean mortar, allowed to cool, reduced to powder, and then treated with strong and pure spirit of wine, or alcohol. This spirit thus acquires a blood-red colouration.

ANOTHER TINCTURE AND MEDICINE OF GOLD.

(GLAUBER, Part I., p. 79, b.)

Dissolve gold in aqua regia. Filter the diluted solution, and with liquor of flints precipitate the gold out of the solution. Then add the excess of the precipitant to the solution of gold. Next place the solution on a sand-bath at a boiling heat for some hours' time, when the liquor of flints will extract the tincture out of the gold, and will be dyed with a fine purple colour. Add pure water, raise to a boil, and the flint will be precipitated (the tincture, of an excellent colour, remaining with the salt of tartar). Evaporate the solution to dryness, and a very fine salt of a purple colour will remain at the bottom of the vessel, out of which may be drawn by alcohol, or spirit of wine, a tincture as red as blood, and little inferior in virtue to potable gold. This golden salt may, in a very short time, viz., in an hour, be perfected with small labour, and transmuted into a wonder of Nature—thus confuting the slanderers of the noble Art of Alchemy.

THE USE OF THE TINCTURE OF GOLD.

(GLAUBER, Part I., p. 26, a.)

The extracted tincture is one of the chief of those medicines which comfort and cheer the heart of man, renew, and restore to youthfulness; and cleanse and purify the blood throughout the body, whereby many horrible diseases, as the leprosy, the pox, and the like, may be rooted out.

Whether this tincture, by the help of fire and art, may further be advanced into a fixed substance, is a question for Alchemy to determine.

How to Prepare a famous Universal Medicine of Gold.

(Glauber, Part II., p. 169, a, b.)

Take three or four ounces of the coagulated and irreducible blood of the Lion, of which the Book of Dialogues treats. Dissolve them, in the dry way, by the help of sal mirabilis, into a red stone, from which, reduced to powder, extract its tincture, by the aid of alcolizate spirit of wine.

This tincture is a famous aurum potabile against many diseases.

It also coagulates living mercury into Sol.

THE PHILOSOPHERS' WATER OF LIFE.

Take one pound of the pure and clean filings of steel. Put them into a glass retort, so that they may occupy a twelfth part of it. Then pour upon them a well-rectified spirit of wine, alkalizate, viz., to every pound of filings from four to six pounds of spirit of wine.

Care must be taken that the glass vessel is sufficiently capacious, or else, when the spirit of wine begins to work upon the steel filings, it will run over. The retort then being placed in sand, and the recipient being ready, add, for each pound of spirit of wine, one ounce of our Alkahest, which will actuate the spirit, so as to dissolve the steel, in which solution the sulphur of philosophers, or the purest tincture of Mars, is let loose, and immediately taken up by the spirit, being assumed with it to the philosophic heaven. But because this soul of Mars has not yet attained to that height of purity which the philosopher desires, therefore it must enter its purgatory, there to put off all the impurities

it has brought over with it, that is to
say, the spirit of wine must, under a
large refrigeratory head, be burnt away,
in which flame the anima martis, or soul
of iron, becomes purified to the highest
degree, the flame carrying the tinging
medicine over in the form of a clear, pellucid water, which is the true water of life
of philosophers, healing all curable
diseases, if daily taken in small quantity.
For this medicine renews the body of
man, and makes old age youthful and
again blooming. Neither do I believe
that a better medicine can be found in
the whole world than this.

It likewise tinges Lune, and coagulates Mercury into fixed Sol.

How to make and prepare the "Atoms" of Gold.

(Glauber, Part II., p. 149, b.)

Dissolve an ounce of pure gold in
strong spirit of salt, or in aqua regia, and
pour upon the solution a pound or two of
pure water, with which must be combined

about one pound of Rhenish wine. Mix them together in a close glass, so that no dust fall therein. Put it aside for some days in a warm place, that the gold may precipitate out of the water, and may settle to the bottom of the vessel in the shape of most curious stars. But if all the gold shall not be precipitated in this time, then set the glass in balneo, and let the solution boil awhile. Then when it is again cool, put by the vessel somewhere that the gold may settle, after which the precipitated gold is to be well washed with pure water.

These most fine and subtle atoms of gold may well be made use of in Medicine as well as in Alchemy.

How Gold is to be Levigated and made Fine.

(Glauber, Part II., 131, b.)

Gold does not by any way more easily admit of being turned into most tender and most subtle atoms than by the following process.

Dissolve pure gold in aqua regia, and, being dissolved, pour thereto as much of the water of tartar as is sufficient; so the clear gold, clothed with a golden colour, will precipitate itself to the bottom of the vessel ; nor will it be a darkish powder, as it is wont to be when precipitated by lixiviums, or by the spirit of urine, but it is light and tender, and shews in brightness like little golden stars ; yea, it becomes so very tender and subtle, that it swims, as it were, in the water, and settles to the bottom very leisurely, and is, therefore, so much worthier than all other calxes of gold, how subtle soever they be, that they may be accounted of small value compared to this.

These shining little golden stars are made so tender and so subtle that they may easily discover and demonstrate their virtues in medicinal use very notably, by the help of other things, and by being dissolved in sundry ways.

THE PROOF THAT GOLD TAKES INCREASE FROM OTHER AND BASER METALS.

(GLAUBER, Part I., p. 197, b.)

Take a small piece of silver, freed from its gold by aqua fortis, that there may be no doubt about the absence of gold from it. To this, in fusion, adjoin so much copper and antimonial regulus, as, being reduced into scoriæ by saltpetre, and again separated from the silver, may leave it malleable and ductile. This, being dissolved in aqua fortis, will leave at the bottom, undissolved, a reddish powder of gold, which it has attracted to itself from the copper and regulus of antimony.

This increase of the gold results so long as fresh copper and martial regulus of antimony and saltpetre are added to the silver (or gold) which is first put into the crucible.

[The use of gold in this operation affords far greater profit than when silver is employed, according to the statement of Glauber.]

Lastly, the greater the quantity of these metals thus employed, and the longer the time they are allowed to remain in flux with saltpetre or nitre, the greater is the profit.

A PROCESS FOR THE CALX OF GOLD.

Put fine gold into a crucible ; let it become intensely hot, and flow by the blast. Project, gradually, philosophical lead upon it, and blow the fumes away with a small pair of bellows. This must be continued until the lead has carried away the body of the gold in white fumes, and lastly there remains " our fire " and " incombustible sulphur," transparent like a ruby. This is the last and first matter of gold--the sophic fire, our sperm and sulphur. This also transmutes silver into gold.

EVAPORATION.

All the antimony has to pass off by evaporating before the gold can in any way be converted into a calx, which calx is regarded by some as the whole secret of the thing.

A Preparation of the Calx Auri.

Take very fine gold, and pass it through antimony. (By passing through antimony is to be understood the process, given above, of projecting the philosophic lead on gold in fusion, and blowing away the fumes.)

Having passed it through antimony, now divide the gold into very delicate leaves, cut into small pieces, and for one part of gold take six parts of mercury, highly purified, and passed through chamois leather several times. Put the gold into a crucible, and let it get red-hot, but take care that it does not melt. When very red, pour the mercury, made hot likewise, over the gold. Then stir the whole with an iron rod, till it gets red, and the gold is ground, amalgamated, and incorporated with the mercury. Then pour the amalgam into a glass of clear water. Take it out and dry it, and again pass the amalgam through chamois leather, pressing the leather very hard, so that the mercury overflows strongly, and so that the mass remains sufficiently hard, which mass must be worked for a long time in a glass mortar with a pestle of the same material, and with double its weight of prepared common salt, till there no longer remains anything of the said amalgam. Then put the whole into a crucible, covered with another, through which there is a hole above, well luted one with the other. Reverberate and calcine the matter well for the space of twenty-four hours, taking care that the gold does not melt. This done, the gold will be found calcined, and the salt and mercury will be evaporated. Then re-amalgamate as before. Then put it, with double its weight of flour of sulphur, into a red-hot crucible, stirring the amalgam till the flowers are burnt. Then take the crucible from the fire, and let it cool. Wash the amalgam with rain water, distilled many times till it be well cleansed. Finally, put it in a glazed earthern pot ; pour S. V. R. upon it, then set fire to the mixture, and burn it two or three times.

Then the gold will be very spongy and attenuated, and will become much more so if the process be repeated two or three times.

––––––

The Preparation of a Calx of Gold (Aurum), of a Beautiful Scarlet Colour.

When three parts of a regulus of antimony and iron, with one part of gold or silver, are melted together in a crucible, a gold or silver regulus is obtained, but neither gold nor silver is destroyed or separated here, like iron, copper, tin, or lead. But if a regulus of gold or silver be treated with Monte Schnyder's " Fulmen " (see " Digby's Chymical Secrets "), there can be separated the solar or lunar sulphur and mercury, and a sharp wine vinegar, or rectified spirit of salt (hydrochloric acid), will make them appear by extraction. In the case of gold there ensues a gold-coloured vitriol, like a topaz ; but from silver there follow crystals like to transparent nitre. In the fæces is contained a gold or silver salt, which can be extracted with water.

When the calx of gold or silver thus produced is put to digest in a bolthead (mixed with highly purified mercury), it is said that it will turn it to gold in about six weeks' time.

THE GOLDEN PURPLE OF CASSIUS.

Dissolve a little gold in common aqua regis Into the solution pour a little of our mercurial water, and mix by stirring or shaking the vessel well. Then the mercury of Jupiter, in a magnetic way, continually attracts to itself the gold from the solution, and tinges the water a blood-red colour. At length the gold with the mercury of Jupiter conjunctively precipitate to the bottom of the vessel in the form of a purple powder. This being washed and reduced with borax, the greater portion of the mercury dissipates, but a small portion remains with the fixed gold, and renders it snow-like and friable : by which it may be seen how great an affinity gold has for tin.

FIXATION.

Yet this is not the way of preparing anything eminent, having efficiency for both. Therefore, if anyone expects a noble product from both, he must with gentle fire fix this purple gold, that the mercury of Jupiter may not fume away, but may remain with the gold.

————

THE OIL OR LIQUOR OF GOLD.

(GLAUBER, part I., p. 7, a.)

Dissolve the calx of gold in the spirit of salt, which should be very strong. From the gold abstract half the solution, and there remains a corrosive oil, upon which pour the expressed and pure juice of lemons, when the solution becomes green, and a few fæces fall to the bottom, which may be reduced in melting.

This being done, put this green liquor in balneo, and draw off the water.

That which remains take out, and put upon marble in a cold, moist place, and it will be resolved into a red oil. This oil may safely, and without danger, be taken inwardly, curing those that are hurt with mercury, etc There is not a better medicine in the exulceration of the glands, and in the ulcers of tongue and jaws, or which does sooner mundify and consolidate. Neither must we neglect necessary purgings and sudorifics, for fear of a relapse, the cause not being taken away.

Neither will there any danger follow, whether it be given inwardly, as in the accustomed use of other medicaments and gargarisms, for it may daily and safely be used at least three times, with a wonderful admiration of a quick operation.

How Gold may be Greatly Increased in Weight.

(Glauber, Part I., p. 178, a.)

Take one part of gold mixed with five or six parts of lead, and drive away the lead again upon a good test until the gold sparkle and shine, when the gold will be found to weigh much heavier than it did at first, the increased weight being from the lead solely.

THE SOLUTION OF GOLD.

(GLAUBER, Part I., p. 264, b. *et seq.*)

Gold is stated to be dissolvable by sal mirabilis, and thence a sort of aurum potabile ensues on distillation, but the addition of a certain vegetable sulphur, or carbon, is said to be quite essential to success.

EXTRACTION OF GOLD OR SILVER FROM LEAD.

(GLAUBER, Part II., p. 29, b.)

Dissolve lead in aqua fortis, and precipitate the lead by salt water. Decant the water, and wash and dry the resulting precipitate. To four parts of this substance add one part of pure gold, or its calx. Melt the mixture of the two substances in a crucible, so that the lead may become a fusile stone ; but the gold calx by this operation is rendered much heavier, and puts on a white appearance.

This whiteness is nothing else than pure and good silver, drawn out of Saturn by Sol, sympathetically, and made visible, whereas previously it lay hidden in the lead in a spiritual and invisible manner.

———

A Good Arcanum.

(Glauber, part I., p. 194, a, b.)

Take of copper one part, of gold or silver two parts, and of regulus martis three parts, all which melt together in a well-covered crucible.

When they are melted, and the cover has been taken off, yet warily, that no coals may get into the crucible, cast in as much well-dried and powdered nitre as there is of copper and regulus in the crucible, care being taken that the salt-petre does not boil over the crucible, a thing that may easily happen, as the mixture swells and rises with the heat.

After the saltpetre has acted on the regulus and copper, and has turned them into reddish scoriæ, which occurs in a quarter of, or half, an hour, the heat must be so increased that the scoriæ will melt completely.

The fused mass is then to be poured into a smelting-cup or cone, which is to be first heated and well smeared with wax on the inner side. In the bottom of such vessel, when cold, there will be found a regulus of pure gold, which, being freed from the scoriæ, will be increased in weight by so much as it has attracted from the copper and regulus martis, or the 50th part of the weight of Sol.

———

THE PRESENCE OF GOLD AND SILVER IN SEA-WATER.

(GLAUBER, Part I., p. 17, b., p. 18, a.)

Fill a great copper kettle with sea water, and pour thereon a little dissolved lead. The resulting white precipitate of lead chloride is to be frequently stirred and moved about, in order that the solution of lead may everywhere be in contact with the sea-salt water. Through this action a spiritual gold adheres to the leaden powder, and subsides to the bottom of the vessel together with it.

This powder, being freed from its salt by washing with water, being then dried, and melted in a cupel, leaves a small grain of gold, as a remainder.

For this extraction silver has the advantage over lead.

THE PHILOSOPHIC STONE : HOW PREPARED.

Dissolve gold in aqua fortis ; add the same weight of our sal ammoniac, and then, by its menstruum, bring the gold into solution.

Gold, being once dissolved with our sal ammoniac, admits not any more melting, nor does it of itself return again into a malleable metallic body, but gets a reddish scarlet kind of colour in the trial (or crucible), and remains an "unfusile" powder. Borax added to this substance, and then exposed to a red heat, melts the gold to a red glass—a clear proof that the gold has been inverted and transmuted by the power of our sal ammoniac.

———

THE SO-CALLED PHILOSOPHERS' STONE.

I. Prepare a quantity of spirit of wine, so free from water that it is wholly combustible, and so volatile that when a drop of it is let fall the same evaporates before it reaches the ground. This constitutes the first menstruum.

II. Take pure Mercury, revived in the usual manner from cinnabar. Put it into a glass vessel, with common salt and distilled vinegar. Agitate violently, and when the vinegar acquires a black colour, pour it off, and add fresh vinegar. Again agitate, and continue these repeated agitations and additions till the vinegar ceases to acquire a black colour from the mercury. The mercury is now, after washing and straining, quite pure and brilliant.

III. Take of this mercury four parts, and of sublimed mercury (corrosive sublimate), prepared with your own hands, eight parts. Triturate them together in a wooden mortar with a wooden pestle, till all the grains of running mercury disappear. This process is tedious, and rather difficult.

IV. The mixture, thus prepared, is to be put into an aludel on a sand-bath, and exposed to a subliming heat, which is to be gradually raised till the whole sublimes. Collect the sublimed matter, put it again into the aludel, and sublime a second time. This process must be repeated five times. Thus a very sweet and crystalline sublimate is obtained. It constitutes the salt of the wise, and possesses wonderful properties.

V. Grind it in a wooden mortar, and reduce it to powder. Put it into a glass retort, and pour upon it the prepared spirit of wine, till it stands about three finger-breadths above the powder. Seal the retort hermetically, and expose it to a very gentle heat for seventy-four hours, shaking it several times a day. Then distil, also with a gentle heat, and the spirit of wine will pass over, together with spirit of mercury. Keep this liquid in a well-stoppered bottle, lest it evaporate. More spirit of wine is to be poured upon the residual salt, and, after digestion, it must be distilled off, as before. The same process must be repeated till the whole salt is dissolved, and distilled over with the spirit of wine. A great work has now been performed; the mercury has been rendered in some measure volatile, and it will gradually become fit to receive the tincture of gold and silver.

VI. Take this mercurial spirit, which contains our magical steel in its belly. Put it into a glass retort, to which a receiver must be well and carefully luted. Draw off the spirit by a very gentle heat, and there remains in the bottom of the retort the quintessence or soul of mercury. This is to be sublimed by applying a stronger heat to the retort, that it may become volatile.

VII. Take common gold, purified in the usual way by antimony; convert it into small grains or fine powder, which may be washed with salt and vinegar till they become quite pure. Take one part of this gold, and pour on it three parts of the quintessence of mercury. Let both bodies be thoroughly well mixed.

FERMENTATION.—Take of our sulphur, already described, one part, and project it upon three parts of very pure gold fused in a furnace. In a moment you will see the gold, by the force of the sulphur, converted into a red sulphur, but of an inferior quality to the first sulphur. Take one part of this, and project it upon three parts of fused gold. The whole will be again converted into a sulphur, or a friable mass: by mixing one part of this with three parts of gold, you will have a malleable and extensible metal.

Project this upon ten parts of mercury and you have a perfect metal.

ALCHEMICAL PROCESS.

I.

Take of crude antimony 16 oz., of small iron brads 6 oz., and ignite to whiteness in an earthern crucible. When in full fusion, inject, gradually, every quarter of an hour, two spoonfuls of pure, dry, pulverised nitre (2 oz. altogether).

II.

Take of nitre 1 oz., or 2 oz., of potassa carbonate 1 oz., of martial regulus of antimony 4½ ozs., of common salt 1½ oz., of tartaric acid in crystals 1 oz. Pulverise each separately, and mix all well together. Put the whole into a large crucible, and let it melt gently in a wind furnace. Stir it with a red-hot pipe stem, and thoroughly unite the ingredients. When well mixed, pour it into an iron cone.

III.

Take of crude antimony 3 scruples (60 grains), of fine gold 1 scruple (20 grains), of steel filings 16 scruples (320 grains). Melt together in a wind furnace. Project, gradually, of Part II., as above, 3 drachms (two spoonfuls at a time, every fifteen or twenty minutes, from a small iron spoon, till the whole 3 drachms are used). The "projection" may have to be repeated ten or twelve times, but nothing should remain except a substance which is red and transparent as a ruby.

MULTIPLICATION.

Dissolve this transparent ruby stone with common purified mercury, and multiply it *ad infinitum.*

THE ALCHEMICAL PROCESS.

Part II.

Take of crude antimony 1 ½ oz., of fine gold ½ oz., of iron or steel filings 1 ½ oz. ; the crude antimony must be powdered. Melt these together in a crucible in a wind furnace, and every quarter of an hour project from an iron spoon, or the bowl of a tobacco pipe, about two teaspoonfuls of "sphera Saturni," or "philosophical lead." Con·

tinue this projection until the residue at the bottom of the crucible remains as a ruby-red, transparent glass.

THE FURTHER TREATMENT OF THE " SPHERA SATURNI."

These pitch-like scoriæ must be changed into amber-coloured scoriæ, by fresh powdering them again finely. Being powdered and weighed, they must be put into a roomy crucible.

Then three times their weight of purified and dried nitre must be projected gradually every quarter of an hour, and the cover put on the crucible.

By this means the pitch-like scoriæ are changed into amber-coloured scoriæ.

The scoriæ must now be " vitrified," which is done by gradually adding the nitre, as above.

The glass which results will then vitrify more aurum in the crucible, and increase it in power.

After this the purified running mercury must be added, and the whole put into a "bolt head," sealed hermetically, and then subjected to a gentle or moderate heat for some length of time.

A PROCESS IN ALCHEMY (PRACTICAL).

Part III.

Having made the "sphere of Saturn," powder it, fuse it in a crucible in a wind furnace, and put to it in fusion the proportionate quantity of gold required. This is supposed to make the gold into a "calx."

The gold will melt entirely, and be no more visible, but the sphere of Saturn is then said to be animated with the "soul" of Sol.

Next weigh what remains to be taken out of the crucible, and then powder it while warm. Now take three times its weight of pure, dry nitre (warm), and project this (two teaspoonfuls at a time) on the powdered and animated sphere of Saturn in fusion (every quarter of an hour) till it is all gone. This operation changes it into amber-coloured scoriæ.

Vitrifaction is the next process, which is done by taking equal parts of orpiment and red sulphur, in certain proportions. Put this mixture into a crucible, and lute a cover on it with a hole in it. The mixture must be fused gradually for eight hours. When the vessel is cool there will be found in it a blood-red glass, which has to be powdered and mixed with purified mercury for the next process.

THE ALCHEMICAL PROCESS.

Part IV.

No. IV. is hardly likely to prove a complete success at first, and may possibly have to be begun again from the beginning.

When the ingredients mentioned in No. III. are in full fusion, projection is made by putting 3 drachms of Sphera Saturni (II.), by two teaspoonfuls at a time, every fifteen minutes, into the crucible   The projection of the 3 drachms (A½ W½) will probably be accomplished only after eleven or twelve times.   This part is said to be the most difficult of the process.   The contents of the crucible have to be brought to a ruby-coloured glass.

One MS. says that orpiment and red sulphur must be added to effect it. Red sulphur is said to be the "chloride of sulphur" (?).

The proportions recommended are "equal parts of antimony, orpiment, and red sulphur."

If this does not succeed at first, then a repetition of this part of the process is advised (the proportions being altered at this stage).

It is of little use attempting to multiply till the ruby-red glass be made (or, at least, the saffron-coloured).

By putting No. III. again into a crucible, and, when fused, projecting warmed nitre (two teaspoonfuls at a time) every quarter of an hour, the amber-coloured scoriæ may, it is said, be readily produced. But the production of a glass might require another continued fusion.

———

THE RUBY-RED TRANSPARENT GLASS, described in the alchemical process, above may possibly require for its preparation the addition of a very pure yellow or red sulphur, and also arsenicum in crystals. These two must be well rubbed into each other, and then put into the crucible, together with the other materials.

According to Paracelsus, it is sufficient to continue projecting the philosophic lead till the mixture turns ruby-red, after which it should transmute silver into gold.

Multiplication is then to be effected by the addition of more gold to the vitrum, when the gold itself becomes changed to vitrum. Then the vitrum is to be dissolved by purified mercury, and this mixture put into a bolt-head, and gentle heat applied for a certain time, when it becomes a red powder, which, being put up in a very small quantity, enveloped in wax, and projected on silver fused in a crucible, transmutes it into the purest gold.

There is a strict connection between the Sb. process and the Hg. process. One is a sequel to the other, and the completion of it.

The gold must be made spermatic, and the production of a calx of aurum is quite essential to success in the prosecution of our Art.

When gold is added to the sphera Saturni, it makes it spermatic.

Vitrification is the next essential step. This is done by first powdering the product, then melting it in a blast-furnace, and projecting, every quarter hour, two teaspoonfuls of pure and dry powdered nitre (the whole quantity of nitre used being three times the weight of the sphera used). This is intended to vitrify it, and it should come to a ruby-red and clear glass, or, at the least, to an amber-coloured glass.

This glass must then be powdered ; when powdered let the purified mercury be mixed with it ; let both together be placed in a bolt-head, and a gentle heat of from seventy to ninety degrees applied, and this for the space of perhaps three weeks, or a full month.

Powdering the sphere of Saturn (to be safe) demands some care ; so, likewise, does the preparation of the purified mercury (by all accounts). The application of a handkerchief to the nose and mouth is by some folk strongly recommended.

The Quintessence of all Metals and Minerals.

(Glauber, Part I., p. 6, b.)

Dissolve gold, or any other metal (save silver), in the strongest spirit of salt, and draw off the water in balneo.

To that which remains pour on the best rectified spirit of wine, and put it to digesting, until the oil be elevated to the top, as red as blood, which is the tincture and quintessence of that metal, being a most precious treasure in medicine.

A Golden Aqua Vitæ, etc.

(Glauber, Part II., p. 150, a.)

Take of the best and purest saltpetre, and of white and pure tartar, each one pound ; of yellow sulphur, half-a-pound. Bring all to a powder, and, having well mixed them, put them into a crucible, and by putting thereto a live wood coal, kindle them, that they may take fire and burn up, leaving a yellow mass behind in the crucible. This, being molten in the fire, and turned forth into a mortar, will yield a fiery, sulphureous Stone, biting the tongue by reason of its sharpness. Now, whilst it is yet warm, powder it, for it presently attracts (when cool) humidity from the air, and admits not of pulverization. Being powdered, pour thereon two or three pounds of the best spirit of wine, and set it by for some days in a cool place, but with this proviso, that you daily shake or stir your matter in the vessel with the spirit of wine. By this means will the alcohol attract a red tincture out of the sulphur, and will withal actuate itself with the salt, by the calcined tartar. Then, let this spirit of wine be filtered, and draw off two-third parts by distillation in a balneum, that so you may have your spirit again, but this time of a very pleasing taste and smell, which it gets from the sulphur, as out of the centre of all odour.

————

THE PREPARATION OF THE VOLATILE SPIRITS OF METALS.

(GLAUBER, Part II., p. 162, b.)

Take of the steel wires which the needlemakers cannot use, one pound, which so heat in the fire that all squalidness and filth may be burnt away. Afterwards put them in a glass body, and pour on them of the elsewhere-described dissolving water, a quantity of four or five pounds. Place the vessel in balneo or in sand, and so apply heat that the water in the glass surrounding the steel may wax hot but not boil. Then the water preys upon the iron to be dissolved. For in this operation the steel is dissolved and fermented like new beer or wine. In this fermentation a certain most subtle spirit of Mars ascends, without any corrosive, breathing a very strong odour, and endowed with a taste vehemently penetrating. For such a spirit so penetrates the tongue that the taste long remains, although a man wash his mouth; yet this taste is not unpleasant. By penetrating the body of him that takes it, it provokes a sweat copiously, opens obstructions of the liver, spleen, and lungs, and comforts the vital spirits and stomach. Likewise it is admirably conducive to the health of such as are accustomed to drink wine mixed with water, because it gives the wine a grateful taste, and that far better than the best of bitter springs are able to perform. This spirit is much improved by rectification.

THE TREE OF GOLD.
(GLAUBER, part I., 7, a.)

Dissolve thin plates of iron in rectified spirit of salt; filter the solution,

which is of a green colour, and evaporate
to dryness on a sand-bath at a moderate
heat. A blood-red mass then remains
at the bottom of the vessel, and its taste
is sharp and biting to the tongue. It is
to be kept in a glass, close-stopped from
the air, lest it be resolved into an oil,
which then becomes of a yellow colour.
That red mass, being put upon the oil of
sand, or flints, makes a " tree " to grow
in the space of one or two hours, having
root, trunk, and boughs. This being
taken out and dried, in the test yields
good gold, which that tree extracts from
the stones or sand. Thou mayest, if
thou pleasest, more accurately examine
this matter.

THE " WHITE WORK " OR LUNAR, OR THE SILVER PROCESS.

It is recommended by some teachers
to begin by trying this process first,
repeating the experiment of projection
with the addition of silver, till the process can be well made sure of, and then

trying the gold process (as performed and recommended by Flamel).

SILVER EXALTED TO THE NATURE OF GOOD GOLD.
(GLAUBER, Part I., p. 177, a.)

This gradation of silver is performed by the help of a certain mineral sulphur, to wit, of iron and antimony, and that in this manner :

Adjoin to silver as much regulus martis, and again let it be separated from it by nitre, which labour is performed in the space of an hour. To the remaining silver adjoin again as much regulus, which is again to be abstracted, and let this labour be repeated 5, 6, 8, or 10 times, which may be done in one day. Afterwards let the silver be dissolved in aqua fortis, for then the gold which the nitre, by means of the silver, has obtained from the regulus, will remain at the bottom, and is to be edulcorated and corporified with borax.

The gold will prove of an excellent quality.

An Universal Menstruum.

(Glauber, part I., p. 163, b.)

Take two or three pounds of menstruum (nitre?) whereof the corrosive nature transmutes, by force of fire, into a nature non-corrosive, and the menstruum is prepared, with which this medicine is to be elaborated, in the following manner.

Dissolve in this menstruum as much of the first ens of gold as it will attract in the heat, and so that a red solution may be made, which digest for some days with its own weight of the dissolving wine. Make separation of the pure parts from the impure by removing the fæces which sever themselves from the medicine by falling to the bottom. This, being concentrated by an easy heat, will be a red pellucid stone, very like to a soluble salt, and is to be carefully preserved.

This medicine will be found second to none, except the Stone of the Philosophers, and will be of the same goodness after a hundred years that it possessed on the first day it was made.

The Preparation of a Most Efficacious Medicine.

(Glauber, part II., p. 152, b.)

Take of new and strong-smelling myrrh, of the purest and clearest aloes, and of the best English saffron, of each one, two, or three ounces. Beat them all into powder, and pour thereon the strong, operative, and volatile spirit of Mars, dissolving as much thereof as will dissolve. To the solution add a little of "my secret ferment," which will cause it presently to ferment. The alembic or retort must be air-tight with the receiver.

As soon as ever the ferment is added to the solution it presently begins to ferment, and the glass being placed in balneo, and heat applied, the volatile spirit of iron ascends readily and nimbly, like spirit of wine, much inferior thereto as to its heat, but yet of a far more penetrating efficacy. The spirit being all ascended, evaporate to the consistence of honey, but yet so gently that the remaining juice may not smell of burning. This done, take out the glass, let it cool, and pour upon the juice, after cooling, the same volatile spirit of Mars which was at first separated by distillation, which spirit will dissolve that thick juice, and this, being dissolved, will become a balsam of a strong odour, of penetrating efficacy, and of a red colour like blood. It must be kept well shut, and may be truly accounted as a balsam of life, for it takes away the obstructions of the whole body, does mightily corroborate and strengthen all the internal vessels and members, and preserves them safe from all corruptions. No other balsam can compare with it.

Dose (after purging and short fasting) : One, two, three, four, to ten or twelve drops.

The Preparation of the Dissolving Water for Metals.

(Glauber, part II., p. 162, b.)

Take of common salt one pound, which dissolve in four or five pounds of common water, and pour upon it half a pound of oil of vitriol, to which superadd some steel wire, fragments, or turnings, and thence, by distilling, separate the water   Then no sharp spirits will ascend with the water, but all the corrosivity will remain with the Mars, and nothing ascend but a subtle spirit, void of corrosion.   This moves to admiration, namely, that of such a hard and fixed metal, with the help of so gentle a heat, should ascend such a flying and penetrating spirit.   But it is more to be admired that this white, volatile, and penetrating spirit, in a few hours' space, is able to change itself into a fixed red tincture.

Fill a glass body above half-full with our spirit of Mars, yet take no more of it than five or six pounds, as that would be more than is needful for probation. Place the body, with its head well luted, in sand, and distil almost all the water by ascent, so that only half a pound may remain in the bottom. Take what ascends out of the receiver, and it will be found to have little more taste than rain-water, and that because the volatile spirit in this abstraction or decoction is separated from the water, and again converted into a fixed body, viz., a most red powder, which red powder is, indeed, a true tincture, yet it has no ingress into metals—unless that be procured to it by the aid of gold.

Hence is fulfilled the precept of the philosopher's teaching : " Make the fixed volatile, and the volatile fixed." N.B.—Ten pounds of the water yield but one scruple of our sulphur.

A Preparation of the Alkahest.
(Glauber, Part I., p. 153, b.)

Take three parts of pure and pulverised nitre, to one part of regulus martis. Place the mixture in a clean glass vessel, and, by a prudent increase of temperature, make it boil gently in a fixatory furnace ; in this degree of heat leave it five or six hours. Then take it out that it may cool, and pour on it pure water and the nitre, which by the regulus of antimony comes out fixt. Wash out, and, lastly, abstract the water ; so there results a fiery liquor, fit for use in metallic operations.

N. B. – This fixation may be as well made in covered crucibles as in glasses, and is good enough, only the management of the fire must be regulated, and the heat at first must not be too intense, lest the nitre evaporate before it be brought to a fixation, in conjunction with the antimony.

THE PRAXIS.

All metals in their proper corrosive menstruums must be dissolved, precipitated, washed, and dried, and then, lastly, with the alkahestic liquor poured on, must be digested, dissolved, and with spirit of wine, separated and reduced into, or brought to, a potability.

A Preparation of the Alkahestic Liquor.

(Glauber, Part II., p. 98, b.)

Take of pure saltpetre, and such as is free from all common salt, one pound, put it into a well-burnt pot or crucible, and set the cover on ; place it in a wind furnace, urge it so long with coals that it may attain unto redness, and all the nitre flow. Now throw in a little powder of good charcoal, so that it burns away at the expense of the saltpetre.

This coal-powder being consumed (converted into carbonic acid), throw in some more of the same, and proceed thus by casting on coal-powder till the said coal-powder no longer shall make fire with the nitre, and the nitre shall appear of a greenish and sky colour. Then pour it out molten into a heated recipient, and allow it to cool. Beat this salt to a powder, and put it into a glass, or else set it in some moist, cool place, and in a short time it will run to a clear and fiery liquor, which bottle and keep for use.

THE PREPARATION OF THE SO-CALLED ALKAHEST.

Take freshly prepared caustic lime, and, if possible, still hot or warm. Powder it quickly in a dry place, and put it into a retort. Add as much absolute alcohol as the powder will absorb, and distil the alcohol at a moderate heat, until the powder in the retort is perfectly dry. The distilled alcohol is now to be poured again upon the lime, and distilled, and this operation is to be repeated ten times.

Mix the powder with the fifth part of its weight of pure carbonate of potassa. This must be done very quickly, and in a dry atmosphere, so that it may not attract any moisture. Insert this mixture of the two powders in a retort, and heat it gradually, after putting about two ounces of absolute alcohol into the recipient. White vapours now arise from the powder, and are attracted by the alcohol, and the heating is to be continued as long as this takes place. Pour the alcohol from the receiver into a dish, and set it on fire. The alcohol burns away and the alkahest remains in the dish. It is an excellent medicine, and is used in the same manner as is the primum ens melissæ.

NOTE.

On account of the great powers contained in the limestone, Paracelsus says that many a man kicks away with his foot a stone that would be more valuable to him than his best cow, did he only know what mysteries were put into it by God, by means of the spirit of Nature.

SPIRIT OF WINE OF THE WISE (ALCOHOL).

(The Physician's Commentary on Basil Valentine.)

Take four ounces of thrice sublimed salt of ammonia, and ten ounces of the Spirit of Wine distilled over salt of tartar, so that it is quite clear. Place in phial over digestive fire, until the spirit of wine is filled with the fire or sulphur of the salt of ammonia. Distil thrice, and this constitutes our spirit of wine.

And over a circulatory fire, it may become a useful and efficacious medicine.

The preparation of a golden Spirit of Wine.

(Glauber, Part II., p. 139, b. 140, a.)

Take white or red tartar, dissolve it in water, and separate all its gross sulphur by a certain precipitating matter (Lixivium). The impurity, thus abiding in the water, is to be separated from the precipitated tartar by pouring out the water. The tartar remaining at the bottom like a snowy sand, is to be well purged by repeated washings with water until the powder itself puts on a snowy whiteness. This process of precipitation and washing must be repeated until the addition of fresh lixivium to the clear solution no longer gives rise to any more black fæces.

Dissolve some pounds of this pure and acceptable tartar in cold water, so as to make it sufficiently acid. Put this solution in some warm place, or in horse-dung, or in a warm balneum, that the tartar may begin to putrefy, may lose acidity, and acquire a sort of sweetness, for which, before it come to be, there is required the time of some months.

After it has lost its acidity, all the water present is to be evaporated per balneum, until it become a thick and black juice, like honey. This being set in the glass in sand, and being urged with a stronger heat than was made in balneo, will yield a fiery spirit, such an one as will mix with gold dissolved in spirit of salt, will separate the pure parts by digestion, attract them to itself from the more gross parts, and so will perform its office in medicine even to most high admiration.

––––––––

FIXATION AND PURIFICATION OF SULPHUR.

(GLAUBER, Part III., p. 3, a.)

Take common yellow sulphur and reduce it to a fine powder. Mix it well with powdered salt in excess. Then distil it, and from it abstract, three times, a most strong aqua fortis, or spirit of salt. So the sulphur remaining in the bottom will be of a black colour. This wash with pure water, and frequently distil the water thence until the same comes off wholly pure, and smells no longer of sulphur.

Then take the sulphur, and reverberate it in a close reverberatory, with antimony. In reverberating it will shew itself first white, then yellow, and then red, as cinnabar.

Having brought it to this pass, thou mayst rejoice, for this is the beginning of thy riches. For this reverberated sulphur, in tinging, renders every silver into the best gold, and the human body into perfect health, more excellently than can be described. Of such great virtue is this reverberated and fixt sulphur.

THE TINCTURE OF SULPHUR

may be exhibited in all diseases, for comforting the heart, the brain, and all the internal members of the body, because it is most excellent, especially in affections of the lungs. Also it is the most penetrating and salutiferous of balms for curing everybody internally hurt, and for restoring all vitiated members to their pristine sanity.

Lastly, it may very well serve instead of an aurum potabile.

How to Fix Common Combustible Yellow Sulphur.

(Glauber, Part II, p. 214, a.)

The whole art of this royal work consists solely in uniting the said sulphur with spirit of wine, and then burning it away under a helm, to catch the incombustible heavenly salt, or permanent water of life, which, with gold, becomes coagulated and fixt to a tinging stone.

This heavenly salt, as soon as, by the flame, it is separated from the sulphur, is true universal medicine against all the diseases of mankind. But, when united with gold, it obtains ingress into and tinges Lune, and coagulates Mercury into Sol.

Now, to join sulphur with spirit of wine (wherein the whole art and mastery consists) is an easy thing, and may be effected in this manner.

For aqua fortis, or for spirit of salt, to have any ingress into sulphur, that is first of all procured by the aid of salts. For then the artist's endeavour will succeed well, and the sulphur in abstraction of the acid spirit will be fixt, and also wax white. But redness is afterward given to it in an open fire, or fire of reverberation. And it will never wax red in a close vessel, how long soever it stands in the fire. When it is thus red, every common spirit of wine extracts not its tincture, because it has no ingress into it, but the fixt red sulphur must first be melted with fixed salt of tartar in a very strong fire. In this way there is given it such an ingress that any spirit of wine can extract from it its tincture.

THE FIXATION OF SULPHUR.
(GLAUBER, Part II., p. 27, b.)

Take one part of yellow sulphur, beaten into powder, and four or five times its weight of concentrated nitric acid, which spirit pour upon the said powder in a glass cucurbite, or retort, and abstract it therefrom several times by distillation. This done, the sulphur gets a red colour, and becomes pellucid or transparent.

If it resolves, in the air, into a fat oil, the operation is well conducted; if not, the process is to be repeated.

HOW TO FIX SULPHUR WITH SATURN.

Take one part of common sulphur; mix it with three or four parts of lead ashes; put this mixture into a strong earthern cementing box, and lute it with a good strong lute that will not crack.

When the lute is dry, put it into a cementing furnace, or into such a fire that in the beginning will only melt the sulphur, so that it may penetrate the lead ashes, and hide itself in them, and thus be initiated to the fire. Then by degrees increase the heat from day to day, till at last the crucible comes to be of a dark red. Then further increase the heat, and continue thus till the sulphur becomes quite fixed with the lead ashes, and constant in the fire.

This requires from eight to ten months' time : during which time the sulphur becomes fixed, and has tinged and fixed its body, the lead, as much as it can, for it is not possible for it to fix all the lead after this manner into gold and silver, but only part of it, yet so that a hundred-fold profit is made out of it by proceeding rightly in the matter.

———

THE PURIFICATION OF SULPHUR (MINERAL).

(GLAUBER, Part II., p. 124, b.)

Take common brimstone, sublime it in the usual way (flowers), or by itself in a coated glass retort, or let it be mixed with decrepitated salt, for so will it be freed from its most crude terrestricity, and be rendered fit for a further mundification by an acid spirit.

Take one pound of these flowers of sulphur, and put it into a strong glass body, coated; then pour in one or two pounds of the spirit of nitre, or of the spirit of common salt, and place it in an earthen vessel in sand. Then put it under a fire, increasing it gradually, until the spirit of salt boils in the retort, and the sulphur melts, when there will swim somewhat like oil on the top of the water.

N.B.—An alembic is to be put on the glass body, lest the spirit of salt, ascending up, disperses in fume, but in the alembic it will be refrigerated, and condensed, and may thus be saved.

This boiling or digestion is finished in some five or six hours, and so the sulphur is mundified, and becomes as clear and transparent as glass.

A PROCESS FOR THE PURIFICATION OF MERCURY.

The purest mercury revivified from cinnabar is to be dissolved in as much aqua fortis as is necessary.

Into the solution pour gradually as much solution of sea salt or hydrochloric acid as is necessary to precipitate the mercury, and the result is a white calx of mercury. Wash this well with water, and dry the calx.

Mix the dried calx with one, two, or three parts of its weight of stone lime, and half a part of rye or wheat flour. Then distil the mixture by means of a retort.

The distilled mercury, unless perfectly clean, may be passed two or three times through chamois leather.

This revivified mercury is bright, like the firmament, and dissolves gold in a very short time, even by rubbing, and without heat. The whole process may, with advantage, be repeated two or three times. Such mercury will be wonderfully pure. The aqua fortis solution must always be diluted with clean water before precipitating   Ordinary mercury contains crudities which it deposits in the water. Weigh the purified mercury, and it will be observed to have diminished by the quarter part or more of its weight, because whatever impurity there was in the mercury (though it be virgin running mercury) remains in the water, and cannot be precipitated.

But, to prove this truth, evaporate the water which was poured off from the precipitate, and there remains a sediment as black as ink.   Purify, therefore, the mercury, and it is fit for all operations, and is a master over all metals.

COMMON MERCURY PURIFIED, AND THEN FIXED.

(GLAUBER, part III., p. 70, a.)

Take of crude mercury and fine Jupiter each one pound. Melt the Jupiter in a crucible, and when it begins to cool pour the mercury upon it, when the heated Jupiter will take to itself the mercury, and become an amalgam, which amalgam must, with dried and purified nitre, be ground upon a stone. This done, take of the strong fluxing powder the same quantity as the amalgam and nitre ; grind them well together, and then the mixture is ready for kindling. But the operation must be so conducted that the poisonous fumes shall be carried away from the operator into the open air. The mixture may be put into a strong earthern pot, and after detonation there remains a mass difficult to flux, which being cupelled, and separated by aqua fortis, affords a considerable quantity of Sol and Lune, abundantly recompensing the cost and labour of the operation.

After the mixture is kindled, the matter must be often stirred with a red-hot iron, so that no part may remain unkindled, but that the whole may be red-hot throughout.

THE FLUXING POWDER.

Take of sulphur one part, tartar two parts, and nitre three parts ; mix them well together. The different substances must be as pure, dry, and fine as possible.

THE MERCURY OF METALS, AND ITS PREPARATION.

(GLAUBER, part III., p. 13, a.)

Take of tartar, calcined to whiteness, one pound, which, reduced to powder, put into a glass retort, well luted. Then apply a receiver, and lute the junctures exactly. When the retort is placed in warm sand, through the tubulure pour about an ounce at a time of the sharp spirit of vitriol upon the calcined tartar, whence will be caused so great an ebullition that, by its own proper power, the spirit will ascend from it. Repeat the injection in the same small quantity till complete neutralisation ensues. When this occurs, administer fire, and by degrees draw forth all the humidity, until the vessel and matter are red-hot. The water that ascends must be rectified, by which the mercury of the vitriol is rendered more subtle and more pure. This pure mercurial water bears in itself, invisibly contained, a living metallic mercury, which is made manifest thus :

Dissolve common gold in aqua regis, and separate the dissolved from the undissolved. Then, leisurely, and drop by drop, pour the subtle and mercurial water upon the solution of gold, until the spirit of the mercury has no more action upon the solution of gold, but ceases, and all the gold is precipitated from the water ; in which precipitation the gold attracts to itself the mercury of the vitriol, from the mercurial water, in such manner that it settles to the bottom of the vessel in the form of slime, or a yellow powder. Next proceed to filter, wash, and dry. The mercury of vitriol is now united with the gold, and both suffer themselves to be fixed into a true tincture for human and metallic bodies.

THE FIXATION OF MERCURY WITH GOLD.

(GLAUBER, Part III., p. 13, a.)

Before the Mercury is put in to be fixt with the gold, it must be proved whether it be prepared duly or not. For, if the mercurial water was rightly prepared, it will contribute mercury enough for the gold, and by this mercury the precipitated gold is so augmented that it is no longer common gold. But if the mercurial water was not legitimately prepared, and consequently could not contribute much mercury to the gold, the gold remains poor, and, as soon as it is sensible of any heat, fulminates, and so is altogether unfit for fixation, being destitute of tinging mercury, which should have converted the whole body of gold into tincture.

Wherefore, after precipitation of the gold and mercury, a small portion of the precipitate must be heated in a small crucible, by way of trial. For, if it fulminates, it is a sign that the mercurial water was not perfect, and could not yield the gold mercury enough. But if, after it be red-hot, it comes forth with a delicate purple colour, it is to be supposed that the gold has imbibed mercury enough, and that they are both fixt together into a tincture.

The fixation is to be effected by placing the matter in a small glass phial in sand ; the heat must be moderate and well sustained, and must be continued for the space of several weeks.

If well prepared, this mercury of metals should tinge a silver plate of a purple colour, when the plate is properly heated.

THE MERCURY OF PHILOSOPHERS.

(GLAUBER, Part II., p. 182, a.)

Take of the filings or raspings of a metal, as Mars, Jupiter, or Venus, one pound, with which mix half pound of our dry salammoniac. If these be well combined, and distilled by retort, the metal will be corroded by the acidity, and the

mercury thereof will be freed from its
bonds, or be separated by distillation,
because the spirit of urine carries that up
with itself, invisibly, but, when the Spirit
is extracted from it, it then becomes
visible.

————

THE MIXED MERCURIES OF MARS AND JUPITER.

(GLAUBER, Part II., p. 182, a.)

Whenever the spirit of Jupiter
(most subtly rectified) is poured upon the
spirit of Mars, the mercuries, both of the
iron and tin, will suddenly combine, and
be so strongly attracted together that,
quitting the water, they will conjunctively
settle to the bottom of the vessel, in the
form of very small golden atoms,
which golden atoms, at the moment in
which they are formed of both the
mercuries, shall be seen to be converted
into constant and fixt gold.

This I take to be one of the greatest
wonders that ever came to hand in all my
chemical labours.

Mercury out of Metals by Tartar only.

(Glauber, Part III., p. 14, b.)

Take of filings of steel, one pound ; tartar, two pounds : common water, twenty pounds. By strong boiling in sand, separate all the water. The tartar in the act of boiling dissolves the iron, and so will volatilise the mercury set at liberty, in such wise that it ascends with the water as a subtle spirit, which, concentrated and made fit by rectification, may be rendered corporeal, by means of solution of gold, or by other means.

By adding to the tartar half as much sal ammoniac, the tartar the more readily preys upon the mercury ; also much more mercury issues thence than by tartar only.

The Common Mercury made Tinging.

Take of common mercury, one pound. Dissolve it in aqua fortis. Neutralise with ammonia, evaporate to dryness, and then heat more strongly.

The mercury then sublimes in the neck of the retort. Such a sublimate is readily dissolved by water. This mercurial water is endued with a power of extracting tinctures from metals, gems, and other stones.

In this work even Proserpine, the wife of Pluto, can scarcely elaborate anything more excellent. Therefore, when this mercury has drawn so much blood from the red lion as to change from white to red, then, indeed, it has acquired the amelioration of a higher degree, but as yet it is able to perform no miracles in tinging. That it may be exalted to so great perfection, the whole process must be repeated ten times, and fixation effected.

A Tinging Mercury out of Antimony.

Take of antimony, saltpetre, and tartar, each one pound, which, pulverised and mixt, put into a crucible, and kindle the mixture with a coal. When the deflagration ceases, melt it, and pour it into a cone. After it is cold, separate the regulus from the scoriæ, which reduce to powder, and dissolve by boiling in water. A red lixivium results, to which add half its weight of sal ammoniac in powder, and put the mixture into a glass retort, tight-fitted to a receiver, and now distil, when a certain most subtle and volatile spirit ascends, in which the mercury is latent, which also, in a solution of gold, may be precipitated, edulcorated, proved, dried, and fixt, as with the mercury of vitriol, and over which antimony has the advantage in point of quantity and of ease of manipulation.

A Tinging Mercury by Resuscitatives.

Take six pounds of vitriol, to which, dissolved in urine, add of sal ammoniac one pound, crude tartar, two pounds, salt of tartar four pounds. Distil from these, in a strong glass vessel, a subtle mercurial water, which, according to the method prescribed, may be made corporeal, and may be fixt with gold into a tincture.

This way of working is easy, and of small expense, so that it may well satisfy the desire of those who are content with what may be acquired by the use of glass vessels.

THE FUNDAMENTAL PROCESS OF ART.

(GLAUBER, Part III., p. 46, b.)

Take one pound of steel wire or filings, more or less, as is convenient. Dissolve it in spirit of salt. Filter the solution, and abstract the water until an oily appearance ensues. Add a like proportion of corrosive oil, or butter of antimony, well mixt together. Distil the mixture, by a sand-bath, in a coated glass retort. When yellow oily drops appear, increase the heat till they shew blood-red. This blood-red oil of Mars and antimony (Proserpine) is the golden branch of Virgil, plucked from the obscure tree, which may be fixed into tincture. When we pour our alkahest upon this red oil, and again draw off the liquor by retort at a gentle heat, and at length give a stronger fire, then the most subtle and purest part of the tincture comes over, and the grossest part remains behind, which is a universal purge.

The subtle portion may yet be made purer and nobler by rectification, and then may afterwards be dulcified from its salt.

Dry the anima martis and antimony. Put them into a strong glass, and with an easy sand heat melt into a red stone. This stone melts as quickly as wax, and has an easy ingress into all metals, even as oil has into dry leather.

This stone has not its equal, for it is better than the fire stone of Basilius, and it is better than Butler's Stone, to which Helmont has ascribed such wonders.

(N.B.—Our secret sal ammoniac answers better than corrosive oil.)

THE COAGULATION OF THE RED OIL OF MARS AND ANTIMONY.

(GLAUBER, Part III., p. 49, b.)

Take a pound or more of raspings or filings of lead, and put them into a glass retort, well coated. Pour on to them half the quantity of the red oil of Mars and antimony. Set in a sand cupel, and give fire gently by degrees, when there will come over no red oil, but only a clear and insipid water, for all the sharpness, with the red tincture, will remain with the lead. In the retort will be found no lead, but this red, tinging, and easily melting stone, of such virtues as those already described.

THE FINAL PROCESS.

(GLAUBER, Part III., p. 50, a.)

Take three or four ounces of our oil of Mars and antimony, coagulated into a red stone by the aid of lead. Grind it to an impalpable powder, and draw off from it ten or twelve ounces of the strong aqua fortis which has been first abstracted from decrepitated sal, and in which is dissolved half an ounce of gold.

Secondly, and thirdly, abstract from it again fresh aqua regis, but without gold. Then the gold radically unites itself with the tincture of the Mars and antimony, and they are constantly fixed together by means of aqua regis. When this is done, pour upon it a good quantity of common water. Let it boil for some hours, and it draws out the sharp spirits which remained with the tincture. This may be once or twice repeated ; then dry it, and it is fit to tinge silver into gold.

This tincture melts as easily as wax. The lead does not hinder it, it is true : it goes into the silver with the tincture, but is easily separated by the cupel. This tincture of antimony and iron, by the help of our Alkahest, might be made into a constant tincture, so that in three or four days' time the said tincture would graduate Luna into Sol.

How Tartar is rendered Pure and Soluble.

(Glauber, Part II., p. 160, b. ; p. 161, a.)

By burning two pounds of tartar, reduce it to a white salt, which, dissolved in water, forms a lixivium. This lixivium, poured upon one pound of tartar, and boiled together with it, dissolves the tartar, and separates the binding or fixing sulphur from the salt. Then pour on one part of common tartar, boil them together yet once, and filter the boiled liquor through paper. Then in the bottom will remain the sulphureous fœces, and the water of tartar will pass through yellowish. Upon this water pour distilled vinegar, to neutralise the lixivium. This being done, the vinegar will also be coagulated with both salts, and will be changed into one salt, which salt is of great use and benefit both in medicine and alchemy.

That feculent slime which adhered to the sides of the filter should not be cast away, but endeavour made to fix it.

For then some admirable discovery may possibly be made, because that is the genuine coagulator of running waters, which it hardens, and it is joined in a singular familiarity with metals, especially with Sol, as has, with admiration, been experienced. For, in a few hours, it tinges Sol with whiteness, and turns it into brittle glass.

SULPHUR TRANSMUTED INTO GOLD.

Dissolve common sulphur, or any vegetable carbon, in common salt. This solution will make the sulphur of a red colour.

Keep this solution for at least one hour's space in the fire, and a little of the sulphur will be found changed into gold. To the red salt adjoin the calx of Saturn. Melt them by fusion into one body, and reduce the lead by cupel, when a grain of gold remains.

How to Imitate Natural Precious Stones.

(Glauber, Part I., p. 412, b.)

Adjoin to the red salt, made of wood or carbon, a little of the powder of white flints. Put them into a crucible, and melt them in a fire that they may become a red glass, resembling almost the colour of a ruby. By continuing the fusion the red colour changes to green, and has the likeness of an emerald. After this comes a sky-colour, resembling a sapphire. Then follows a yellow, not unlike a jacynth. Then, after a long continued heat, it becomes black, and like to an agate.

The Preparation of the so-called Primum ens Melissæ,

Take half-a-pound of pure carbonate of potassa, and expose it to the air until it is dissolved (by attracting water from the atmosphere). Filter the liquid, and put as many fresh leaves of the plant melissa, or balm, into it as it will hold, so that the liquid will cover the leaves. Let it stand in a well-closed glass, and in a moderately warm place, for a period of twenty-four hours. The fluid may then be removed from the leaves, and the latter thrown away. On the top of this liquid absolute alcohol is to be poured, so that it covers the former to the height of one or two inches, or until the alcohol becomes of an intensely green colour. This alcohol, or spirit of wine, is then to be taken away and preserved, fresh alcohol is put upon the alkaline liquid, and the operation is repeated until all the colouring matter is absorbed by the alcohol. This alcoholic liquid is now to be distilled, and the alcohol evaporated until it becomes of the thickness of syrup. This is the primum ens melissæ. But the alcohol which has been distilled away may be used again and again.

The liquid potassa must be of great concentration, and the alcohol of great strength, else they would become mixt, and the experiment would hardly succeed.

A VEGETABLE ELIXIR.

In the proper season of the year, when the herb is at its full growth, and consequently its juices are in their highest vigour, gather, at the fit time of the day, a sufficient quantity of balm. Wipe it clean, and pick it. Then put it into a stone mortar, and, by laborious beating, reduce it into a thin pap. Take this glutinous and odoriferous substance, and put it in a bolt-head, which is to be hermetically sealed, and then place it in a dunghill, or some gentle heat equivalent thereto, where it must digest for forty days. When it is taken out, the matter will appear clearer, thinner, and have a quicker scent. Then separate the grosser parts, which, however, are not to be thrown away. Put this liquid into a gentle bath, that the remaining gross particles may perfectly subside. In the meantime, dry, calcine, and extract the fixt salt of the grosser parts, separated as before mentioned, which fixt salt is to be added to the liquors when philtered. Take next, sea salt, well putrefied; melt it, and by setting it in a cold place, it will run and become clear and limpid. Take equal parts of both liquors, mix them thoroughly, and, having hermetically sealed them in a proper glass, let them be carefully exposed to the sun in the warmest season of the year, for some six weeks. At the end of this space, the primum ens of the balm will appear swimming at the top like a bright green oil, and this is to be carefully separated and preserved. Of this oil, a few drops taken in a glass of wine, for several days together, will bring to pass those wonders that are reported of the Countess of Desmond, and others ; for it will entirely change the juice of the human body, revive the decaying flame of life, and restore the spirits of waning youth.

A GOLDEN-YELLOW TINCTURE FROM WHITE NITRE.

(GLAUBER, Part II., p. 169, a, b.)

Take of the hairs of a sound man, or of any animal, well washed and cleansed, four ounces. Upon which pour of most strong and well rectified spirit of nitre, one pound, and the spirit will totally dissolve the hairs. Upon this solution pour by degrees so much oil of tartar as will be sufficient to neutralize the spirits of nitre, and totally deprive them of their corrosive power. But the addition of oil of tartar should not cease till the acid spirit acquires a rich golden colour. This being so, filter the solution through paper. If now from this liquor, in a glass vessel set in balneo, all the water be extracted, in the bottom of the glass will remain a red salt, from which, if there be added good, strong spirit of wine, an almost clear solution results. Further, if one-half of the spirit be abstracted from the tincture, then a yellow oil is obtained, which, if it be rubbed upon good silver, the metal acquires the yellow colour of Sol.

The fixation of this tincture will amply repay the time bestowed upon it.

A SPECIES OF SOPHIC STONE FROM CARBON.

(GLAUBER.)

If any mercurial salt be added to charcoal in a due weight, and be closed with it in a crucible but one day, and kept in the fire, the coal will be changed into a red, fiery, and heavy stone, more metallic than vegetable, and possessing admirable virtues which the tongue cannot declare.

THE WHITE SWAN OF BASILIUS, OR THE FULMEN OF JOVE.

(GLAUBER, Part I., p. 201, b.; p. 202, a.)

Take one part of tin, melt it in a crucible, and when it is melted, take the crucible out of the fire. Pour out the melted tin into another earthen vessel, and mix therewith one part of quick-silver, which will be presently absorbed by the tin, but the tin will become so brittle and friable, that it may be ground to fine powder upon a stone.

With this fine powder mix two parts of pure and dry saltpetre, by grinding them well together, till the amalgam cannot be known from the nitre, but one white powder is made of both.

This fine powder, or impalpable mixture, divided into equal portions (not exceeding one oz.) is to be cast into a red-hot vessel, or retort, the resulting vapours allowed to condense, and then another powder follows. The mass remaining in the bottom of the retort may be brought to metal by reduction with carbon, the process with nitre being repeated, till half the original regulus be brought to scoriæ. But if now gold be added to the metals thus employed, then a purple anima of gold and mercury results, which, digested to fixation, may be made to furnish the salamandar constant in the fire. The purple anima of gold and mercury, which has passed into the receivers, I free from the flowers of tin by washing with water, filtering it through paper, coagulating it, and then fixing it into a tinging stone. And I doubt not but that some good thing will thence proceed.

THE PREPARATION OF THE OIL OF SAND OR FLINTS.

(GLAUBER, Part I., p. 44, b. ; p. 45, a.)

Fuse together (at a red heat) one part of powdered sand or flints, and three or four parts of pure and dry potassium carbonate, until the mixture comes to be a clear, transparent glass, wherein lies hidden a great fire and heat. As long as it is kept dry from the air, the same cannot be perceived in it, but if water be poured upon it, then its secret heat discovers itself. If this fused and transparent clear glass be powdered in a warm mortar, and then exposed to the air in a moist place, it melts and runs into a thick and fat oil. This fat liquor or oil of flints, sand, or crystal, may not only be used inwardly and outwardly by itself, but it also serves to prepare metals and minerals into good medicines, or to change them into better by chemical art.

Tincture of Venus appears in the form of a deep red salt, which tincture performs whatsoever has been attributed to the tincture of Mars. In the same way a fixed tincture may be had from common combustible sulphur in three days' time. ———

A RAPID FULMEN, CHANGING IRON AND STEEL INTO GOOD GOLD.
(GLAUBER, Part III., p. 71, b.)

Take of fluxing powder four or five drachms ; mix with it an ounce of aurum fulminans, precipitated from aqua regia, not with salt of tartar, but with salt of ammonia. With this fulmen and steel needles make S S S in a crucible.

Let not the needles be above one ounce weight, else the fulmen will not be able to graduate them wholly into Sol, or gold. ———

A RED TINGING STONE.
(GLAUBER, Part III., p. 3, b. ; p. 4, a. ; and p. 82, a.)

Take either sea coals or wood coals, powdered ; good saltpetre ; common salt ; and oil of vitriol, of each a like quantity. Put these four things into a glass retort, well coated. Fit a receiver to it, and in an open fire distil off all the humidity. Urge it at length with the strongest fire, and a green liquor of sulphur comes over, which the ancients called the " Green Lion," and the same dissolves gold. When they are digested a good while, or the green liquor is often abstracted from the gold, then they are fixed together, and the liquor of sulphur, together with the gold, turns into a red tinging stone.

Is it Carbon, or is it only a Vegetable Sulphur ?

(Glauber, Part II., p. 48, b.)

Put the green or white juice of the wood or coals extracted by the sal in a glass retort, with some sal ammoniac ; draw off all the water by distillation, and the spirit of the sal ammoniac brings over the vegetable sulphur of a golden colour. It is a most penetrative spirit, and of wonderful efficacy in medicine and alchemy.

Being very volatile, it must be carefully secured.

————

A Red Carbuncle Prepared from Charcoal and Sal Mirabile.

Melt two or three ounces of sal mirabile in some pot or crucible, and throw in a piece of wood-coal or charcoal. Put on the cover, and let the mixture flow for half an hour, or an entire hour, so that the salt may dissolve as much of the coal as it can, and may leave the rest of it undissolved. Then pour out the matter, and there appears a red stone of salt, which has a hot taste, as most alkaline salts are found to have.

This red carbuncle, being dissolved in water, yields a green solution, which, being filtered and let stand for some hours, appears of a white colour, and, on further standing, acquires a yellowish colour. One drop thereof gilds over an imperial even as sulphur does, if it be therein put.

If any acid be poured into the white solution of the coals, and that little by little, until the alkaline salt be neutralised, a sediment will precipitate in the form of a white powder, which, separated from the salt, and washed and dried, burns away, and answers exactly to the mineral sulphur.

ANOTHER MODE OF DEMONSTRATION.

Take the red carbuncle out of the melting-pot, beat it into a fine powder, and mix therewith half its weight of sal ammoniac, powdered. Draw off by a glass retort, so that the sal ammoniac may bring over with it the said sulphur. Wash off this red matter with ordinary water.

YET ANOTHER.

First of all, exactly melt the coals by the sal mirabile in a melting-pot, so that the salt be accurately alkalizated by the coals, and taste sharp. Now treat the powdered mass with anhydrous alcohol, and put the glass to digest in hot sand. Well shake the vessel now and then, so that the spirit of wine may extract the sulphur, and leave the salt untouched. The alcohol becomes as red as blood. Exhaust the matter with fresh spirit. Now distil the extract, and there results a sweet oil of a blood-red colour, an excellent medicine of sweet odour and taste, and little inferior to that named potable gold. This oil has its use in Alchemy as well as Medicine.

THE PREPARATION OF THE SWEET OIL OF VITRIOL.

(GLAUBER, Part I., p. 21, b.)

Commonly in all fat soils or clayey grounds—especially in the white—there is found a kind of stone, round or oval in form, and in size like to a pigeon's or hen's egg, and smaller also, viz., as the joint of one's finger. On the outside this stone is black, and is therefore not esteemed when it is found, but cast away as a contemptible thing; but if it be cleansed from the earth, and beaten to pieces, it looks within of a fair yellow, having streaks, like a gold marcasite, or a rich gold ore, but there is no other taste to be perceived in it than in other ordinary stones, and although it be made into powder and boiled a long time in water, yet it does not alter at all, nor is there in the water any other taste or colour than there was at first (when it was poured upon the stone) to be perceived.

Now this stone is nothing else but the best and purest minera (or ore of vitriol), or a seed of metals, for Nature has framed it round, like unto a vegetable seed, and sown it in the earth ; out of this there may be made an excellent medicine, as follows :

Take this ore, beaten to pieces, and for some space of time lay or expose it to the cool air; within twenty or thirty days it will magnetically attract a certain saltish moisture out of the air, and grow heavy by it ; at last it falls to pieces as a black powder, which must remain there further still until it grow white, and until it do taste sweet upon the tongue like vitriol. Afterwards put it in a dry vessel, and pour on so much pure water so that it shall cover it by one or two inches. Stir it about several times in a day, and after a few days the water will be coloured green. This you must pour off. Add more pure water, and proceed as before, stirring it often until that also come to be green. This must be repeated so often till no more water be coloured by standing upon it. Then let all the green waters poured off run through filtering paper, to purify them, and then, in a glass body, cut off short, let them evaporate till a skin appear on the top. Hereupon set it in a cool place, and there will shoot out little green stones, which are nothing else but a pure vitriol. The remaining green water evaporate again, and let it shoot as before, and this evaporating and crystallising must be continued until no more vitriol will shoot, but in warm and cold places there will remain still a deep green, pleasant, sweet liquor, or juice, which is the true, sweet, and green oil of vitriol, and has all the virtues elsewhere related.

But now this green oil may further be reduced (many fair colours appearing meanwhile), without fire, to a blood-red, sweet, and pleasant oil, which goes far beyond the green both in pleasantness and virtue, and is, by comparison, like a ripe grape to an unripe one.

It is to be admired that this ore or metallic seed, which may justly be called the gold of physicians (as so good a medicine can be made of it), is not changed or altered in the earth, like other things that grow in it, but always keeps the same form and shape until it comes to the air. For first it swells and grows as a vegetable seed does in the earth, while this grows out of the air. For within four weeks at furthest it turns black, and a fortnight after it becomes white, and then green, and lastly the fairest red, and a most pleasant medicine.

Our Secret Sal Ammoniac.
(Glauber, Part II., p. 178, b.)

Take of oil of vitriol, excellently well deflagrated and rectified, one pound, upon which oil of vitriol leisurely pour so much highly rectified spirit of urine as may completely neutralise the acid spirit.

In this conjunction, from two contraries, arises a neutral salt.

This operation being rightly performed, there results a sharp and penetrating liquor, in which there is a power of carrying upwards with itself the purest essences of animals, vegetables, and metals, which is what no other entity in Nature is able to perform, as remains to be shewn. Therefore, if a pure, dry salmiac be wished for from this salt liquor, then the solution is to be evaporated at a gentle heat, and the water abstracted, when a fair white salt remains at the bottom of the dish, which is our secret sal ammoniac. By benefit of this wondrous works may be performed, both in Medicine and Chemistry.

To Make all Corrosives Sweet.
(Glauber, Part II., p. 69, b.)

Vitriol, distilled with salt, yields a corrosive spirit, but if coal dust be mixed with them they give a sweet spirit, which graduates Luna into Sol, when digested therein.

A Sweet, Graduating Spirit, for Bettering Metals.

The various metals mixed with coal dust and sal mirabilis, yield, by distillation, a sweet spirit, exalting some metals into Sol.

The Volatile Salt of Animals.

The volatile salt of animals, and especially of man, purifies all things by its volatilising virtue, as appears in our most secret sal ammoniac.

The Tinctures of Mars and of Antimony.

If we precipitate these tinctures of Mars and antimony with the solution of

Sol, and then edulcorate and dry the same, we do by this means obtain a dry graduating water, which, being molten with any white or red metals, makes them yield good gold and Luna on the cupel, to the great profit of the artist.

THE SIGNED STAR OF ANTIMONY.

Take one part of the regulus of antimony, and four parts of pure tin. Melt them in a crucible, pour them out, and let them cool. The said mass makes all iron and steel fusible. This alloy of tin and antimony, added to twice its weight of iron or steel, heated to redness in a crucible, quickly brings out fusion on still further urging the heat to perfect whiteness.

This substance is hard enough to strike fire with flint.

A PANACEA OF ANTIMONY (STIBIUM).
(GLAUBER, Part II., p. 107, a.)

The preparation does for the most part consist in the calcination by nitre, which corrects and changes the venom and immature quality of the antimony. Then, subsequently, the pure part is extracted by spirit of wine, and becomes a tender and light red powder, which can effect those things that have been ascribed to it. It should be taken of a morning fasting, some hours before meals.

Dose: one, two, three, or four grains.

A Good and Useful Medicine of Antimony.

Pulverise antimony, and put it in a clean and dry glass retort. Distil it over a strong fire, three or four times, till it be a red powder. Extract it with vinegar, and circulate extract ten days over a gentle fire. Then remove vinegar by distillation. Transfuse what remains, by a skilful process, into the oil.

N.B.—This extract must be made volatile with spirit of wine.

Let the humidity of this oil be removed by circulation, so that it becomes a dry powder.

Four grains of this oil, taken with St. Benedict's Cordial, cures quotidian, tertian, and quartan fevers, if the patient be well covered and perspire freely.

The same dose is an efficacious remedy against the plague, when it is taken with vinegar or with spirit of wine, according as the disease makes itself felt by an excess of heat or cold.

THE PRAXIS, ETC.

Mingle and melt so much regulus of antimony with the imperfect metals as may render them friable and brittle, that they may be pulverised.

With this mix three parts of the purest nitre, and put the mixture, closely stopped up, upon a fire, in glass or earthen vessels, for some hours, in order to fix. Afterwards take them off, and, as they are melted, pour them out that they may yield the regulus, which is to be taken away, and put with lead (plumbum), into a cupel, and reduced to dross. Then that gold and silver which the imperfect metal or mineral got in the fixation stays in the cupel, and may be examined by the lesser weights of probation, whence it will appear how great a fixation so little time will produce.

An Experiment with Mercury of Antimony.

(Glauber, Part II., p. 183, a.)

Take of antimony, pulverised, one pound; of our sal ammoniac, half a pound. These, well mixt, distil by retort, and our salmiac will come off, and, by the alembic, will carry with itself the most pure mercury and sulphur of the antimony, of a black ash colour, which sublimate is named the head of the crow. For, if a little of it be thrown into pure water, the sal will melt, and the mercury and sulphur will remain in the vessel as a grey powder, which, when dried and then touched, appears as thin, light feathers, whence it has acquired the name of the crow's head. Heated to redness in a crucible, it melts into a red stone.

Put the grey sublimate, or crow's

head, which did ascend, into a glass body, and upon it pour so much of my tartar as is needful for neutralisation ; then lute a head thereto, closely fitting a receiver, and administer fire in sand until all the humidity shall ascend. This being done, the acidity remains with the salt of tartar, and the spirit of urine ascends alone, carrying upwards with itself the most pure invisible mercury of antimony, which then, by the aid of Sol or Lune, becomes fixt and visible.

From one pound of the mercurial water scarcely three or four grains of the corporeal mercury will ascend.

Nevertheless, the subjects whence it is extracted are cheap, and enough of them may always be had.

———

THE CROW'S HEAD.

(GLAUBER, Part II., p. 183, a, b.)

Now, returning to our crow's head, let us see whether it may be made white, by a lotion of a sharp lixivium. If you take the glass out of the sand, after you have once thence extracted the mercurial water, you will find your black crow turned into a white swan. For, in the glass you will find a snow-like salt, which, if you take out and put into another round glass, or philosophic egg, and set it in a fixatory furnace to be fixt, then the white colour in twenty-four hours waxes yellow, and a little after puts on a blood-red colour. Yet it is not then so well fixt as that it may be taken out, but must be suffered to stand for some time in burning coals, with this caution always, that the fire be no stronger than that by which the red stone may be liquefied, like an oil. For it melts as easily as wax, and neither the mercury, nor the sulphur, nor the salt, will evaporate. Which is that which affects the mind with admiration. Whence it may be concluded that the same operation may be done, and such fixation made, in an open fire, in a covered crucible.

After it is fixt, it may be used with admirable profit in Medicine and Chemistry.

TRIAL.

Put an iron wire into the liquefied mass, and take up a small quantity for proof. Wash away the salt from it, and cast the red powder upon a silver plate red-hot. If it fume not, but enters and tinges the silver, not with a black, but with a yellow colour, then the mercury with its sulphur is fixt.

TRIUMPHAL CAR OF ANTIMONY.
(The Physician's Commentary on BASIL VALENTINE.)

Take best Hungarian, or other, crude antimony. Pulverise it. Spread it on an earthenware dish, provided with a low margin. Place dish on a calcinating furnace over the fire (which must be at first moderate). As soon as the antimony begins to fume, stir it about with an iron spoon. Continue the stirring until the fumes entirely cease, and the antimony adheres together in the form of small globules. Remove the whole from the fire, pulverise it again, place on

fire, and stir until there be no more
fumes (as before).

This calcination must be continued
till the antimony gives out no more fume,
does not conglomerate into globules,
and has the appearance of pure white
ashes.

Place the calcined antimony in a
crucible, such as goldsmiths use for melting gold and silver. Set it over a
violent fire till the antimony becomes
liquid like pure water.

To prove whether antimony has
acquired its proper glassy transparency,
dip into it an oblong piece of cold iron,
and examine the antimony which cleaves
to it carefully. If it be clear, pure, and
transparent, it is all right, and has attained
its due maturity.

Glass, whether prepared from
metals, minerals, or any other substance, must be subjected to heat, until
it has attained to maturity, and exhibits
a clear and pellucid transparency, else it
is unprofitable for any other medicinal
development.

When antimony has become vitrified in the way described, heat a flat, broad, copper dish over the fire, pour the antimony into it in as clear and thin a state as possible, and there results a pure, yellow, pellucid glass of antimony.

This preparation of what is called glass of antimony is the best, simplest, and most efficacious known.

A Safe Medicinal Preparation.
(Ibid.)

Take the above-mentioned glass of antimony. Melt it in a crucible until one-third part evaporates. Pound it fine. Pour on it rectified spirit of wine. Close, and allow to circulate for three months. Extract spirit of wine by distillation, when it will be red, and may then be kept as an excellent medicine.

This substance, dissolved in a glass of wine, acts as a gentle purgative, or as an emetic.

The dose must be adapted to the strength of the patient.

THE EXTRACTOR : THE BALM OF ANTIMONY, ETC.

(The Physician's Commentary on BASIL VALENTINE.)

Take pure glass of antimony, prepared in the best way. Pound it as fine as the finest flour. Place it in a broad-bottomed glass vessel. Pour over the antimony some highly-rectified vinegar. Subject it to digestive fire, or in summer time expose it to the sun. Shake and agitate it several times a day.

Let this slow digestion be continued until the vinegar assumes a red or yellow colour, like unto that of purified gold. Now pour off this clear and pure extracted substance. Add more vinegar. Repeat the process till no more gold-coloured tincture can be extracted.

Mix all the extract; place it in a vessel; put on the cover; distil off the vinegar, till there remains at the bottom a gold-coloured powder.

Pour on this powder distilled rain water; let it evaporate by distillation;

add more pure water; repeat this till all the acidity is washed out, and there remains a sweet and pleasant powder.

N.B.—The size of the vessel should not be larger than the quantity of the extract requires.

When two-thirds of the tincture have evaporated, change the vessel, and distil the remaining tincture in a smaller vessel, till there remains a thickish paste. If the powder be drained altogether of moisture, it is better.

The method by which it may be known whether the powder is as sweet and free from acidity as it should be, is to take and taste a little of the water which has been drained off by evaporation. Great care must be taken to distinguish between the acidity of the vinegar and that of the antimony, which latter constitutes the strength of the same.

This sweet powder should be pounded in a hot mortar, put into a glass vessel, and highly rectified spirit of wine poured on to it. Expose it to a gentle digestive heat, as above, and there then results a beautiful red tincture, with an earthy sediment at the bottom of the glass.

The extract is sweet and pleasant to the taste.

The sediment still retains its poisonous character, but the tincture is a wonderfully potent external remedy.

Dose : Three or four grains of this medicine cure leprosy, and the French disease. It purifies the blood, dispels melancholy, resists all poison, removes asthma and all chest complaints, and relieves the stitch in the side. It restores the whole organism to the most perfect health.

NOTE.

The tincture described in the text has all the virtues attributed to it, but its use should be continued for some time, in order to secure its full benefits

The yellow powder mentioned above, from which the extract has not yet been made by means of alcohol, should be pounded on a stone (hot) and placed in an egg, boiled hard, from which the yolk has been taken out.

Leave the powder in a humid place till it is dissolved into a yellow liquid. This tincture, used as a liniment, is an excellent remedy for all wounds and bruises. After application, bandage with clean linen.

GLASS OF ANTIMONY BROUGHT TO AN OIL.

(Physician's Commentary on BASIL VALENTINE.)

Take glass of antimony, and pound it to a fine powder. Extract the tincture by means of distilled vinegar. Remove all traces of acidity by washing and distillation of the water. Add to the residue some of our spirit of wine. Circulate the solution in a pelican vessel for the space of a month; dextrously distil it, without the addition of anything else. The result is a red oil, from which the fire stone is afterwards formed. It is a sweet, pleasant, and wonderful sort of medicine. This oil is the quintessence, or the highest form, of antimony.

There must be four preparations before antimony is perfect. The first preparation is calcination and liquefaction into glass ; the second is digestion, by which the extract is perfected ; the third is coagulation ; the fourth is its distillation into an oil (separation of subtle from gross).

Then follows fixation by the last coagulation, and thereby there results the pellucid fiery stone, which can operate on metals only when it is fermented and rendered penetrative.

The distilled oil accomplishes all purposes for which it can be employed by the skilful physician.

This oil, if properly used, is truly a universal medicine.

The said medicine acts like magic, especially in all kinds of fevers. Dropsy is completely cured by it, if two doses of the said oil be taken in daily doses of four to eight grains, morning and evening.

It restores youth, dispels melancholy, and the hair and the nails are renewed.

————

GLASS OF ANTIMONY BROUGHT TO AN OIL OF GREAT VALUE IN SO-CALLED ELLIPTICAL CASES.

(Physician's Commentary on BASIL VALENTINE.)

Pound the glass of antimony to a fine powder; add omphacium; digest for some. days in a broad-bottomed vessel, well closed from the air. Continue this until all the moisture is abstracted. Pound it with a double quantity of clarified sugar, moistened with spirit of vinegar. Put the mixture into a retort, and distil, at the end, with a strong heat. Then there appears a red oil, which must be clarified with spirit of wine.

To this oil add a little spirit of salt, and pour the whole into a subtle preparation of calx of gold (described in my other works: B.V.).

When they are distilled together it assumes the tincture of gold, and it leaves the body intact.

THIS IS HOW THE OPERATION WAS CARRIED OUT IN THE YEAR OF GRACE 1665.

The red oil in the retort was rectified, and a white oil was obtained, of a pleasant acid taste. To it was added half as much spirit of salt. The mixture was next digested together in a retort for the space of a month, and then still further amalgamated by distillation. It was afterwards poured on the calx of gold, and digested for one month's time, until it was of a golden colour.

Thereupon I removed the liquid, sweetened the powder with distilled rain water, and again extracted the tincture with spirit of wine.

Then I restored that winged red dragon, gave him his tail to eat for six entire months, and obtained a most sweet and pleasant tincture, eight grains of which remove, by means of perspiration, the morbific matter of every curable disease.

The solvent which is employed must not only be sweet and free from corrosive properties, it must also be of a nature homogeneous with that of the substances on which it is poured, in order that it may extract from the mercury thereof a good and pure sulphur. Rectified spirit of wine is the most congenial to the sulphur of our substance, which does not amalgamate with the spirit of salt.

The tincture is very precious ; but it has mostly the colour and little of the weight of the potable gold of the sages.

When the fermentation (described in the text) has taken place, the medicine which results is wonderfully efficacious.

When you have brought antimony to this pass, you may justly boast that you have solved the enigma of the sages, and that you have learnt the Magistery— a Magistery known but to few.

Triumphal Car of Antimony.

(Physician's Commentary on Basil Valentine.)

Take one part of pulverised antimony, and one part of Armenian sal ammoniac. Mix, put into a retort, and distil together.

(Note, that the retort should consist of A, furnace; B, retort; C, receiver; D, tube between receiver and alembic, E. F is a furnace which sublimes by its moderate heat all that is in the receiver into alembic E. Thus the substance which is distilled from the retort (B) is immediately sublimed by the heat of the furnace (F).

On the product of the distillation now pour hot distilled rain water, and so remove every salt and acid taste. Then the antimony will be of a pure, feathery white. Dry with subtle heat, and place in the circulatory vessel called pelican. Pour on it highly rectified spirits of vitriol, and circulate till they be properly amalgamated.

(Note, that this union should be so close that, in distillation, the two shall rise together. Amalgamation in alchemy is not merely mixing two liquids. The union must be inseparable, and the ingredients must really change and modify each other. The union should, in fact, be like that of male and female seed, which produces a real organism, and that is something more than a mere mixture of the two ingredients.)

Then distil together ; add to mixture spirit of wine, and circulate again. Remove the sediment, and you will have the antimony thoroughly amalgamated with the spirit of vitriol and of wine.

One drop of this tincture, mixed with rose-water, has greater medicinal efficacy than a whole pot-full of herbs. It proves a good appetiser and digestive, purifies the blood, and cures colic as if by magic.

The Elixir of Antimony of Basilius.
(Physician's Commentary on Basil Valentine.)

Pulverise some good (mineral) antimony with half as much salt of ammonia ; put all that is sublimed into a glass retort ; distil three times, always removing sediment. Remove salt by means of water, and reverberate the antimony over a moderate fire in a well-closed vessel, till it becomes red. Add strong distilled vinegar of wine ; extract its redness ; remove vinegar, till there remains a powder (by means of the water bath). Extract with spirit of wine, so as to remove the sediment. You will then have a clear and pure tincture. Place the spirit of wine with the tincture in a broad-bottomed distilling vessel ; add some tincture of corals and quintessence of rhubarb, and administer a dose of three or four drops.

It acts as a painless purgative, and has an exhilarating effect on the animal spirits.

AN ARCANUM OF ANTIMONY FULLY DESCRIBED.

(Physician's Commentary on BASIL VALENTINE.)

FIXATION.

Pulverise some antimony, and put it in a broad-bottomed distilling vessel. Pour upon it aqua fortis, to the height of some inches. Close stop the vessel, and expose to gentle heat for a space of ten days ; decant the extract thus obtained ; free it by filtration from all fæcal impurities ; place it in a glass vessel, and remove the aqua fortis by means of distillation.

There will then remain at the bottom a dry, yellow powder of antimony. Pour on it distilled rain water ; expose it in a glass vessel to moderate heat, and there results a red tincture, or extract.

Filter ; distil the water gently in a water bath, and there remains a red powder. Pour on it strong distilled vinegar, which in time is coloured red, like blood, and deposits a sediment.

Distil this vinegar, and again there remains a red powder. Reverberate this powder continuously for three days over an open fire, and extract from it the tincture with spirit of wine Strain off the sediment that remains from the spirit of wine or tincture. Again separate, by distillation, the alcohol, by water bath. and there now remains a fixed red powder of wondrous efficacy.

This fixed red powder proves a most useful medicine in chronic diseases, especially where it is important to excite perspiration, and in such cases it is said to produce the most wonderful effects.

Dose : half a drachm, thrice daily. It renovates the whole man.

THE BLOOD-RED OIL OF ANTIMONY, ETC.

(Physician's Commentary on BASIL VALENTINE.)

Take good, friable (not crude) antimony. Pulverise it, and pass it through a fine sieve. Place it in broad-bottomed distilling vessel (cucurbita). Add to it vinegar distilled from its own proper mineral, and digest it, at moderate heat, for thirty or forty days.

The vinegar will then be tinged, as it were, with blood. Pour this red tincture into a retort ; gently separate the vinegar by distillation ; and make extract of the remaining powder with spirit of wine. The extract now appears of a blood-red colour.

Pour it into a circulatory vessel, which is most suitable for this purpose. Digest the extract in the water bath, until the tincture is seen to rise and pass, in a volatile state, through the alembic.

Place the whole substance in a glass cucurbite ; distil the spirit, and when it passes through the alembic it will be of a blood-red colour.

Remove the spirit, and there remains a thick and heavy oil.

This oil proves a most efficacious universal medicine. It utterly consumes all sorts of morbific matter.

Hence the physician should not grudge the time and care which must be given to the preparation of this remedy.

THE TRUE BALM OF LIFE, OR ROYAL RED OIL OF ANTIMONY.
(Physician's Commentary on BASIL VALENTINE.)

Place pulverised Hungarian antimony in a glass cucurbite, or retort ; add true vinegar of the sages, rendered more acid by means of its salt ; close cucurbite, and plunge it in horse-dung, or the water bath, for forty days. The vinegar then turns a deep red colour.

Decant the vinegar, and keep adding more, till no more red colour can be extracted. Strain all the vinegar, and pour it into a clean vessel. Again plunge in horse-dung or use the water bath, as before. Allow the digestion to continue for thirty or forty days.

Then the body is again dissolved, and the substance becomes as black as ink. This is the sign that true solution has taken place, which will ultimately effect a separation of the elements.

Place this black substance in another cucurbite, and put on its alembic. Distil over the vinegar at a moderate heat.

The vinegar now rises as a clear fluid, and there remains at the bottom a dirty-looking substance. Pulverise this ; wash with distilled rain water ; dry gently, and place it in a long-necked circulatory vessel.

(The circulatory should resemble three hollow balls, placed one on the other, and communicating by means of tubes, with a long neck at the top.)

Add highly rectified spirit of wine, so that it covers the substance to a height of two or three inches. Close the vessel well, and expose it to gentle heat for two whole months. The spirit then becomes of a bright red colour. Pour out the extract ; filter ; place in cucurbite, and remove the black sediment.

Place the alembic on the cucurbite ; distil gently. The spirit of wine carries the tincture of antimony upwards ; the elements are separated, and the alembic and receiver both present the aspect of bright gold.

Place the red substance, which by distillation has passed into the receiver, in a circulatory vessel, for a space of ten days. By means of this circulation, separation has taken place, for the oil has thereby acquired gravity, and sinks to the bottom, while the spirit is limpid, as at first, and floats at the top. Then separate the oil from the spirit, in a separatory.

This is the substance of which all the sages and alchemists have written. This is the goal of all alchemists—the oil of antimony—the great, coveted treasure. This oil is of remarkable sweetness, most pleasant to use, and free from all corrosiveness.

No one can understand or comprehend the incredible virtue and potency of this royal oil. I call it the balm of life, because it can help those whom all physicians have given up.

It renews a man's system, just as though he were born again, purifies the blood, and, in conjunction with tincture of corals, casts out leprosy, drives away melancholy and sadness, braces up the joints and the heart. It improves the memory, and is our great sheet anchor in consumption.

———

THE MERCURY OF ANTIMONY ELICITED. (The Physician's Commentary on BASIL VALENTINE.)

Take eight parts of the king of antimony, one part of salt from human urine, clarified and sublimed; one part of sal ammoniac, and one part of salt of tartar. Put the well-mixed ingredients into a glass vessel, add strong vinegar, close up with the lute of wisdom. Digest salts with vinegar a whole month over gentle fire; put the whole into a cucurbite; distil vinegar on sand, and mix with salts thus dried three parts of Venetian earth. Distil, at a strong heat, the contents of the retort, and there results a marvellous spirit, which add to the pulverised regulus of antimony. Let them digest for two months, then distil the vinegar gently, and mix with what remains a four-fold weight of steel filings.

Distil, at a strong heat, the contents of the retort. The spirit of salt then carries the mercury with it in the form of vapour. Let it be drawn into a large glass receiver containing water; the spirit of salt mingles with the water, but the mercury is precipitated to the bottom as true mercury.

This is the way in which running mercury is prepared from antimony.

The Mercury Resolved into Oil.
(The Physician's Commentary on Basil Valentine.)

Take one part of this mercury, and four parts of strong oil of vitriol. Extract the oil, and there remains its spirit with the mercury. Sublime at a strong heat, and place all that is sublimed again at the bottom of the vessel. Pour on it as much of the oil of vitriol as before, and repeat the process three times. At the fourth time, place all that is sublimed with the sediment. Pound, and it is pure and bright as crystal. Place in circulatory, add the same quantity of oil of vitriol, and three times as much spirit of wine ; circulate till mercury be resolved into oil, floating on the rest like olive oil.

Separate this oil from the rest, place it in a circulatory, pour on it some strong distilled vinegar, leave it for twenty days, whereby the oil recovers its gravity, and drops to the bottom, while all that is poisonous in it remains in the vinegar.

This oil itself possesses marvellous efficacy in the amelioration of metals, and yields only to the King of Kings Himself.

This oil of mercury is the fourth pillar of Medicine. It stimulates the vital action of the brain, makes men active, and cures leprosy and paralysis.

If anyone has been suffering from chronic disease, and uses this oil daily for some time, his nails and hair drop off and grow again, and his whole frame is rapidly renovated, his blood purified, and all morbid matter radically expelled.

A Certain Balm, or Oil, of Antimony.

(Physician's Commentary on Basil Valentine.)

Sublime one part of antimony with a fourth part of sal ammoniac. The salt raises the sulphur of antimony to a bright red colour.

Pound the sublimed substance, and to each pound of antimony, add six more ounces of antimony. Sublime, as before, and dissolve the sublimed substance in a moist place. Wash away the salt added to it, dry gently, and there results a sulphur which burns away like that of the apothecary.

Extract its tincture with distilled vinegar. Separate the vinegar gently, at a moderate heat, transtil the remaining powder very gradually, and, if no error have been committed, there ensues an excellent oil, sweet, pleasant, and grateful in its use, without danger or corrosivity.

This oil cures consumption and all

pulmonary complaints. It relieves asthma and difficulty of breathing.

Dose : Take two grains in spirit of wine in the morning, and in the evening before retiring to rest. It purifies the chest, purges out all phlegm, and clears away every obstruction.

THE SO-CALLED VINEGAR OF ANTIMONY.
(The Physician's Commentary on BASIL VALENTINE.)

Pulverise the ore of antimony, place it in a round glass vessel with an oblong neck, pour on distilled rain water, so as to half fill the cucurbite, close well, and plunge in horse dung for putrefaction, or make use of a steam or water bath, until the ore begins to effervesce, and produces a foam on the surface. Then it is time to take it out, as it is a sign that the body has opened.

Place again in a cucurbite ; close well, extract water, which has an acid taste. When all the water is distilled, increase the heat, and the substance will be sublimed.

Pound again with the sediment, add the same water, and again extract, when it will be much more acid.

Repeat the operation until the water be as acid as ordinary vinegar. The oftener the operation is repeated, the less there is of the sublimed substance.

Pour this vinegar over some more of the raw ore, to the height of about three inches. Digest, in pelican, for twelve days, till the vinegar becomes red, and more acid than before. Decant, and distil by sand heat or water bath, when the clear vinegar will rise, while the red powder will remain at the bottom.

If an extract be made with spirit of wine, it forms an excellent medicine.

Rectify the vinegar once more, in balneo, to free it from its oiliness; dissolve it in its own salt, *i.e.*, one ounce in four ounces; sublime in ash, and the vinegar will be more acid, and acquire greater strength and efficacy.

THE STAR OF ANTIMONY.
(The Physician's Commentary on BASIL VALENTINE.)

Take two parts of Hungarian antimony, one part of steel, and melt, with four parts of burnt tartar, in an iron ladle or basin, such as is used by goldsmiths for refining gold.

Allow all to cool ; take out the regulus ; purify ; pulverise ; add to it three times as much burnt tartar ; melt ; pour into basin as before.

Repeat this three times, and the regulus becomes highly refined and brilliant. If the fusion has been properly performed—which is the point of greatest importance—there results a beautiful star of a brilliant white colour.

N.B.—In the third fusion the fire should be most intense, so as to remove any remaining impurity. The star is as distinct as if a draughtsman had traced it with a pair of compasses.

This star, with sal ammoniac, is brought to a red sublimate, for the tincture of iron ascends.

The said sublimate may be dissolved into a liquid of highly medicinal quality.

This sublimate, before being placed in a cave or cellar for dissolution, should be purged of its salt with pure water.

The alchemist has, then, a hot and ignitable substance, in which wonderful possibilities are latent.

It is dissolved into an oil, which should be purified by transfusion and distillation.

THE FIRE STONE PREPARED FROM THE OIL OF ANTIMONY.

(The Physician's Commentary on BASIL VALENTINE.)

Take equal parts of the ore of antimony and of nitre ; pulverise ; mix well ; place over a gentle fire, and bake dextrously. There remains a blackish substance. Out of this prepare glass ; pound ; extract its red tincture with strong distilled vinegar (made of the same ore). Separate the vinegar by distillation.

There remains a powder, from which should be made a second extract with highly rectified spirit of wine. We then have a beautiful, sweet, red extract, of great medicinal value. This is the pure sulphur of antimony.

If there be two pounds of this extract, take four ounces of salt of antimony ; pour over this the extract ; circulate, for at least a month, in a well-closed vessel, when the salt will unite with the extract of sulphur. Remove sediment ; extract spirit of wine in balneo ; sublime the powder which remains, and it will be distilled in the shape of a many-coloured, sweet, pellucid oil.

Rectify this oil in balneo, and when it is perfect it will be of a deep red colour.

Then take living mercury of antimony ; pour on it red oil of vitriol ; separate, by distillation, the viscidity of the mercury, and there results a precious precipitate of a glorious colour, which is of the greatest medicinal value.

Take equal parts of this precipitate and of our oil of antimony ; put the mixture into a well-closed phial. If exposed to gentle heat, the precipitate will gradually be dissolved, and fixed in the oil. For the fire consumes its viscidity, and it becomes a red, dry, fixed, and fluid powder, which does not give out the slightest fume.

This is the great medicine.

THE PREPARATION OF THE TINCTURE OF GOLD AND ANTIMONY.

(GLAUBER, Part I., p. 78, b.)

Take of pure gold ½ oz. Dissolve it in aqua regia. Precipitate the solution with liquor of flints, and wash and dry the same. Take regulus martis, beaten fine, with which mix three parts of the purest nitre. Place the mixture in a crucible heated to low redness. Let the heat be now much increased, till the mass becomes rich purple. Grind the cooled mass very fine, and to four parts of this mixture add one part of the

aforesaid golden calx. Put the ingredients into a strong crucible, with
cover on, and give a heat of fusion, when
the calx of gold will assume the antimonial nitre, and a mass of an amethyst
colour will result. Allow this substance
to remain fused till it puts on the clear
redness of a ruby. Nitre or tartar may
now be added, in a small quantity, in
order to promote fusion.

Lastly, pour forth the matter, when
it shall have come to the utmost redness of a ruby, and suffer the heated
mass to thoroughly cool. The oriental
ruby-coloured mass is now to be
powdered, while still warm, and the
tincture extracted by the addition of
spirit of wine. The gold, together with
the antimony, will remain very white (like
the finest talc), and may be washed with
water and recovered by precipitation.

The coloured tincture proves a
sovereign remedy in many respects.

THE END.

SOME MODERN ALCHEMICAL
EXPERIMENTS.

SOME
MODERN ALCHEMICAL
EXPERIMENTS.

CONTENTS.

———

6   *Contents.*

MODERN ALCHEMICAL EXPERIMENTS.

THE PREPARATION OF MAGNESIUM BY ELECTROLYSIS.

The metal may be readily obtained from a fused mixture of four at. chloride of magnesium, and three at. chloride of potassium, with a little sal-ammoniac.

A simple and convenient mode of effecting the reduction is to fuse the mixture in a common clay tobacco pipe, over a lamp: the negative electrode being formed of an iron wire passed up the pipe stem, and the positive electrode of a piece of gas coke, just touching the surface of the fused chlorides.

THE PREPARATION OF CERTAIN METALS BY MEANS OF ELECTROLYSIS.

The positive electrode is formed of the inner concave surface of a carbon crucible, filled with muriatic acid, and standing within a porcelain crucible. The liquid to be decomposed is contained in a small porous cell, standing in the carbon crucible, and the negative electrode is formed of a wire or narrow slip of platinum dipping into the liquid. The whole is heated over the sand-bath.

A concentrated solution of chrome, or of manganese chloride, subjected in this manner to the action of a four-pair Bunsen battery, quickly yields large lumps of the metal, chemically pure.

DEPOSITION OF THE EARTH-METALS BY ELECTROLYSIS.

Corbelli has deposited aluminum, or other earth-metal, by electrolysing a mixed solution of rock alum, or sulphate of aluminum, and chloride of sodium, with an anode of iron wire, coated with an insulating material, and dipping into mercury placed at the bottom of the solution, the negative pole of zinc being immersed in the solution. Aluminum is then deposited on the zinc, and the chlorine set free at the positive pole unites with the mercury to form calomel.

DEPOSITION OF THE EARTH-METALS BY ELECTROLYSIS.

Aluminum, or other earth-metal, is deposited by the single cell method from a dilute solution of the chloride. The liquid is to be placed in a jar, in which is immersed a porous cell containing dilute sulphuric acid. An amalgamated zinc plate is immersed in the acid solution, and a plate of copper in the chloride solution, the two metals being connected by a copper conducting wire. At the end of some hours the copper plate becomes coated with a lead-coloured deposit of the earth-metal, which, when burnished, presents the same degree of whiteness as platinum.

ELECTRO-DEPOSITIONS OF THE EARTH-METALS.

An American process consists in depositing the earth-metal from a solution of a double salt of the earth in question, and potassium, of the specific gravity 1·161, employing a current from three or more Bunsen cells, the bath being worked at 140 Fahr.

PREPARATION OF THE EARTH-METALS BY REDUCTION.

This process consists in forming a solution composed of freshly precipitated earth, dissolved in a boiling solution of cyanide of potassium.

A MODIFICATION OF THIS PROCESS IS THUS DESCRIBED.

Calcined alum is dissolved in a solution of boiling cyanide of potassium.

REDUCTION OF THE EARTH-METALS BY MEANS OF POTASSIUM-CYANIDE.

The chloride, iodide, or bromide of the earth-metal to be reduced is brought in contact with either the melted cyanide or its vapour. A portion of pure anhydrous oxide may be added to increase the product.

REDUCTION OF THE EARTH-METALS FROM THE SULPHIDE.

The earth-metal may be reduced and obtained from the sulphide, either by heating it in hydrogen, or by heating it with the pure earth of the metal to be reduced; or with its sulphate in such proportion that the oxygen contained in that compound is just sufficient to convert the sulphur into sulphureous acid.

The earth-metals may also be obtained by decomposing the sulphide with an ordinary metal, such as iron, copper, or zinc. _____

ELECTRO-DEPOSITION OF THE EARTH METALS.

Aluminum is deposited upon a plate of copper in a solution of the double chloride of the earth and ammonia, by using a strong current, the deposit being susceptible of a brilliant polish.

_____

ELECTRO-DEPOSITION OF CERTAIN EARTH-METALS.

A strong current of electricity will deposit magnesium from an aqueous solution of the double chloride of magnesium and ammonium, upon a sheet of copper, in a few minutes ; the deposit will be homogeneous, strongly adherent, and readily polished.

ELECTRO-DEPOSITION OF ALUMINUM OR GLUCINUM.

Bunsen electrolised the fused chloride (or fluoride) of aluminum and sodium in a deep, covered, porcelain crucible, divided by a partition of porous porcelain which extended half way down the vessel. Carbon electrodes were used, and these were introduced through the opening in the cover. He used a current from ten cells of his zinc and carbon battery. The salt will be fused at the boiling point of mercury, and readily yield the metal. The temperature of the liquid should then be raised to near the melting point of silver, when the particles of liberated aluminum fuse and unite together into globules, which, being heavier than the fused salt, deposit at the bottom of the crucible.

SEPARATION OF THE EARTH-METALS FROM THEIR SALTS.

Cryolite (fluoride of Al. and Na.) 5 pts.
Sodium chloride . . . . . . 2½ ,,
Sodium . . . . 2 ,,

The pulverised mineral is well mixed with half its weight of well-dried common salt, and the mixture is arranged with sodium, in alternate layers, in an earthen crucible (lined with pure carbon), a layer of pure cryolite being placed at top, and the whole covered with a stratum of " decrepit " salt. The mass is rapidly heated till it melts completely, and is then left to cool, after being stirred with a clay or iron rod.

The aluminum is generally found in large globules.

SEPARATION OF THE EARTH-METALS FROM THEIR SALTS.

Fluoride of glucinum & potassium 5 pts.
Sodium chloride . . . . . 2½ ,,
Sodium . . . . 2 ,,

The pulverised double fluoride is mixed with half its weight of well-dried common salt, and the mixture is arranged in alternate layers with clean sodium in an earthen crucible, lined with pure carbon, a layer of pure double fluoride being placed at top, and the whole covered with some well-dried common salt.

The mass is thoroughly heated to the point of fusion, and then allowed to cool, after being stirred with a clay or iron rod.

The glucinum is generally found in large globules.

SEPARATION OF THE EARTH-METALS FROM THEIR SALTS.

Chloride of aluminum and sodium 10 pts.
Fluor spar, or cryolite . . . . 5 ,,
Sodium . . . . 2 ,,

The different ingredients, perfectly dry and pure, and finely powdered, are placed, together with the sodium, in alternate layers in a carbon crucible, which is moderately heated till the action begins, and afterwards to bright redness, the mass being stirred with a rod of iron or clay, and afterwards poured out.

If the process goes on well, the aluminum is obtained in a compact mass, and partly in fused globules encrusted in a hard mass.

SEPARATION OF THE EARTH-METALS FROM THEIR SALTS, ETC.

Chloride of glucinum and sodium 10 pts.
Fluor spar . . . . 5 ,,
Sodium . . . . 2 ,,

The different ingredients, perfectly dry and pure, and finely powdered, are placed, together with the sodium, in alternate layers in a carbon crucible, which is moderately heated till the action begins, and afterwards to bright redness, the melted mass being stirred with a rod of iron or clay, and then poured out.

If the process goes on well, the glucinum is obtained in a compact mass, and partly in fused globules, encrusted in a hard mass.

PRESERVATION OF
KALIUM, NATRIUM, ETC., WITH BRIGHT
METALLIC SURFACE.

Place the pure metal in a basin containing absolute alcohol, till it acquires a perfectly bright surface : then quickly transfer it to a basin containing chemically pure petroleum ether, and finally to a third containing a saturated solution of chemically pure naphthaline in petroleum ether. In this last solution the sodium or potassium remains unaltered.

PREPARATION OF THE TRI-OXIDE (CALX) OF GOLD.

Gold tri-oxide is a blackish-brown powder, obtained by heating the hydroxide to 100 degrees (C). If this be more strongly heated, it gives off oxygen, and is converted into a brown powder of metallic gold.

Gold tri-hydroxide is obtained by heating a solution of gold tri-chloride with an excess of magnesia, and well washing the precipitate with nitric acid.

The gold solution may also be treated with caustic potassa, till the precipitate formed is re-dissolved, and then the dark brown solution is boiled till it becomes of a light yellow colour, a slight excess of sulphuric acid being added, and the precipitate washed. The hydroxide thus prepared always contains a little potassa, and for this reason it is dissolved in strong nitric acid, again precipitated by water, and then dried (in vacuo).

A better plan, perhaps, is to warm a dilute solution of gold tri-chloride with caustic potash, and precipitate the brown solution by Glauber-salt, when it is obtained in a form resembling precipitated ferric hydroxide.

A solution of gold with muriatic acid in excess yields, with an excess of potash bi-carbonate, an olive green precipitate. If, however, the gold solution contains excess of nitric acid, then an orange-red precipitate separates out of the solution.

Silver Transmuted into Gold by the Action of Light.

In the focus of a burning-glass, twelve inches in diameter, place a glass flask, two inches in diameter, containing nitric acid, diluted with its own volume of water.

Pour into the nitric acid, alternately, small quantities of a solution of nitrate of silver and of muriatic acid, the object being to cause the chloride of silver to form in a minutely divided state, so as to produce a milky fluid, into the interior of which the brilliant convergent cone may pass, and the currents generated in the flask by the heat may so drift all the chloride successively through the light.

The chloride, if otherwise exposed to the sun, merely blackens on the surface, the interior parts undergoing no change : this difficulty, therefore, has to be avoided. The burning-glass promptly brings on a decomposition of the salt, evolving, on the one hand, chlorine, and disengaging a metal on the other. Supposing the experiment to last two or three entire hours, the effect will then be equal to a continuous mid-day sun of some seventy-two hours. The metal becomes disengaged very well. But what is it? It cannot be silver, since nitric acid has no action upon it. It burnishes in an agate mortar, but its reflection is not like that of silver, for it is yellowish, like that of gold.

The light must therefore have so transmuted the original silver as to enable it to exist in the presence of nitric acid.

THE END.

Printed in the United States
84983LV00006B/40/A

9 781564 593443

Enjoying Wildlife

Fifty years with the British Naturalists' Association in Hertfordshire

Edited by Graeme Smith
Line drawings by Chris Doncaster and Michael Clark

GW00630517

Published by Training Publications Limited

3 Finway Court, Whippendell Road, Watford, Hertfordshire, WD1 7EN

Cover photographs:
Painted lady butterfly, *John Stevens*
Badger, *Michael Clark*
Great crested grebe, *John Stevens*
Southern marsh orchid, *John Stevens*
Greater spotted woodpecker, *Chris Doncaster*
Corn poppies, *Graeme Smith*
Fallow deer, *Michael Clark*
Frogmore Gravel Pits, Stevenage (background), *Graeme Smith.*

Text set in Bookman, 9 point on 11

ISBN   1 84019 001 9

1st Edition

Printed by Training Publications Limited

Motorway verges form a happy hunting ground for kestrels

There is a pleasure
      in the pathless woods,

There is a rapture
      on the lonely shore,

There is society,
      where none intrudes,

By the deep sea,
      and music in its roar.

I love not man the less
      but nature more.

Byron 1788-1824

CONTENTS

Foreword
Richard Mabey

There has been much wistful speculation over the past year or so about the demise of the amateur naturalist. Today fieldwork has become hard-edged and statistical, driven by the demands of a career structure or by the important but necessarily sombre needs of conservation. Where are the naturalists who roamed and stared and counted for the sheer joy of it, the ecstatic but meticulous obsessions with the 'minute particulars' of nature? Gone along with the water meadows and nightingales maybe.

But I have never shared these pessimistic regrets, and this collection of memoirs, anecdotes and manifestos by members of the Hertfordshire Branch of the British Naturalists' Association decisively proves the amateur naturalist to be alive, well and still in thrall to the natural world, at least in this patch of the Home Counties. And what a picture of passionate enthusiasms they conjure up. A commuter to the City of London in the 1950s regularly seeing a dozen black redstarts in his lunch-hour. Minute studies of everything from smuts to whole woods. Fungus forays in Epping Forest, cross-county treks, and night-long rambles to take in owls, the dawn chorus *and* a good breakfast. One unvarying field characteristic of amateur naturalists is the sheer fun they have from their occupation.

Of course there is much to be sad about too, and as this book is shot through with an elegiac sense of just how rich the countryside of the late 40s and 50s was compared to today. I too can remember when the streams not only still flowed through the chalk, but were sparkling clean, when most villages had their barn owls and most heaths their nightjars. No wonder, perhaps, that there are now more professional conservation biologists than field naturalists. But I am sure that behind their earnestness still beat the hearts of children who were enraptured by their first sight of a water spider's diving bell, and that they are better and more compassionate scientists because of it.

But there have been gains as well as losses in Hertfordshire, and the field naturalist understands better than anyone just how adaptable and inventive nature can be. There are new habitats and new species, motorway verges and muntjac deer. Badgers prosper and our celebrated bluebell woods cock a snook at an increasingly unpredictable climate. And stealing amongst them, through Northaw Great Wood or Panshanger or along the Mimram, can still be glimpsed the enthralled figure of the native Hertfordshire naturalist, searching for horse-stingers and devil's darning needles.

© 1998   Richard Mabey

Introduction
Graeme Smith

Enjoying wildlife is as easy as you make it. It can be done from an armchair, while pottering around the house and garden or while shopping in town. With a little more effort, a trip to the countryside will provide more interesting, perhaps rarer or more ancient experiences. Search for wildlife or let it visit you. Sit quietly in a wood for half-an-hour and it will certainly come to you; birds will become curious, shrews and mice will be less cautious in their grassy runs, spiders, beetles and ants will pass by and camouflaged beasts and bugs will reveal themselves. I remember once sitting in Derry's Wood, near Wormley Wood, and watching a few yards away a grasshopper warbler, whose back end shook vigorously with the exertion of singing. Study a particular group in detail and the wonder will last a lifetime. The subject matter is endless and the beauty is more than skin deep.

The Hertfordshire Branch of the BNA has been grubbing and poking around the County for over 53 years. From the start, reports of rambles and members' observations have been brought together in our so-called *Bulletin*, a worthy historical and social document and local wildlife record. This book celebrates the 100th edition of our 'nature log'. In this special edition, we have dropped the usual accounts of walks and we have elicited essays from our members reflecting our interests and reminiscences. I hope some of this enthusiasm rubs off. If you would like details of the Hertfordshire BNA please write for details to Mrs C. James, 56 Back Street, Ashwell, Baldock, Hertfordshire. SG7 5PE. We have a very varied programme of events, with a ramble or indoor meeting about once a fortnight.

Finally, none of this book would have been possible without the efforts of our tireless *Bulletin* editors and their helpers. We owe them a great debt. They have been:

1950-66	Eileen Aspden
1966-69	Ann White
1969-74	Trevor James
1975-81	Frank Lancaster
1982-85	Angus Bell
1985 to present	Graeme Smith

Acknowledgements
Graeme Smith

Many enthusiasts have contributed in various ways to our small, but beautiful book. First thanks must go to those BNA members who sent in articles, sometimes unbidden, for our enterprise.

This book was produced by a small committee and I am especially grateful to Chris Doncaster for helping edit several drafts, for producing the superb line drawings and not least for his fund raising activities. The Revd Tom Gladwin arranged a publications grant of £1,200, offered financial advice, stimulation and made sure deadlines were met. Chris James, as Branch Chairman, ensured the Branch's needs were considered and Barry Peck provided valuable liaison with the publisher. Peter Alton undertook vital publicity.

Other contributions and facilities for which we are grateful are; calligraphy from Pat Lancaster, the *Foreword* from Richard Mabey, a hornbeam and other drawings by Michael Clark, typing from Kathy Hall and scanning and OCR software support from Whitby Bird & Partners. We also are indebted to the publishers Training Publications Ltd. for generous and professional advice, several experts who refereed articles (Steve Brooks, Colin Plant, Raymond Uffen and Trevor James), and Dr. D. Applin, editor of *Country-side* for permission to print the butterfly eggs article.

1. **In the Beginning**
John Pearton

A founder member of the Hertfordshire Branch of the British Naturalists'
Association recalls our early days.

During the second world war I joined the British Empire Naturalists' Association (BENA) and went out once or twice with the Ruislip Branch. Then came the end of hostilities and Richard Ward, who had been transferred from London to the Liverpool office of the shipping company for which I worked, came back to Barnet and bought a bungalow in Potters Bar. We then found out that we both belonged to the BENA.

It was then, around 1945, that Dick Ward and his wife Margaret invited BENA members to their home one Saturday afternoon to form a new local branch, the North Middlesex branch, later the Hertfordshire & North Middlesex Branch and then just the Hertfordshire branch. In essence, the North Middlesex Branch was formed around the nucleus of BENA Ruislip Branch members who lived in or near North London. The rambles programme was arranged to suit train and bus timetables with fortnightly meetings alternately Saturday afternoon/all day Sunday with a cafe tea before the return home. However, afternoon walks in winter were not thought worthwhile because of the early dusk; most of us worked on Saturday mornings in those days. Many of the areas visited were very local and would now seem rather suburban, such as Whitewebbs Park, Scratchwood, Hadley Wood, Elstree Reservoir and the country around Potters Bar, Cuffley and London Colney.

The *Bulletin* was started by Ken and myself in 1950 and was a light-hearted and simple affair with articles ranging from the serious to the flippant. How gratifying it is to know that it has been kept up all these years. I think the Branch has been remarkable for its continuity of membership and for managing to remain small and friendly, and yet attracting new members to prevent stagnation. May the Branch and its *Bulletin* continue to flourish.

With best wishes

2. The Bulletins
Jennifer Beeston
and Diana Furley

This is a review of the Bulletins up to 1996. In the early days the Society was called "British Empire Naturalists' Association" and at that time we were the "North Middlesex Branch."

Looking back it is satisfying that the people who were the first members in the BNA from its early days in the fifties, the Peartons and Honnors, the Gladwins and Sages, and from the sixties Frank Lancaster and Trevor James, members who have contributed so much to its history and development, are still part of the group or in close touch with it. This gives a valuable sense of continuity.

In the fifties the group was small and growth was initially slow. By 1959 there were only 26 members. It was not until the later sixties that membership roared away, reaching 61 in 1969, the year when 31 people turned out for the Ouse washes meeting. Rather too much of a good thing perhaps! This small membership did not matter. There was tremendous energy and enterprise in the variety of activities which were undertaken. For example, the two studies of Trent Park and Northaw Great Wood described later, were major achievements in which Bryan Sage was the prime mover, giving the group direction and aim at this time.

June and John Pearton along with Ken Honnor and Eileen Aspden did so much to keep things going in the fifties. Long-serving committee members such as Mary Blake, L.C. Pagniez or "Pag" and Graham Horsley gave us good service, likewise Ron Freeman, who joined in the mid-sixties and is still a member. Ray and Phil White did crucial work on the Trent Park survey. A central figure of the fifties was Mr. F Clarke, the first president until his death in 1958, highly knowledgeable in botany and mycology.

In the early days, copies of the bulletins were posted from member to member, a system that continued until 1983 when personal copies were at last available. They included not only rambles reports but also a wealth of other items such as quizzes, puzzles, articles contributed by branch members and even some excellent watercolour miniatures by Mr. Clarke.

Gordon Vaughan worked in the City of London. In 1950 he wrote about the bird populations of London's bombed sites including the black redstart which he describes as being quite common - "one can see up to twelve in one lunch hour. I first heard its autumn song on September 28th ... and I have heard it on several occasions since." - The appearance of this species breeding on these sites is well recorded elsewhere, but it is fascinating to read it here as a contemporary account by a BNA member.

Looking at the rambles reports and seeing what they reflect of their times, there is plenty of food for nostalgia here. Most members travelled to meetings by bus or train whether within Hertfordshire or further afield. The ladies walked in wellies it's true, but usually wore skirts and coats while the older gentlemen wore peaked caps and were called 'Mr.'. And then, ah, the dear lost world of the tea-room! How the members loved the reviving cuppa before catching the bus home! And they usually found one whether served by cafe or public house. By the later sixties most members were using cars and the teatime habit lapsed. According to the *Bulletin* in July 1968, members had a different indulgence, the lunchtime pint! Nowadays we are very austere and have neither. Here is a nice teatime quote dated October 11 1953 after a fungus foray in Epping Forest. "During tea at a very crowded scruffy cafe the occupants wondered what on earth the queer toadstools were for. Mr. Briggs was heard enlightening the proprietor by confiding that he took them home and made jam of them."

Since the bulletins of this early period offer sufficient distance in time for patterns of change to appear, comparison between the records then and now are interesting. Differences in land use account for so many changes in the life of wood, field and stream. For example, many birds have decreased in numbers and/or range over Hertfordshire since then. One lamented loss has been the nightingale, "a fairly common summer visitor ... where there is suitable cover" (B. Sage, *Bulletin* 1959) and recorded regularly on rambles. Likewise nightjar, snipe, corn bunting, tree sparrow, grey partridge, barn owl; and these trends sadly continue locally and nationally, viz. recent alarm over skylarks.

Conversely, some bird records have altered little through fifty years. For example, a golden plover flock has always been recorded on the regular winter ramble in the London Colney area. Some birds, as is well known, have increased in number like the jay, magpie, sparrowhawk and blackcap. Some 'new' birds have established themselves in this time like the collared dove and Canada goose or changed habits like the cormorant.

Many magpies do not make up for a retreating red-backed shrike. It is a poor exchange! This shrike, which still remained a fairly common bird in certain areas of North Hertfordshire (B. Sage, 1959) was recorded irregularly in the *Bulletin*, viz., in May 1951 near Hertford; in September 1953 seen on a ramble to Ashridge; in 1960 twice - in May at Goose Green and in June again in the same area. In July 1968, a pair with two young were watched on Telegraph Hill and a female was seen later in the Pegsdon area.

How difficult it is to choose either interesting records from among so many of the different kinds or a day particularly memorable. The BNA visited both Therfield Heath and Bramfield Forest regularly and in April 1965 they were delighted by the sight at Therfield of pasque flowers "not in hundreds but in thousands" and in April 1968 they recorded 77 bird species in Bramfield on an exceptionally hot day in "woodlands teeming with birds." cirl buntings and crossbills were seen with nightingales and grasshopper warblers. There were summer migrants, together with winter visitors such as fieldfare (singing) and brambling. Lastly at Lilley Hoo, August 1967, Mike Ingram records Venus's looking-glass and 13 species of butterfly. There are many other such reports.

Reading through these old reports there is an impressive variety of events and activities that have taken place over the years. Some of these were discontinued after a while, others became traditional practice. Two that had a short life were the all-night ramble and the camping weekends. The last were short breaks usually over the August Bank Holiday, either in the Brecks, on the East Anglian coast or sometimes the New Forest. They ran from 1955-62 and produced some very full lists. The idea was revived again in July 1969 with another trip to the New Forest where Mike Clark had organised some deer watching for everyone.

The all night rambles ran from 1950-55. The *Bulletin* does not explain their demise. They were an annual walk through the night over different routes and took place in mid-May so that the group could monitor the dawn chorus before walking to their nearest hotel breakfast. They were much enjoyed and the lists produced were tabled in the *Bulletin* and compared over the years. But there was no further night ramble or dawn chorus for years. In 1969, Mike Clark led a combined evening ramble for nightjar/nightingale and subsequent dawn chorus, members to take a nap in between. Revived and successful, the dawn chorus featured regularly later in conjunction with an evening badger watch. This Mike Clark had also introduced to the group as an interesting activity in June 1968. Torrential rain ruined this first occasion but branch members were not deterred. Badger watching is still a favourite BNA activity, twenty-five years on. Mike was unlucky with weather and feared that the night ramble/dawn chorus would also be ruined by rain (it wasn't). He wrote a wry account of the mid-evening stage describing the rain and Keith Wheeler's attempt to attract some moths as the others were settling down in cars.

"The plan was to sleep in the cars until just before dawn and Keith took the opportunity of taking his portable moth kit for a round of the woods by Chrishall Common. It was feared that the brilliant white light might attract keepers/police or farmers of two if not three counties. There was even a risk of bringing in an aircraft or two. But the exercise ended in increasing rainfall when one moth, out of sympathy, collapsed into the portable screen."

The weekends away (first one Maldon 1952) and the indoor meetings usually at members' houses (first reference is March 1962) have given so much pleasure to all over the years and provided so many stories, of which the best known is that of Scolt Head Island, May 1956. It was a chapter of accidents for all who took part, ending in the party being stranded and finally rescued by some gallant locals in a sailing dinghy.

On occasions this branch has set itself demanding targets, in particular the study of specific sites over a period of time. The first such was the Trent Park survey 1956-59, an ecological comparative study of two ponds initiated by Bryan Sage and carried through successfully. Bryan was also prime mover and largest contributor in the Northaw Great Wood survey undertaken in 1962. The object of collecting the material was to produce a book that would be of value to teachers using the Hertfordshire School Camp. As described elsewhere in this book, *Northaw Great Wood* was published in 1966. Maxwell Knight the naturalist wrote in the foreword as follows, "the whole book just goes to show what a body of amateur naturalists, all members of one society, can do ... this work bears the stamp of a most essential quality - dedication in the best sense of the word."

The Branch takes itself seriously but also has much fun. Such as the time when Tom Gladwin's bike blew up or when members shinned up trees on one April 1st, or were marooned on islands or took on the hazards of the English countryside. There were many close encounters of the waspish kind and where gins and snares were found on paths and carried off; gamekeepers, whistle-blowing wardens and furious farmers were met and matched (well, some of the time). Last, but never least, were the struggles against that oldest British adversary, the weather. Many a leader waxed rueful over it. Trevor James wrote vividly of Mersea, April 1967, as follows: "we proceeded to the gloom of the windswept mudflats by Coopers Beach, where scarcely a feather flapped in the gale-force wind." He describes feelingly the dilemma of "Four stalwarts of the branch and two poor unbeknowing guests" on a drenching day in the Beane Valley, Sept 1967. "At Tonwell there was much debate as to whether to turn back but, no, we plodded on with the comforting thought that we may as well be completely wet having followed the walk rather than soaked by going back." Hertfordshire mud, glorious mud - now there's a potent memory for everyone. Not one of the walks is without interest and I can remember some of them as though they had happened yesterday.

The bulletins are a happy mixture of light-hearted enjoyment, as in Trevor James's accounts of hilarious winter weekends in snowy Holkham in the seventies, and the serious admonitions of our editors to the effect that we enjoyed ourselves too much and did not do enough serious recording work. Flowers, birds, butterflies, and mammals have formed the backbone of the reports, but we have always had at least two fungus forays a year, sometimes under the leadership of outside experts such as Margaret Holden or Peter Holland. Enthusiasms are now developing for mosses, beetles, spiders, hoverflies and dragonflies and most recently and paradoxically for marine life.

Walks, which take place fortnightly and therefore must number 1,250 in a period of 50 years, necessarily form our principal group activity. Small numbers on walks were often commented on; in fact they usually ranged from 3 to 21. The smallest number on the last trek was one, Frank Lancaster himself, the instigator of this arduous event, which took place five times. We think Trevor

James also went for a walk by himself in the snow one winter's day, when driving was difficult.

Indoor meetings have continued since earliest times and we have enjoyed some outstanding evenings, such as Bryan Sage's account of wolves, caribou and moose in Alaska in 1970, Trevor James's talk on Nepal and *The Birds of Israel* by Tom Gladwin in 1983. There were slides of flowers shown by Patrick Rawlinson on several occasions. Hospitality and good food in members' houses have always been traditional although we have also held some meetings in halls and had non-members join us.

The *Photograph Album*, containing winning entries from our annual photographic competitions, was resurrected as an institution in 1976. Our annual dinners were started in 1973. Camping weekends, which used to be a feature in our early days, were reintroduced with the glorious weekend in the New Forest in September 1981. Except for another happy occasion near West Mersea in September 1990, these more or less died out again after the hurricane near Arundel in September 1983! The Boxing Day ramble led by Ron Freeman, whose birthday coincides with it, has also been a notable and convivial occasion, ending as it does with soup and sandwiches in a friendly pub. The first of these rambles was in 1974.

When Trevor James was editor his own enthusiasm and ever-increasing knowledge inspired everyone to enjoy themselves and develop their own expertise. There were frequent reprimands to leaders of walks for not sending in reports and exhortations to all members to send in notes of things they had seen in their own back gardens. When Frank Lancaster took over as editor, he issued forms to leaders for their reports and, with one sweep of his new broom, this problem seems to have been solved. However during Frank's era there were still frequent chidings about lack of individual records. Angus, with executive efficiency, seemed to have conjured up interesting notes from lots of people (especially, perhaps, bird notes from Betty Edwards), and bulletins appeared with clockwork regularity. Trevor still acted as scientific advisor and Shirley Bell did all the typing.

The present editor, Graeme Smith, has been making the *Bulletin* even better and more sophisticated ever since 1985. He has used computer technology to great effect and has introduced occasional short articles, such as Chris Doncaster's on fleas, bugs and house martins and Peter Alton's on chimney-sweep moths near Monken Hadley. The format has also been greatly enhanced by the splendid sketches and drawings by Chris Doncaster and Betty Edwards, and continuing Frank's tradition, the insertion of quotations and snippets of wisdom.

Mention must also be made of the many memorable holidays we have enjoyed; Ireland, Wales, the Lake District, Exmoor, Dorset, Derbyshire, Somerset, the Wyre Forest, the Western Isles and, more recently, France have all provided memorable holidays. One can tell how much they have been enjoyed by the careful, loving accounts of them and the wonderful lists of things seen, far beyond the range of our native Hertfordshire and often providing material for talks with slides later on.

To conclude is difficult! Writing this article has made us realise how essential a *Bulletin* is for a Group like ours. It puts on record our own experiences in a way that a national wildlife magazine does not, and gives a feeling of togetherness and participation in a thoroughly enjoyable and worthwhile activity. I hope the *Bulletin* and the Branch will still be thriving in 50 years' time.

A short toed eagle seen on the French holiday in 1992

3. **Where have all the Sparrows gone?**
Revd. Tom Gladwin

House sparrows raiding wheat at harvest

The view from my childhood bed embraced a distant rookery and the red-tiled roof next door. Here, warmed by the early morning sun, congregated great numbers of house sparrows. I found interest in those birds. The soft warmth of their colours, conversations and habits such as their shrinking away under the tiles at the onset of rain, fascinated me. I loved those sparrows.

The Hertfordshire countryside into which I had been born in 1935, which delighted members of the newly formed Hertfordshire Branch of the British Naturalists' Association in 1946, was more diverse, more vibrant, and very much more tranquil than that of today. Railways were at their peak, few people owned cars, there were no motorways and no intrusive jet aircraft. As audibly evident each dawn, many back gardens still housed a few chickens. Horses ploughed, hauled barges, drays, and the daily deliveries of bread and milk, and continued to do so well beyond the end of the Second World War. Other products sometimes deposited by these dutiful animals were quickly removed to the vegetable garden!

16

Seemingly filled with life, it was a different countryside then. Through summer the meadows, hedgerows and woodlands, wherever one went, were alive with a joyful choir of humming insects. Fingers of crystal-pure chalk streams emerged from the foot of the Chilterns and flowed year-long to fill the palms of the Colne and Lea. From chalk downland to lowland river valleys existed extensive areas of verdant flower-rich pastures. In season many would be solid gold with meadow buttercups, broken only by a few willows often marking some of the many farm ponds that still existed. There were few flooded gravel pits and only three open waters, Aldenham and Tring Reservoirs, and Panshanger Lake, containing significant populations of waterfowl. Most farms comprised a mosaic of small fields enclosed by winding networks of long established, stock proof, well managed, species-rich hedgerows. Arable was rarely extended to the margins, cereals were harvested later in September and there were plenty of gleanings and seed bearing winter weeds to sustain large flocks of finches, buntings, and sparrows, until ploughing and sowing began in the following spring. There were corners, and a liberal scattering of dense copses which provided cover for mammals, and from which nightingales and other birds sang. Indeed there was a general randomness and lack of uniformity of great benefit to wildlife. These were halcyon days before the wildlife capacity of our County was imprudently depleted by agricultural chemicals, the conversion of ancient meadows once thick with flowers to arable, and the ripping out of hundreds of miles of hedgerows. Even now, by spraying set-aside inspring, some farmers are effectively stating "there can be no place for wildlife".

Change was already affecting our deciduous woodlands. Large quantities of oak and other hardwood trees had been felled to meet the demands of the war. Some were converted to charcoal, and remnants of the burners' camps and equipment used can still be seen in a few places such as Alexander's Wood (Bramfield). Following the war, those oak/hazel and oak/hornbeam coppice woodlands from which most of commercially useful timber trees had been felled were classified as derelict woodlands and assigned to be clear felled and planted with exotic coniferous species such as douglas fir, sweet smelling European larch, Corsican pine, Lawson's cypress, Norway spruce, Scots pine and western hemlock. Never as rich in wildlife as the native semi-natural woodlands they replaced, the young plantations initially attracted species such as nightjars, tree pipits and grasshopper warblers. Later, as they matured, they benefited species such as goldcrests and coal tits.

From first awakenings I was willingly apprenticed to two fine naturalists, my father and paternal grandfather. Both had comprehensive collections of birds' eggs from the Hertford area, including those of land rails (corncrakes) taken on The Meads (Hertford Meads). I too had a collection at a time when it was still a respected interest. How grateful I am to have had such caring and devoted mentors.

Most weekends there were country walks, some of which were annual events.

In March, for example, we would visit a laneside verge at Great Amwell to pick lesser celandines which were locally scarce in that period. A little later, in April, one from every newly completed clutch of four peewits' (lapwing) eggs would be collected from The Meads for that day's tea. One dawn in late May or early June would find us at Hertford Heath listening for, and then watching, the wrynecks that nested in an old orchard. On several but not every visit we also listened to musical woodlarks which I was told sang through the night. Later, in June, we would picnic in Broad Riding Wood (Broxbourne) enjoying purple emperors, fritillaries, hairstreaks, and other butterflies. There were wood warblers in Broad Riding Wood, and redstarts in most of the woods around Broxbourne, Brickendon and Hertford Heath. Other species of particular interest included red squirrels regularly seen along Walnut Tree Walk when we visited great grandparents in their flint cottage by Great Amwell Church.

Many summer and autumn days were spent beside local waters. Here I graduated from catching innumerable minnows with bread paste on bent pins, to tempting gudgeon, dace and roach in the New River, chubb in the Lea, brown trout and grayling in the lower Beane and Mimram, and finally large carp in private lakes. Listening to the plop of furry water voles, I learnt the names and seasons of the main aquatic plants and insects.

My boyhood home looked across the great expanse of The Meads. Flooded in winter, the haunt of breeding lapwing, snipe and redshank in spring, and a brilliant carpet of meadow buttercups in summer, here was the cradle of my lifelong love of wildlife and countryside. Lazily grazed by cattle and horses at all seasons, flowers from The Meads decorated our home. Milkmaids (lady's smock), shirt buttons (stitchwort), cowslips and even a few blooms of green-winged orchids, appeared in season among gatherings from the garden.

There, too, were birds in abundance. Whinchats and yellow wagtails nested commonly on the floodplain, butcher birds (red-backed shrikes) in scrub along chalk slopes carpeted with cowslips and pyramidal orchids, Redstarts in ancient oaks by the Lea under Ware Park, and gossiping colonies of tree sparrows in long-ago pollarded willows. Yellowhammers called for a 'little-bit-of-bread-and-no-cheese', and turtle doves rang many never to be answered telephones. We threw small stones which bats caught and expelled, barn owls quartered the meadows at dusk, and nightingales and sedge warblers sang well into the night. As evident from the bulletins, these were all species regularly encountered on BNA rambles through and in some cases beyond the 1950s.

There were always surprises. In 1953 a pair of stonechats stayed on after winter and nested in a remnant of gorse heath by Hertford Sewage Farm. The following year two pairs of wheatears nested in rabbit burrows on the slopes above Chadwell Spring. In some years pairs of common sandpipers were present by the Lea throughout the summer but, despite optimistic observation, it was not until 1961 that they were proved to have bred. Elsewhere in Hertfordshire in the fifties, BNA members were recording stone curlew breeding around Barkway, crossbills at Oaklands (Welwyn), and cirl buntings along the upper Mimram Valley.

Like most young naturalists in the years after the war, I did not have the benefits of modern field guides, binoculars and other optical aids which are now accepted without question as essential standard equipment. The first field guide, Roger Peterson and others' *A Field Guide to the Birds of Britain and Europe*, was not published until 1954. Further there was no definitive publication on the birds of our County until Bryan Sage's *A History of the Birds of Hertfordshire* appeared in 1959. Most of us had to make do with examining copies of T. A. Coward's *The Birds of the British Isles and their Eggs* and Witherby's *The Handbook of British Birds* in the County Reference Library on wet Saturday mornings. I still recall the feelings of great privilege as the librarian unlocked the cabinet in which these treasured volumes were housed, and handed them to me. The Hertford Public Library held few natural history books, but was always pleased to borrow them from other libraries. As a result of their kindness and interest, I became an avid reader of authors such as BB (Denys Watkins-Pitchford), E.W. Hendy, W.H. Hudson, Richard Jefferies, Henry Williamson, and Viscount Grey of Fallodon. It is true to say that I fed off their gifted descriptions, insights, and interpretations of the countryside and wildlife. Their works, forever at hand, continue to excite my spirit as much as they did fifty years ago. How impoverished is the naturalist who has not explored these classics.

As indicated above, few young naturalists in the immediate postwar period could afford, or even had access to, binoculars. For most this remained the case until the early fifties when government surplus stocks became available. These instruments, mostly 6x30 models with individual eye-piece focussing, and heavy 7x50 glasses, lacked the crispness, sharpness, width of field, and light transmitting capabilities of modern equipment.

The years that followed were to see rapid and accelerating changes. Some of the birds mentioned so far have long passed from, or become scarce, in our County. There have, however, been compensations in new arrivals including the softly plumaged collared dove and, with the increasing number of flooded gravel pits, species such as gadwall, ringed plover, little ringed plover and common tern. For the latter reason waterfowl populations have increased by over 800% since 1948/9. Other birds whose populations have increased include stock dove, green and great spotted woodpeckers, grey and pied wagtails, long-tailed tit, blackcap, chiffchaff, magpie, chaffinch and greenfinch. Sparrowhawks and hobbies have returned to our woodlands where, in contrast, marsh and willow tits and hawfinches have become very scarce indeed. There are fewer swallows and spotted flycatchers, but where, we should ask, have all the sparrows gone?

The greatest changes of all have been down on the farms. Habitat destruction, the use of agricultural chemicals, and increase in arable, have resulted in a catastrophic decline of many once abundant species and much-loved songsters. There are silent areas where no skylarks or song thrushes sing, where there are no grey partridges or tree sparrows, and where there remain just small remnants of the once great flocks of finches, buntings, and house sparrows. Given the opportunity nature is quick to heal its wounds and wildlife populations to recover, but will government find the political will to change things before it is too late? In the meantime no house sparrows come to the table scraps and seed scattered daily for the birds on our Digswell lawn. May they soon return, for I still love those sparrows?

Stone curlews at Icklingham, Suffolk

4. **A Weekend at Holkham, Norfolk**
Trevor James

Chris Doncaster

Hen harriers - regular winter visitors to East Anglia

*The Hertfordshire branch of the British Naturalists' Association has a long
tradition of weekend breaks birdwatching on the Norfolk coast.
This is a report of one of the more eventful and memorable meetings
which took place in January 1972.*

The cold wind of Friday blossomed into fine snow squalls in a north-easterly
gale on Saturday as we proceeded to patrol the shingle banks by Salthouse
and Cley. The air was thick with salt spray as we jogged downwind along
Eastern Bank. The birds, though, were quite spectacular and were to remain
so for the whole weekend. Three Bewick's swans, 170 or so brent geesw, two
gadwall, two sanderling and some 50 teal were among our first encounters.
Odd single snow buntings flew past us on the wind's edge and a kestrel fought
to hover over the shingle. Near the Cley Nature Reserve, ducks wafted down
onto the lagoons and we recognised 50 gadwall, with five or six shelducks, ten
goldeneye and 20 wigeon amongst others. Having tottered the length of the
bank to Cley, however, we made off to a slightly less exposed landscape on
Salthouse Heath, but were rewarded for our pains only by a green woodpecker.

The dense, misty atmosphere of the morning cleared in the afternoon and
revealed a racing sky of tall clouds in a yellow sunlight, as we explored Stiffkey
Marshes (pronounced 'Stewkey', I am assured). Over the saltings we went,
much to the horror of some who bogged down half-way over. When we reached

the roaring sea and its wader flocks, the sight was not one to be forgotten. To left and right stretches of yellow glowing marsh; on the mud flashing hoards of knot and dunlin, sanderling and oystercatcher. But most spectacular was the flying of a flock of some 250 brent geese, which rose as we approached and made off to another patch for safety.

The idea of warmth and dinner seemed to distract some from the enjoyment of nature. In any case we were all keen on the Victoria Hotel's catering when we arrived back. They dished up wild duck, probably from the marshes.

Sunday awoke to a rigor mortis of ice and a dusting of snow in the ditches and fields. But at least the sun was shining and the wind had run away. We marched out, down the long track at the hotel's doorstep, towards Holkham dunes and their curtain of pines. We did not get far before the birds erupted around us; snipe and a flock of geese, including 50 Canadas and some 30 pink-foots, all rising into the crystal air. Some feral Egyptian geese attracted derision, but they were still handsome; while farther on red-legged partridges, wigeon and mallard appeared. Someone yelled "Hawfinch!" at the edge of the pines, and we believed them.

Following the inland track behind the trees, we wound along the dune edge, unaware of the towering clouds out to sea. We enjoyed ourselves watching willow and coal tits, goldcrests and treecreepers in the trees and a woodcock which rose from its leafy nook. A pond sported dabchicks and a weary rabbit at its edge, too tired, in the cold, to run away. At one point I snatched a brief view of a large falcon over the fields, possibly a peregrine, and we increased our pace to the end of the treeline to try and find it. We never did get over the fence though, to follow it over the grassy dunes. As we approached the edge, the wind suddenly rose, snow flaked down in lumps and the black towering clouds enveloped us in a raging blizzard before we had time to hide. Over the dunes a kestrel hovered in the howling gale. We hid behind the dune ridge and the snow careered over its edge until everything, including us, was two inches deep in snow.

The snowstorm boiled away as soon as it had come, leaving a kind of gap of silence. In the path, the only footprints where we had trodden were those of a weasel. Through the delicate tracery of the pines and dunes we dared scarcely touch a frond for fear of spoiling it, until we looked out over the arctic desert of Holkham beach. The sea seemed to float, in a distant roar, above a white mirror. Most of us stayed to watch, and eat, but I walked out into the horizon of sea and snow to look at its vastness and the birds it still contained. By the water's edge were three or four bar-tailed godwits. On the sea some common and velvet scoters, with gulls and numerous groups of common waders. Another member joined me and as we returned a pair of pintail flew above our heads to land nearby. Finally, against more black clouds, we watched a flock of shore larks flying high along the coast; about 38 altogether.

After that, lunch was pretty rushed. We soon moved back through the trees, leaving the desert to its silence. Over the fields behind the trees, we came across a pair of whooper swans in one field, and a large flock of about 80 white-fronted geese, with some pink-foots and brents. A sparrowhawk was seen being mobbed by crows and we recorded more common partridges, snipe, corn bunting etc.

Some of us went into Holkham Park, while others returned to base joyful at the sight of a great grey shrike en route. Holkham Park is always an anticlimax after the coast. But its herds of fallow deer were splendid in the snow and the lake held numbers of heron, cormorants and various duck, including goldeneye, pochard, the two pintail and eight pairs of goosanders. A sadder note was struck though, by our discovery of a dead red-necked grebe on its bank.

After such a weekend, it is not surprising everyone felt more keen of wit, more alert and energetic, than our urban life usually allows. Perhaps it was fortunate, for the drive back was hazardous enough to require all the concentration our drivers could muster.

Goldeneye at Holkam Park

5. **Badger Watching**
Michael Demidecki

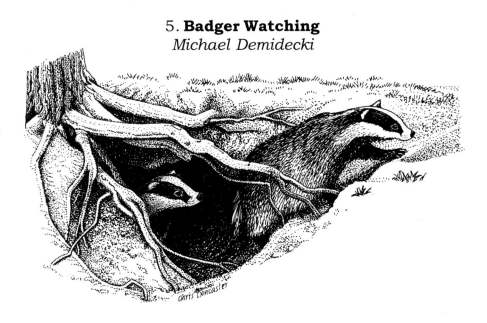

Badger watching is always entertaining and a good event in which to recruit new members for any natural history society. Such an evening gathering can yield theatrical delights.

When organising a watch the leader has several things to arrange. Getting everyone to the sett in time is important, watchers should be in position and quiet say half an hour before sunset, then there is an hour when you can see fairly well, though good light gathering binoculars are needed owards the end of that time and afterwards. I use a pair of Zeiss Dialyt 7x42, which are renowned for their optical quality. When choosing binoculars, you should bear in mind that, up to a point, the greater the number achieved by dividing the diameter of the objective lens (e.g. 40mm) by the magnification (e.g. x8), the brighter will be the potential image. However as the diameter of the pupil of the average adult can widen to not more than about 5mm, a factor of 5 is sufficient. Beyond that it will make no difference. Dull, dark, rustle-free clothing should be worn for badger watching, gloves conceal the outline of the hands and a veil (netting) over the head breaks up the moon-like appearance of the face. If it is likely to be a midgy evening, don't forget the insect repellent!

We have tended as a group to combine a badger watch with an overnight stay somewhere and a dawn chorus for the next morning followed by breakfast. With the help of Ron Freeman (former Deputy County Scout Commissioner for Hertfordshire) we have had some excellent scout accommodation on several occasions, though we slept in our cars or in the open in Ashridge in 1981 and at the author's home in Berkhamsted in 1988. Staying in scout accommodation has not been without its amusing side. Once I had forgotten to bring a bread knife for breakfast toast; we had just returned from our dawn chorus foray and everyone was starving. Elliot Ungar saved the day by slicing the loaf with a scout wood saw which made an excellent alternative!

After everyone has assembled in the evening, we have made our way to various setts, in groups of no more than say four to a sett. In 1988 to my dismay we were beaten to a sett at Ashridge by other watchers so I had to organise an alternative venue and with the light fading fast a certain amount of panic ensued.

It is a good idea to ensure that the landowner has no objection to your watching the chosen sett. In 1974 we were in position at one sett at 8.20p.m. (sunset was 9.08p.m.) when the farmer spotted us. He came over at 8.30 and banged his stick hard on the ground as he remonstrated with us. We made our peace with him and I am pleased to say he let us stay, but I was sure that with all the disturbance we should not see a thing. However our *Bulletin* report records events afterwards as follows: "10.15 - boar badger emerged, walked slowly over the spoil heap and left via well trodden path. 10.25 - sow emerged, sniffed the air, passed more quickly across the sett entrance and eventually left by the same path. 10.45 - another sow emerged, passed quickly over spoil heap and disappeared into the wood at the other side."

To encourage badgers to stay longer by their sett after they emerge, you should pre-bait near the entrance holes or scratching tree with peanuts. However this needs to be done a few times on alternate nights prior to the watch and also after arrival at the sett on the night of the watch. It is vitally important when watching at a sett to make sure that whatever wind there is blows into your face and not from the watcher towards the sett. One of the first things a badger does on emerging is tentatively to sniff the air and if there is the slightest human scent about the animal will retreat and perhaps remain in the sett until the watchers have gone.

After the sun sets and the birds become quiet there can be a magical, even theatrical atmosphere at a badger sett. You never know what exactly is going to happen, or what you are going to see. I quote from Frank Lancaster's account of the BNA badger watch in 1974 in Broxbourne Woods: "The theatre was situated some fifty yards inside a deciduous wood and our seats could best be described as fifth row centre of the dress circle. The stage setting was a main badger sett at bottom right, whilst hidden in the wings at top right were two secondary exits. The back of the stage was fringed with thick undergrowth, but the front stage was devoid of any furnishings and was set out in light relief as a barren sandy platform fifteen feet by eight feet - the result of many years of badger activity.

"The canopy of the trees was not unusually high, nor for that matter was the cloud base. The wind was threatening rain, and a steady force two wind gave us immunity from scent detection from members of the cast.

"An avian chorus of evensong off stage rewarded the quiet vigil of the watchers. For the record I had been previously informed by Robert (the late Robert McCready) that the land hereabouts had in medieval times and later been part of the wealth of the Westminster Diocese.

"The waning light was a signal for the songsters to 'tuck their heads under their wings' and the weight of the silence reminded me of the quiet whispers of the cloisters. During this hour of composure and disciplined silence one was made aware of the infinite beauty of nature. All this was free to man, but alas he is regrettably fettered to materialistic chattels.

"Nature waits for no man, and in a rapidly failing twilight the stage was alive. This was not according to the programme. Act 1, scene 1, should have been a very wary and slothful entry by the principal character, who in turn would dictate whether other members of the cast would be permitted to grace the stage.

"From the left wings, a ballet without sound or music, tumbling and rolling, tig and chase, hide and seek, all impromptu in fun and game, filled the stage. In fact such was the exuberance of the three youthful performers that they trespassed into the dress circle to look and stare, ears pricked to the sky like the pyramids of Egypt. The sharpness of their profile depicted an alert and intelligent turn of mind which they would need to exercise every day of their lives to outwit the hunter, who is bent to kill under the guise of sport.

"Their departure was as unexpected as their entry. They were swallowed up into the darkness. They had performed for fully five minutes under the soft red lights of our filtered torches homing onto them from the dress circle. There was no applause, coughing or rustling of programmes, but an unspoken thank you for having been honoured to watch a 'Prelude of Fox Cubs at Play!' "

6. **The Special Studies**
Trevor James

Petty whin and sampling freshwater life at Hertford Heath

Over the years the Hertfordshire Branch of the British Naturalists' Association has tried to extend its activities to more than searching for and recording interesting species of wildlife in the County. Looking at the ways it has gone about this and the value of these studies over a period is an interesting exercise, because it brings clearly into focus several things that the group has achieved and enjoyed.

The Trent Park Survey

At the Branch AGM in 1956 there was a discussion about supplementing the usual programme of rambles and bird weekends with a new project aimed at getting to know more intimately a smaller area of countryside, and Trent Park at Enfield was suggested as the venue. Thus was born the idea of *Special Studies* - and right from the start it was aimed at trying to focus the group's natural history interests on more co-ordinated studies of such habitats, their ecology and even the kinds of management strategy for which to aim.

The first report of this, in the *Bulletin* of 1956, highlights a dilemma in doing this kind of thing, because, although the Branch gained permission from the Principal of Trent Park to do the study, he asked them to give a list of objectives. This we did not find easy to supply, since at the time we were not very clear what we wanted to achieve. However, the group eventually focused on three things: making a comparative study of two ponds; putting down a quadrat; and making a mycological survey. No less than one Saturday per month from March to October was given over to this. Considering that Saturday working was then the norm amongst ordinary folk, this was some commitment. Eventually we had to economise and to concentrate our efforts on studying a single pond. The mycological list was limited to what Mr. Clarke, who died in 1958, was able to bring together in a series of seven visits in 1956 and 1957.

Our initial comparative work between the two ponds - Moat Pond and Lime Grove Pond - had shown some differences in fauna; in fact the wooded Moat Pond had a somewhat more diverse microfauna than the open pond. However, there were apparently some changes at the Moat Pond during or after the 1956 season and this led to the study being changed into one looking closely at the flora and fauna, including microscopic fauna, of Lime Grove Pond only. This survey was pursued with some vigour and enthusiasm. In a short report on the project in 1957, Bryan Sage pointed out that "our results may well prove to be of considerable scientific value, for Dr T. T. Macan writes that 'as far as I know nobody has ever made a thorough survey of a lowland pond...a good survey of the type of pond which you are investigating would therefore be valuable'." Measurements of water temperatures and pH were made, a map of the vegetation was compiled in 1956, and a series of line transects of vegetation was carried out the following year, along with notes on flowering periods of the species of flora. Most impressive of all though was a tabulation of the aquatic fauna (and some algae), with months of occurrence of species. Helped by Macan's then recently published book on freshwater biology, as well as John Clegg's *Wayside & Woodland* series book on freshwater life, the group was able to tackle some of the myriad different groups which inhabit even such a small habitat. Access to Ray and Phyllis White's home with microscopes also helped.

The study carried on throughout 1957, 1958 and 1959, but the last year in particular proved problematic because of drought. A range of planned studies was abandoned because of the lack of water. Mary Honnor's final report to the Principal of Trent Park makes it clear that the group would not be continuing, other than with casual observations. Nevertheless, the study did make some very useful and interesting observations. Not the least of them was that the pH of the pond varied dramatically through the season - from pH 8.5 in March 1958, to pH 6.5 in June, back up to pH 8 in August, and back down again to 6.5 in December. While the plant list suggests the pond to have been rather acidic, quite typical of this part of the country, from the point of view of its flora and also evidenced by its general paucity of aquatic snails, it shows that simple pH readings belie a much more complex relationship with time of year and rainfall etc, all of which no doubt affected the microscopic fauna. Some of the recorded species are particularly interesting too. The great crested newt was obviously quite numerous and the flora included such relatively uncommon species as marsh pennywort and lesser spearwort.

The study also had other effects - not least a much greater knowledge amongst our members of aquatic life, as well as a general grounding in the use of microscopes, scientific keys and field equipment. That it remains one of the few attempts by anyone other than a scientific institution to carry out a really detailed pond study is a testimony to the difficulty of doing even this kind of thing. It also forms a valuable body of information about the state of such a pond at a time before environmental degradation and pollution really took a hold, and when field ponds were still used for watering stock. Trent Park College is aware of this and more scientific, comparative studies are again under way using the BNA's information as a background.

Special Studies in the 60s

The one really major study carried out corporately by BNA during the 1960s, was the work which culminated in the production of the book on Northaw Great Wood. The production of the book as such is described elsewhere by Bryan Sage, but the work of getting information together for it was spread over several years, this time not just on fixed Saturdays during the year, although some Branch field meetings were held to help the study along. Several members happened then to be living around the Northaw/Potters Bar area and others were only slightly further away. The result was that individual studies supplemented a sheaf of information gathered together by Bryan, and with his whip hand behind the group, much was accomplished fairly rapidly. This time, the study was much broader ranging and not so specialised. It also tended to focus on those wildlife groups in which the Branch was more accustomed to deal: birds, mammals, plants, fungi and the more obvious insects. Based on quite simple tabulation of species, the work was able to document the richness of the wood, but did not really attempt to go into its ecology in any original way. What it did do, though, was to paint a picture of the wood's wildlife as it was before it became generally overgrown and then over-run by visitors, both of which have changed its character dramatically in the 30 years which have followed.

Some of the studies for the Northaw Great Wood book involved considerable amounts of work. For the mammals, Michael Clark, then just beginning a career as a student of the County's mammals, spent long hours in the wood with his dog, finding badgers' setts or carrying out small mammal trapping. Peter Chance spent many hours compiling the first accurate path map of the wood as a guide for other people in their work. Bryan Sage had collected detailed bird data on the wood during the 1950s and early 1960s, but this was massively supplemented by a detailed study of the less common breeding birds, involving the plotting of all singing males, carried out mainly by Trevor James and John Lines during 1962-4. Early butterfly data, which had shown a rich fauna, including such unlikely rarities as the high brown and pearl-bordered fritillaries, was supplemented in 1964-5 by repeated searches by Trevor James, often accompanied by hordes of biting mosquitoes and millions of irritant flies. Graham Horsley, Ken and Mary Honnor and Eileen Aspden made many repeated visits to look for flora and fungi etc, the latter then being a splendid spectacle every year.

While there was no other properly organised study of a site during the rest of the 1960s, two other sites did receive some attention of a similar kind shortly after. One was Northaw Marshes. On 26th July 1970 a special field study day was held, when 22 members who attended were used to map the overall flora of the marshes. The approach was quite idiosyncratic at the time, but it did have the effect of producing a series of plant maps which quite clearly showed the variation in species-composition across the site according to the kind of land use each area had. These were written up in number 49 of the *Bulletin*. It also forms a snap-shot of the habitat of a site which has since undergone many changes but which remains important, although no longer quite the old-fashioned grazing marsh that it once was. The study remains the only published account of the site.

The other site was slightly less *ad hoc* in its selection. On 15th November 1970 the first of what was then hoped would be a series of meetings was held to study Lemsford Springs, recently acquired by the Herts & Middlesex Trust for Nature Conservation and wardened by Branch member, Tom Gladwin. The first meeting spent half a day looking at freshwater life, especially fish. Later, in May 1971, habitat and site mapping was carried out, followed by some work on transects in June the same year; these were incorporated in the site records. The site later developed as one of the best documented nature reserves in the County.

Wateringplace Green

It appears to have been 21st May 1972 that the group, led by Robert McCready, made its first chance visit to Wateringplace Green at Ardeley, although the County's botanists had known about the place for a long time, under one or other of its other names: Bury Mead, or Moor Hall Meadows. Unbeknown to the BNA, it was also already a Site of Special Scientific Interest. That brief visit produced a pair of snipe, evidently breeding, and enough was seen of the flora to show a rich site which was almost 18th century in appearance, a most unlikely locality in the agricultural expanse of northeast Hertfordshire. A further visit, also led by Robert McCready, took the party back that way on 1st July 1973, when common spotted orchids were obvious. By 1974, discussions within the Branch had revived the idea of a special study and it was proposed that the Branch spend some time documenting the wildlife and habitats of Wateringplace Green.

This study did serve to capture members' attention and to make the group try harder at identification. It also had as its aim the creation of a biological record of the site, at a time when it was beginning to become apparent that the only way to conserve wildlife was to document it in some detail and use that documentation as informed ammunition to influence the way a place is managed. This turned out to be very timely.

The original intention had been to make four field visits by the Branch during 1974, but in the end only two materialised, although two members, Michael Demidecki and Trevor James, made a private visit in May. A habitat map was drawn up and standard habitat record cards made out, as well as some recording of species, one or two of which, like the green-winged orchid, have not been seen since. Later in July 1974, however, the first 'official' visit was a disappointment because parts of the site had been sprayed with weed-killer! Nevertheless, further recording was carried out, and again for fungi etc. in October the same year.

The study continued to accumulate information, both from organised field visits and from special visits by individuals, throughout the period 1975-1980, with detailed attention being given to flowering plants, birds, mammals (with live trapping carried out) and a range of insect groups. The body of records acquired gave a very thorough insight into this rich and almost unique site in Hertfordshire, which has been added to the files of the County's biological records centre. The information gleaned proved essential in halting planned agricultural 'improvements' and ultimately in influencing management agreements organised through the Nature Conservancy Council and the Herts & Middlesex Wildlife Trust. The records also included some important ones for understanding the site's ecology, such as a rare ground beetle *Bembidion clarki* which specialises in living in fenland springs, and one of the County's last records of common cotton-grass, which has since succumbed to a combination of drought and poor management both here and at all its other sites. In fact, the study spanned that period in the mid-1970s which seems to have marked a watershed in the climatic and habitat characteristics of the County when the 1975/76 drought came upon us, after which habitat enrichment from agriculture has had a dramatic effect.

The Hertford Heath Special Study

The group had made the occasional excursion to the Hertford Heath area over many years, but mainly to walk further afield - down to the Broxbourne Woods, along Ermine Street etc. A visit to find nightingales in June 1979 is recorded in the *Bulletin*, and then in early 1982 there was a meeting which was supposed to have been a task day to help the Hertford Heath Nature Reserve warden, Tony Oliver, in his work. In the event, this was cancelled, but this background was to form the basis for the group's next special study during the period 1982-1988.

Hertford Heath Nature Reserve, run by the Herts & Middesex Wildlife Trust, is an area of ancient common land and a Site of Special Scientific Interest owned by Haileybury College and split into two areas - Goldingtons and The Roundings - north and south of the main Hertford-Hoddesdon road. Goldingtons was already heavily scrubbed up in the late 19th century, with some remaining droves and clearings, as well as some ponds, one of which, Crabtree Pond, is very old. The Roundings, by contrast, was quite open heath and rough grazing as late as the 1950s, with one ancient pond - Brides Farm Pond - and some more recent water-filled excavations called the Brick Ponds. The whole area is obviously acidic and has some relict rare plants for Hertfordshire, although many species formerly present have disappeared.

The Branch's first real study visit was on 12th June 1982, led by Trevor James, when an attempt at mapping the habitat on both areas was carried out. This was followed in September the same year by a fungus foray which revealed several uncommon species, including what was taken to be the rare *Amanita eliae* on the Roundings. In May 1983, a meeting, followed by a supplementary visit by one member, was given over to mapping the breeding bird species found on the site. This came up with a list of 28 species in all on The Roundings and 29 in Goldingtons. Work on flora, fungi and birds was later supplemented by more detailed studies of the invertebrates, especially of the main ponds. With only one or two meetings a year, however, and with only a handful of people actively involved, the ability of the group to do anything other than build up a basic species list was limited and no further work on mapping vegetation or birds etc. was carried out.

The Branch's work was written up by Trevor James in 1985 and presented as an interim report to the Wildlife Trust, with a résumé compiled by Graeme Smith published in the *Bulletin* in the following year. From the start, the aim had been to compile information to try and influence the site's management, because little account had been taken of the requirements of the site's rarer species in management work. This has proved to have been valuable, for it focused attention on the two main habitats of special importance - the ponds and the remaining areas of heathland, both of which have since been the special focus of management. It also showed the problems of trying to maintain these interests because droughts have taken their toll of the former and, despite much active work, the real heathland component of the latter has continued to decline. The fungi interest, also seen to have been important in the early 1980s, has not been sustained, probably also because of drought.

The other aspect of the group's interest in Hertford Heath was its involvement in active site management. This was encouraged especially by Frank Lancaster who, with his scouting background, had long urged that members put a bit back in 'payment' for their leisure interests and enjoyment of the countryside at large. This met with a varied response. On one memorable day, 13th November 1983, the group, fired up with Frank's enthusiasm, attacked the rapidly encroaching scrub for the first time around the trig. point on the Roundings. Vast stands of brambles and regenerating birch trees were removed to re-unite two minute vestiges of heath, which have since formed the nucleus of a much larger area of open ground. Other tasks were spent clearing Crabtree and Brides Farm Ponds and scrub around the Brick Ponds and along the main rides. However, the latter was apparently too late to save the Petty Whin, which disappeared in the late 1980s from its main site on the Roundings.

Some of the group's studies turned out to be unproductive - such as the projected mammal study on 8th July 1984 when 33 live mammal traps produced one solitary field vole. Some limited moth trapping was carried out in July 1985, centred on the warden's house, while Graeme Smith and others later concentrated on mosses. The last real effort at recording insects was made in 1987 but some further work parties returned in 1988. However, by then there was a consensus that the *Special Study* had done its bit at this site. Although the interim report was never followed up by a formal final report, as hinted at in *Bulletin 89*, the information gathered allowed a deeper understanding of the site's interest. The Wildlife Trust's work has continued with more formal habitat monitoring now in place. Nevertheless, there remains the need to make a continued update of such studies to follow changes and to build up continuing understanding of the responses of a wide range of species groups to the effects of management.

Panshanger

It was proposed in 1989 that the BNA should move onto another site. This time though, rather than try anything very intensive, the aim would be to gather together general information within a fairly informal visit. The large landscaped parkland at Panshanger, west of Hertford, was thought to be a good venue; it was both a nature reserve with some long-standing known information, and also was the subject of intended gravel extraction by its owners, Redland Aggregates. They had obtained permission as long ago as 1981 but had not yet started operations. It was also large enough to allow a ramble as well as spending time studying one aspect of natural history. It was therefore seen as an opportunity to focus attention on the detail in an attempt to try and influence where excavation and associated workings could do least damage. As such, it was a tall order and there is no way that a group like the BNA could attempt to bring together anything like a complete study on its own. For this reason, as well as a need to involve as many people as possible, most of the meetings tended to be joint field meetings with other organisations, especially the Hertfordshire Natural History Society.

A first visit was made on 23rd July 1989, mainly aimed at being a reconnoitre, but also to produce a preliminary plant species list (the work also contributing to the projected new *Flora of Hertfordshire* being worked on by Trevor James). Despite a hot, sultry day, much useful work was done, including a look at the newly set-aside arable north of the river Mimram. The meeting report, though, did stress the difficulty of defining habitats across an area as large as Panshanger, and this has been the focus of quite a bit of work in the subsequent years.

There have since been one or two visits to Panshanger by the Branch every year until the present (1997). Again, work has focused on various different aspects, either different geographical areas of the Park or on different wildlife groups. A very useful freshwater study day was carried out on 3rd October 1993, followed by a somewhat less useful one on 3rd July 1994, but it was then shown just how important the old course of the river Mimram is and how relatively impoverished the recently cleared out section of the Broadwater had become. Several field visits have been carried out looking at the flora in various areas and comprehensive plant lists have been compiled for many of the more important areas of the Park. A large-scale compartment map has been drawn up to focus recording into manageable units and individuals doing their own studies can use this.

A couple of fungus forays have been carried out, of which the one on 20th October 1991 was the most important, when not only did the Hertfordshire Natural History Society join the group but also the British Mycological Society. Several new County records were made and one species was recorded for the second time only in Britain. An important finding was the importance of the wetland margins, especially old alder stands, for this important group.

Panshanger Park has long been known for its ancient trees. Its famous Panshanger Oak is reputed to be the finest maiden-stem oak in Britain, but the Park has also got a large number of other old trees. While several of the BNA visits have looked at some of these trees, especially for insects, it was down to Trevor James and the Branch Vice-President, Bryan Sage (coming by then from Norfolk), to spend many weekends mapping and recording the condition etc of all the old trees on the site. Old trees were defined as anything with a diameter at breast height of greater than a metre, as well as other obviously older specimens of species like hawthorns. The study found no less than 501 trees of 16 species. A dendrologist from the Forestry Commission, Mr. John White, was brought in to give an opinion on some of these. His examination suggested that, while the Panshanger Oak was maybe upwards of 519 years old, there were other trees far older. One decrepit pollard oak was dated at 918 years! An ancient gnarled field maple near the western side of the Park, undateable, was reckoned to be one of the oldest trees of its species in the country. Bryan Sage presented a report on these trees to Redlands and it is planned to produce a more detailed paper on the work later.

The Panshanger study is continuing, but will need some concerted effort to bring it to a conclusion if such a thing is really possible. This highlights the one main difficulty with all these projects - drawing them to a useful conclusion and ensuring the results are made full use of. While most of the data have been submitted to the County biological records centre and have made positive contributions to management policies, too few of the *Special Studies* have been followed up by comprehensive final reports. The book on Northaw Great Wood is a fine exception. This shows the importance of trying to establish at the outset what the objectives really are; to have a worked up programme of activity and a timescale. In that study, the Hertfordshire Branch of the BNA showed what a local group of enthusiasts could do just on their days off. After all, the Branch can now boast of having some of the better naturalists in the County, who have learnt their trade in part through just such studies, while the Branch *Bulletin* has remained one of the few places where some of these accounts have so far been published for posterity.

Wood mice

Old Broken Tree, Cr wood

7. **Favourite Trees**
Michael Clark

Most naturalists have favourite trees.
Hertfordshire has many ancient trees to treasure.

The best known examples of historic stands of trees are probably the distinguished field oaks, *Quercus robur,* in Hatfield Park. It is reputed that the oldest medlar, *Mespilus germanica,* in Britain is a feature of the historic gardens here and, not far away near Welwyn, the Panshanger Oak is special not only for being one of the finest oaks in the land but because it is one of the only ones not to have been pollarded.

Oaks were certainly dominant around where I grew up in South Hertfordshire and the most exciting childhood tree climbing was into the mighty field oaks. In one, near Hertford, I saw my first barn owl and during another climb along a bough of a big beech, *Fagus sylvatica,* I came across my first tawny owl nest. The eggs were about to hatch and the parent birds had collected a selection of small mammals, stored next to the eggs, with which to feed the nestlings as soon as they appeared.

Aged yews, *Taxus baccata,* were popular because they were the easiest of the high old trees to climb, but the hornbeam, *Carpinus betulus,* must have been of special appeal for its character very early on in my life. This character, real or imaginary, of hornbeams seemed to become indelibly registered somewhere in my subconscious from the first time I was shown Arthur Rackham's illustrations of pollarded trees with human characteristics in childhood. Whether he was picturing willows, hawthorns or hornbeams, Rackham could breathe character and life into them of a very special kind. Until I was given my first bicycle, I walked to school through the Home Wood part of Northaw Great Wood, an ancient South Hertfordshire oak-hornbeam wood. Perhaps as a result of this I have never felt concerned about walking in woodland on the darkest nights whilst badger or deer watching.

The woodland management which produced the strange, high branched old shapes of the great pollarded specimens has largely disappeared, but it is occasionally practised where woodland owners recognise the beauty of these very old trees and keep them going by cutting back to the convoluted trunks.

I have made a particular effort in the past two years to seek out and photograph these old hornbeams in our local woodlands for fear that they may disappear as woods, are partly cleared or heavily coppiced without concern for the ancient specimens present. We are rich in this species, native to SE England only, and many Londoners will be familiar with the extensively pollarded hornbeams of Epping Forest.

Some of my first sketches as a schoolboy in Northaw Great Wood were of outstanding hornbeam specimens and many of these trees still survive in the school camp part of the wood. It will take careful management to ensure that many future generations will still find these trees. Perhaps visitors will be reminded, as I always am, of Rackham's illustrations and be left with a deep affection for this hardy tree in its most romantic form. Even when Rackham drew tree studies for their own sake, somehow his fantasy image of the 'wood imps' and 'little folk' seemed to creep in and appear amongst the hollows around the roots. If you watch at a badger sett or fox earth at twilight, below the intricate form of a pollarded hornbeam, you can also let your mind wander and begin to imagine trees taking on human forms from the twisting boughs and branches over your head - the eternal character of wild woodland at its most appealing.

As well as enjoying a lifetime of visiting the hornbeam woodlands of Hertfordshire and Essex, where probably the purest stands exist, I have walked many miles of woodlands in Kent where hornbeams also provide cover for woodcock and shade spectacular carpets of bluebells.

Years ago, during coppice and pollarding work on nature reserves, I quickly noticed how hornbeam, compared with other trees, would soon blunt my chain saw. It seemed appropriate that the traditional handles of wood-working tools should be made from this wood and it is always amazing how these trees respond to harsh layering to produce superb hedgerows which are both attractive and valuable for wildlife. Vedel & Lange (1965) explain that the 'beam' in the name is closely related to the German 'baum', which is an old Anglo-Saxon word for 'tree', so that 'hornbeam' signified the tree with the hard or horny-textured wood.

The very slow growth of the tree in woodland was demonstrated to me by pictures taken in 1939 of Hopkyn's Wood nature reserve, not far from Welwyn, which show two woodsmen removing the coppice to leave one stem only. These trees have now grown with fine single trunks, yet nearly sixty years on still have slim girths. Whatever happens to them - whether left as mature 50m (or higher) standards or coppiced or pollarded - the practices of sympathetic woodland management can make our hornbeams almost immortal.

Reference:

Vedel, H. & Lange, J. (1965) *Trees & Bushes* Methuen, London

8. **The Northaw Great Wood Book**
Bryan Sage

NORTHAW GREAT WOOD
Edited by Bryan L.Sage FZS

Northaw Great Wood was a frequent venue for the British Naturalists' Association field meetings in the 1950s and 1960s. In addition to group outings many individual members pursued their own special interests in the wood. Encounters with school teachers, their pupils and other visitors led to the birth of the idea of a book on the natural history of the wood and to a greater appreciation of the wood and its wildlife.

In those early days virtually all of the wood was leased to Hatfield Rural District Council and was used for public recreation, as is the case today. One exception was an area in the northeast corner which was controlled by Hertfordshire County Council and used as a base for natural history and other rural studies. It contained a number of camp sites which were used by a succession of school groups throughout the spring and summer. Those of us who spent a lot of time in the wood could not fail to notice the steady increase in the numbers of visitors. In talking to some of these it became clear that many were genuinely interested in the birds and other wildlife that could be seen there. Others had different reasons for being in the wood, one such being a gentleman who from time to time appeared on a Sunday to practice playing his bagpipes because, he explained, his neighbours did not like them! I also often encountered teachers with groups of children from the camp. Their level of interest in natural history was very considerable and I was frequently asked to identify bird songs or sundry insects. It was these encounters that led to the birth of the idea of a book on the natural history of the wood that could be used by visitors and, I hoped, lead to a greater appreciation of the wood and its wildlife.

Within the local BNA group was a lot of expertise and a large volume of records. It is one thing to have an idea but quite another to bring it to reality; the key question was "Who would finance the book and publish it?" Obviously this was beyond the resources of our BNA group. Since the primary purpose of the proposed book was educational I decided to approach Hertfordshire County Council, specifically the then Chairman of the County Education Committee to seek his support. The day of my appointment at County Hall duly came and I arrived armed with a brief synopsis of the proposed book. It proved to be a highly successful meeting and the gentleman in question, whose name I cannot now recall, embraced the idea of the book with enormous enthusiasm. At a subsequent meeting of the full County Council the project was accepted as worthy of support and it was agreed that it would be financed and published by the Council.

This was the moment of truth; the local BNA group now had to produce the goods! A number of meetings were held, mostly, as I recall, at my home, and some flesh was put on the skeleton. It was agreed that the title of the book would be *Northaw Great Wood - Its history and natural history*, and responsibility for the various chapters was allocated. Despite the volume of records to hand it soon became evident that more work had to be done. An obvious gap in our combined knowledge was the question of soils; none of us had the necessary knowledge to tackle this aspect, yet it was of fundamental importance. Outside help was clearly needed but would have to be voluntary since there was no budget for the payment of fees. I approached my friend Mr. D.W. King of the Soil Survey of England and Wales and he rose to the occasion magnificently. He worked through the wood very thoroughly and kindly wrote the soils chapter. The accompanying map was drawn by that organisation's cartographer. The services of one other outsider were utilised; Dr Lewis Lloyd-Evans of Ware had been studying the snails and slugs (*Mollusca*) of the wood and he generously contributed a chapter on them.

The various groups of members involved now got to work and the sequence of chapters was decided upon, starting with a historical survey by Trevor James. This was followed by an introduction to woodland ecology by me and I also wrote the chapters on geology, birds, amphibians and reptiles, beetles and woodlice. Trees and shrubs were dealt with by Graham Horsley and wild flowers by Eileen Aspden. We were fortunate in that Ray and Phil White were fungi experts and were thus able to tackle that difficult subject. Likewise, Ken and Mary Honnor had the knowledge required to deal with the lichens, mosses and liverworts. Finally, there was Michael Clark, our mammal expert, and Trevor James who also dealt with the butterflies.

It is important to remember that we were not trying to produce a scientific treatise, but simply an introduction to the general ecology, fauna and flora of the wood that could be used and understood by youngsters as well as interested adults. This being the case, it was essential that the book be adequately illustrated. It was here that the artistic abilities of various members came to the fore. The excellent line drawings of the buds and leaves in the chapter on trees and shrubs were drawn by Graham Horsley and those for the fungi chapter by Ray White. All the other drawings were done by Michael Clark and these embraced mosses, liverworts, mammals (including tracks and skulls), beetles, slugs and woodlice - truly a monumental effort. Then there were the maps, all of which, except those for soils and geology, were drawn by Peter Chance. These included a map of the footpaths network and another showing the distribution of the main tree species; both involved Peter in many hours of detailed survey work in the wood. As far as I can recall, I drew the geological map. There were also three black and white photographs - the frontispiece was mine, Eric Hosking kindly donated those of redstart and hawfinch, and John Markham that of lords-and-ladies. For the more serious minded reader we provided checklists of the various groups.

For reasons that now escape me, Watford Technical College was charged with the design of the book. In due course they produced a cover design that was truly awful – khaki in colour with two vertical lines (or was it one?) of beetles near the right-hand edge of the page. This showed a total lack of imagination and would do nothing for the book. I then asked Michael Clark to come to the rescue and he produced what proved to be a winning cover design – black with the face of an owl in white on the front, bled into the bottom and sides, and on the back three lines of animal tracks. Standing in a shop window this striking design attracted immediate attention.

In 1966 the great day finally arrived for publication; a thousand copies had been printed. This figure had literally been plucked from the air since nobody really had any idea of what the demand would be. A certain amount of chaos ensued! This resulted from the fact that nobody had thought out the mechanics of the actual marketing of the product and County Hall announced that they had no means of undertaking this. In the event the 1,000 copies arrived at my home and all enquiries made to County Hall about the book were referred to me. It quickly became apparent that the demand was going to be far greater than we could possibly have imagined. My wife Audrey and I spent hours each week packing and mailing copies (costs refunded by County Hall) not only all over the British Isles, but also to meet orders which came from Canada, the United States, Australia, New Zealand, South Africa, Holland and elsewhere in Europe. In due course we were able to arrange for a shop at Cuffley, called Novelties, to stock copies and others were placed in the Rural Studies Camp in the Great Wood. The first printing rapidly sold out and a further 1,000 copies were printed in 1967. Who would ever have imagined that a book about a small wood in Hertfordshire would be in such demand? Looked at in the context of 1966, however, this was a quite unusual concept and it coincided with an upsurge of interest in environmental matters generally. The checklists that we provided have, of course, all been extended since as a result of further research that was perhaps largely encouraged by the appearance of the book. The wood itself has changed much in the past 30 years so the book now represents a valuable historical record.

Early in 1972, some six years after the book was published, Hatfield Rural District Council announced plans for radical changes to the wood, including the eradication of large areas of bracken and the removal of dead trees. It was stated that these and other proposed actions were necessary because the wood was a fire risk. The public reaction to this nonsense was massive and immediate, partly perhaps because of the interest in the wood generated by the publication of our book. Letters by the hundred were received by HRDC, I publicised the issue in the *Barnet and Potters Bar Press* and even appeared on a TV programme with Richard Baker (who then lived at Hadley) which was filmed in the Great Wood. In the event HRDC were forced to modify their proposals.

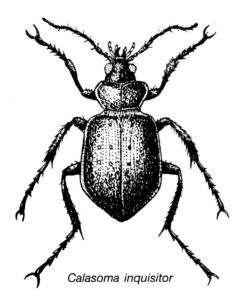

Calasoma inquisitor

9. **Rusts and Smuts**
Kerry Robinson

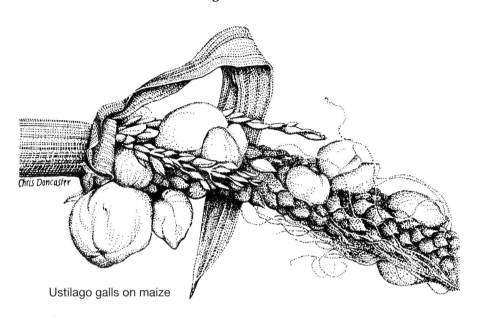

Ustilago galls on maize

Chris Doncaster

Gardeners often come up against rusts and smuts when they find their plants sickening in their gardens. Suddenly the leaves of a plant start to look a bit pale or reddish spots appear on the surface. On turning the leaf over a rust may be revealed.

Rusts belong to a group called *Uredinales* that include many common genera such as *Phragmidium*, *Puccinia* and *Uromyces*. There are approximately 275 species recorded in Britain, although many are rare and others more commonly found in Scotland.

The life cycle of a rust is complex, with up to five spore stages. Some rusts require two hosts to complete their life cycle and these species are termed heteroecious, while those requiring only a single host are called autoecious. Despite their complex lives, many rusts are fairly easy to identify as they grow only on particular plants; these are termed host specific. By knowing your plants you can identify many rusts without the aid of a microscope, although there are a few exceptions.

Some of our most common species grow in our gardens and one of the commonest is *Puccinia lagenophorae*, which is parasitic on groundsel. It forms

43

what are termed cluster cups in bright orange on stems and leaves. Amazingly, this species, native to Australia, was not known in Britain until 1961, when it was discovered at Dungeness. Now it can be found in almost any garden with a patch of groundsel.

Antirrhinums are frequently attacked by the rust *Puccinia antirrhini*. The surface of the leaf develops pale yellow-green spots and underneath the leaf a ring of dark brown spore masses can be seen breaking through the epidermis, each surrounded by a white halo. This rust was first definitely recorded in Britain in 1933 in Kent, but there are unconfirmed reports of its occurrence in 1921.

Probably the most infuriating to gardeners is rose rust, caused by two species, *Phragmidium tuberculatum* and *P. mucronatum*. In May small yellow spots can be found on the surface of the leaf and underneath, the orange spores begin to appear. As the rust's life cycle proceeds, black teliospores are produced, each with a sticky stalk which attaches itself to anything close by and waits until the next spring to start the cycle again. Other garden rusts include *Cumminsella mirabilissima* on Oregon grape and *Melampsora euphorbiae* forming an orange-yellow rust on the leaves of various spurges, *M. hypericum* attacks the leaves of tutsan and *Puccinia malveraceum* which is to be found on hollyhocks and lavatera.

Woodland plants also suffer from infection by rusts of which one of the earliest is *Uromyces ficariae*. This forms a chocolate brown spore mass on the leaves and stems of lesser celandine, eventually distorting the plant. Growing with this, the orange cluster cup rust *U. dactylidis* may be found. It is not confined to lesser celandine and is commonly found on other species of *Ranunculus* and other hosts, including such grasses as *Dactylis*, *Festuca* and *Poa* species.

Among bluebells you may notice pale yellow patches on the surface of the leaf. Underneath will be found dark brown concentrically arranged spore clusters. This is the rust *U. muscari*. Dog's mercury suffers from an orange rust called *Melampsora populnea*. This species is heteroecious (= two host species) and completes its life cycle on white poplar and aspen. *Puccinia punctiformis*, a very common rust on creeping thistle, gives off a strong sweet honey-like smell at the beginning of its life cycle in April. Later the plant takes on a spindly appearance and the leaf surface becomes covered in a thick dark brown mass of spores.

There are many more common rusts, far too numerous to list in a short paper. Two rare species I have found in Hertfordshire and consider worth mentioning are *Uromyces junci* and *Milesina kriegeriana*. I have found *U. junci* on both of its host plants. One is common fleabane, where purple spots appear on the surface of the leaf and orange spores underneath. The second is hard rush, where golden brown spores first show, followed later by the overwintering stage when a dark brown mass of teliospores is produced. Until I collected it at Norton Common in Letchworth it was believed to have been confined to Cambridgeshire, Norfolk, Suffolk and Yorkshire.

Milesina kriegeriana is an inconspicuous rust found on the underside of buckler fern but it is clearly visible on the dying fronds where it forms a white powdery spore mass. It can be found on other species of fern from autumn to early spring or on species of fir, its alternative hosts, from June to September. There are eight other species of rust that occur on ferns, but this is the only one so far recorded in Hertfordshire.

Smuts have a simpler life cycle than rusts. They form blisters and swellings on plants and can also cause black scabs or yellow patches to form on the leaves. Sometimes the spores can stick themselves to seeds and grow with them. Smuts belong to a group called *Ustilaginales* and there are about 90 species in Britain, although I have seen only 13 in Hertfordshire. All British smuts are parasitic on flowering plants, being commonest on grasses and sedges, but they also occur on the anthers of flowers and on their leaves.

One of the commonest is *Ustilago violacea*, which attacks the anthers of campion, coating them in a pinkish-purple spore mass which easily comes off on one's fingers when touched. This smut can sow its spores on the ovaries of the flowers so symptoms will show in the next generation. Infection of seedlings and underground shoots can also occur. *Urocystis anemones* is another smut which is to be found on leaves and stems of wood anemone. This produces blister like swellings that break open to expose a thick black spore mass. Similarly on the leaves and stems of creeping buttercup a smut called *U. ranunculi* might appear, again bursting through to show a mass of black spores.

A species that superficially doesn't resemble a smut is *Entyloma ficariae*. Here the spores are embedded in the leaves of lesser celandine. Its presence first becomes noticeable when pallid yellowish spots appear on the surface of the leaf and, as the smut develops, it produces a whitish area on both sides. Eighteen species of *Entyloma* smut occur on other plants and, as with rusts, they are host specific.,

Common grass smuts include *Ustilago nuda*, the loose smut of wheat and barley, which is blackish-brown in colour and, when mature, very powdery. This eventually leaves the plant tissues bare. The smut enters the plant through the young ovary and then moves to the growing point where it remains dormant until the seed germinates. *Ustilago longissima* forms elongated blister-like swellings on the leaves of sweet grass species and the blisters break open to expose a brown powdery spore mass. *U. striiformis*, known as stripe rust, is found on various other grasses and *Ustilago avenae* on false oat grass. Early in June the inflorescences become covered with a black-brown powdery mass of spores. This, like *U. nuda,* can completely destroy the ovaries and leave the rachis quite bare of flowers.

One of the more interesting species is *Ustilago maydis*, which grows on sweet corn; a fairly recent addition to the County list, its appearance is due to the dry hot summers of recent years, as it depends on having temperatures of between 26° and 34°C for development. It produces silvery white 'galls' about 10mm in diameter, which later split to expose a dark brown powdery mass of teliospores. These can overwinter in the soil and still re-appear up to eight years later. The young galls are sugary and aromatic and in Mexico are considered a delicacy; some are sold commercially and canned. A word of caution, however, if the galls are not very young and the spores have begun to mature, they are extremely poisonous!

10. **The Magic of Mushrooms**
Chris James

Fly agaric fungi

As early as 1950 in the very first edition of the Bulletin, *the interest of several members in the study of mycology was clearly evident. This was long before the modern fascination with this sphere of natural history was popularised by the plethora of field guides, coffee table books, recipe books and cookery series on colour television.*

Throughout fifty years of field meetings, this interest has never really waned and the Branch has almost always had one member, at least, who could go some way towards interpreting the mysteries of fungi to other members. Only during the early and mid-1970s did there appear to be a time when the membership struggled to identify and record the names of species, even though the fascination was there.

That the Branch's early interest got off to such a good start must be attributed to Mr. F. Clarke, who provided lists of species for no less than eight field meetings during 1950. These early forays were undertaken in woodlands that were easily accessible to members living in North Middlesex and which could be visited by London Transport or the Hertford North Railway Line. Popular sites were Scratchwood, Broxbourne Wood, Whitewebbs Park and Northaw Great Wood. Several of these outings recorded fungi which were abundant during July and August, for Britain did not then always experience the summer droughts that are a phenomenon of the 1990s. 1956 appears to have been an especially wet year and many of the reports on the summer rambles record heavy downpours. However, the damp conditions through July and August produced good shows of species of *Collybia*, *Pluteus* (a group normally found growing on fallen wood), *Russula*, *Hypholoma* and *Bolbitius* and resulted in 44 species being identified on a foray near Bayford in mid-August.

Not only did Mr. Clarke identify fungi but he also painted them beautifully in water colours and the first *Bulletin* includes three colour washed drawings of species occurring on cow dung - very small species easily missed by those not trained to look in the right sort of places! In 1951 Mr. Clarke provided the information which produced pages of lists of both edible and toxic fungi - a nightmare for those stalwarts who were valiantly typing individual copies of the *Bulletin* at the time.

An intriguing quotation from the foray report for October 5th 1952 reads: " A Mr. Reid of Kew was very co-operative and helpful during our foray at Northaw Great Wood, held jointly with the Hertfordshire Natural History Society, although it was difficult to keep such a large party in order." Dr. Derek Reid is now one of the country's foremost field mycologists - what a great thrill it must have been to have such an expert in our midst! Dr. Reid's expertise produced a list of 85 different species, unsurprisingly the highest total of any foray held by BNA during the 1950s.

A special foray was held in Epping Forest, Essex, to celebrate the Golden Jubilee of national BNA in 1955. The published guide to the forest at that time confidently asserted that as many as 68 different species of fungi could be found, but Mr. Clarke estimated that there were at least 300! After more than forty years of further discoveries, what must the total be now? The careful laying out and labelling of the fungi found on this foray much impressed the author of the report, as did a splendid exhibition of Mr. Clarke's paintings. The point was made that BNA is truly a field natural history society.

Mr. Clarke was elected the first president of the Branch in 1953, a position he held until his death in 1958. He was very much missed by our members who were, however, delighted that his large collection of paintings, drawings and field notebooks was accepted by the Royal Botanic Gardens at Kew as a respected contribution to mycological studies.

During the next fifteen or so years, the Branch's interest in fungi fluctuated and there were fewer forays included in field meeting programmes, although two enthusiastic followers of Mr. Clarke led the forays and recorded fungi whenever they were able. The acquisition of a ciné camera also ensured that both fungi and forayers were recorded for posterity! Without the enthusiasm of John and June Pearton, the Branch's interest in fungi might well have faded.

In September 1974 the Branch again ventured over the County border to Epping Forest, following a comment at the Annual General Meeting that not enough was being done to promote the study of fungi. The foray was led by a local man and 50 species were identified during the morning. The *Bulletin* records that "Epping Forest is a mycologist's dream and a beginner's nightmare"!

Activities livened up again in 1976 when a foray in Northaw Great Wood ended with tea and a display of collections in the village hall, followed by a slide show. Then in 1977 the first big foray for many years was held in two ancient woodlands in northern Hertfordshire - new territory for many. Forty-five people from several natural history societies attended and were led by Miss Margaret Holden, County Recorder of fungi for the Hertfordshire Natural History Society. The final total of species found in Wain Wood at Preston was

120 and these were the first records for the wood since the 1840s. Eighty species were collected from Hitch Wood nearby and half of these were new records for the wood.

Miss Holden was invited to lead another foray in October 1978 following a lecture with colour slides borrowed from the library of the British Mycological Society. The foray was held in a part of East Hertfordshire new to both the Branch and to Miss Holden, and records collected on this occasion helped to fill in several gaps in our knowledge of the distribution of fungi in the County.

It is at this point that I hope that readers will forgive me becoming personal. I have to attribute my own interest in fungi to the encouragement given by Margaret Holden. During the very late 1970s and early 1980s, it was Margaret who patiently repeated the Latin names each year as the common species reappeared in their magical way. Margaret also impressed me with her foraying basket complete with its dropper bottles of chemical solutions which, when applied to the appropriate species, turned fungus flesh pink, green or blue! She reassured me that the first ten years of study would be the worst but that the names would eventually stick.

At the Annual General Meeting in 1982 I agreed to become the Branch's recorder for fungi, although this followed only four years of amateur and very part-time study - I still had a long way to go. Each year since then the field meeting programme has included at least two forays, sometimes three, of which one has usually been held in one of Hertfordshire's fine ancient woodlands and the other in a less well-known area of countryside, including habitats other than woodlands.

On several occasions the Branch has been given permission to foray in woods not normally accessible to the general public, including Hatfield Park and Knebworth estates. At Hatfield, on October 2nd 1988, we were joined by members of both the Hertfordshire Natural History Society and the Cheshunt Natural History Society, thus creating a combined foraying party of thirty people. The final list of species found on that day totalled 142 and included the unfamiliar (to us) names of several myxomycetes - small species better seen with a hand lens or through a microscope! These were identified by Peter Holland and by a young and already very skilled mycologist, Kerry Robinson. Kerry became a BNA member in about 1990 and the branch has benefited enormously from her knowledge and methodical recording. Kerry's first properly ordered list of species appeared in the *Bulletin* for a meeting held at Scratchwood, Middlesex, on March 5th, 1989.

Another memorable foray was held at Panshanger Park on October 20th 1991. Here again the Branch had gained permission from the owners, Redland Aggregates, to explore various habitats, especially the damp woodland and osier beds on the valley floor. Thirty-five people attended which made the logistics difficult during the day - some folk were lost, 'never to be seen again' - but the total list made the day worthwhile. The *Bulletin* report reads:

"Despite the dry season, and therefore low expectations, our resident experts recorded no less than 189 species. A good number of these were made up of 'lesser fungi', the rusts, smuts, mildews and micros, but nevertheless a significant aspect of the day was the number of important finds that were made. Of the larger fungi (*Basidiomycetes*), *Galerina autumnalis, Lactarius obscuratus* and *Lepiota subalba* were new to Hertfordshire. *Russula brunneoviolacea* was the second County record and *Naucoria escaroides* was a re-discovery confirming an old record. The brackets and other related fungi also came up trumps - one of them was none other than a second British record. It is of note that a good number of these rare species, as well as other interesting finds, were associated with the damp ground along the river Mimram. This ancient habitat is already known to be amongst the most important in the Park."

One of the experts present at Panshanger was Alan Outen, who has since taken over from Margaret Holden as County Recorder for fungi and who has also helped to identify collections of fungi found on BNA forays.

In order to provide a focus for our forays, the distribution of fungi has been mapped on record cards for each species and, where possible, historical information from early bulletins added. The map of Hertfordshire on the card includes the grid lines dividing the County into 2km squares; a dot indicates the presence of the species in question within its appropriate 2km square. These dot maps have been a standard method for recording distributions of wildlife species for some twenty years and are a relatively cheap and easy way of storing biological information. Modern developments in information technology have revolutionised the systems, but the dot map is still incorporated in special biological data handling programmes.

For several years Margaret and Alan have been researching and writing a book on the fungi of Hertfordshire. It is good to know that much of the information gathered so painstakingly on BNA forays and on private outings by BNA members will make a contribution towards this book which is eagerly awaited.

In the meantime, it is good to be able to record that interest in fungi is still strong amongst Branch members and others are also making notes about species found and, importantly, where they are found. Without an accurate map reference we cannot put that all important dot on the map!

For those whose interest has been slow to kindle, or for whom foraying is physically arduous (progress is often very slow!), Hertfordshire BNA has provided armchair foraying in the form of slide lectures. The most recent was given in 1991 by Fred Boardman, a member of the BNA and Associate of the Royal Photographic Society. Sadly, Fred died not long afterwards and so we felt especially privileged to have seen just 80 species out of a possible 400 that Fred had photographed over the years. He enjoyed his sorties to other parts of the country, especially to Scotland, which is of great interest to mycologists, many species found there are not found further south. Not only were members treated to Fred's superb slides but they were also entertained with little yarns about the habits and folklore of fungi. So to finish this article about the magic of mushrooms, here is a quote from Fred's own report of his talk in the *Bulletin* for October 12th 1991.

"One very memorable species is the fly agaric, *Amanita muscaria*, which has red caps with white spots on them. When eaten by humans, the fungal toxins induce a 'high' during which the unfortunate victims think they can fly; people have been known to jump out of windows failing to prove their ability. Of course we know that they have to vomit after eating them, but that reindeer can eat them with impunity. This is why they can fly and why Father Christmas wears a red cloak with white trimmings to remind us of this fungus."

11. **Wild about Flowers**
Graeme Smith

Searching for and enjoying wild flowers has always been one of the most popular pursuits of the British Naturalists' Association. Flowers are easy to observe and identification guides are readily available. From the earliest days the Bulletins are packed with floral lists and the Hertfordshire Branch has made significant discoveries and visited many important sites for flowers.

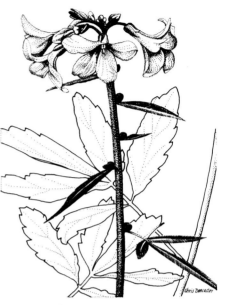

Coralroot bittercress

Two things are noticeable from the early bulletins. The first is that English names of wild flowers have changed, sometimes to an extent where it is now difficult or impossible to be sure what was originally intended. In June 1950, for example, a visit to Scratchwood uncovered goutweed, yellow loosestrife, dyer's rocket, blue and yellow scorpion-grass. Upright St. John's wort and marsh club rush. Goutweed is now better known as ground elder. Yellow loosestrife poses the problem that it could be four species, yellow loosestrife, wood pimpernel, creeping jenny or dotted loosestrife. However, in July 1950 on a visit to Northaw Great Wood, both yellow loosestrife and yellow pimpernel were recorded. In the 1950s I don't think that dotted loosestrife would have been thought worth recording as a wild plant. *Bentham and Hooker* shed no further light on the dilemma and I conclude that in this instance sloppy recording has muddied the waters. Yellow loosestrife is rare in Hertfordshire and Middlesex, so I guess that our yellow loosestrife that was is now creeping jenny. Dyer's rocket is now more commonly known as weld. Blue and yellow scorpion grass is plainly a forget-me-not and *Bentham and Hooker* confirm the most obvious answer; changing forget-me-not, *Myosotis discolor*, with its bright blue and yellow flowers. Upright St. John's wort is now common St. John's wort, *Hypericum perforatum*. And marsh club rush; perhaps bulrush?

On 16th July 1952, our Branch visited the Bayford area when yet more upright St. John's wort was found, along with square-stemmed and trailing St. John's worts. Mountain crane's bill (now Pyrenean crane's-bill) was also seen together with musk mallow, sneeze wort, fleabane, cow wheat and great valerian. The valerian presents a difficulty. Is the great valerian reported just common valerian or the taller, more unusual Pyrenean valerian, an escapee from cultivation? *Dony* does not record the latter, but this would not be expected of him with an alien species. However, common valerian is recorded near to Bayford in *Dony's Flora*, in fact the area between Bayford and the river Lea seemed to be a hot spot for the species. It will be interesting to see if the Flora 2000 project uncovers the plant in all its original sites.

True marshwort, *Apium inundatum*, is an uncommon Hertfordshire aquatic plant. However, the marshwort recorded in July 1952 would probably be marsh woundwort. The same goes for the records of marshwort at St. Albans in July 1957 and at London Colney in the same month. It is interesting that common cat's-ear was recorded in 1952 as long-rooted cat's-ear. An intriguing and unlikely entry is madwort at Hatfield in September 1956. It could have been lesser dodder which, after all, is a weird creation, or more likely it was field madder, *Sherardia arvensis*. Dodder was confirmed on a visit to Chorleywood Common in 1961 and this record made its way into *Dony's Flora*.

The second thing of note in the early bulletins is the casualness with which now rare plants were then reported. In some instances these records are strongly suspected as being in error, although the records cannot be entirely disregarded. A prime example is shepherd's cress, *Teesdalia nudicaulis*, now a rare cruciferous plant of heathy soils. This was first mentioned in the bulletins in a list of 43 plants found in June 1950 at Enfield Chase. It was 'discovered' by the BNA in June 1952 at Hertford and in June 1956 at Wheathampstead (with corn gromwell). The plant gets no special mention in these cases and probably shepherd's purse was the proper identification. Shepherd's cress was extinct in the County after about 1920. In August 1976 shepherd's needle, *Scandix pecten-veneris,* a rare arable plant, was found in a field near Westfield Common, but was noted as being increasingly rare. The next BNA sighting was not until April 1995 when many plants were discovered at a field edge at Scales Park near Nuthampstead. The author also saw a few plants in 1997 at the edge of a horse gallop near Hill Farm, Radlett; there are several old records for shepherd's needle in this area.

Another odd plant that is rarely seen now but which got blasé treatment in early bulletin reports is longleaf. In fact this is a garden escapee and is like a pignut but with strap-shaped serrated leaves. Longleaf first appears in the bulletins in August 1950 between Broxbourne and Little Amwell. It was then seen in September 1952 at Wormley Woods and then the year after in June on a walk from Broxbourne station to Hoddesdon via Hertford Heath and Little Amwell. These records are a little suspicious as the plant prefers the chalk. Perhaps the culprit was greater burnet saxifrage. The next sighting of longleaf was in September 1978 on the Long Trek when it was seen in Reed Chalk Pit along with common hound's-tongue. The Branch has not seen it since, although the author found it in a grassy area on the Walkern Road in 1994, a well known, long established site.

Cornflower gets a mention in August 1957 when a large patch was discovered in a corn field near Oughtonhead Common. This is now almost never seen in a native situation, although major roadworks may throw up some dormant seed. Cornflower is a regular inclusion in wild flower seed and the scattering of seed in the countryside may give spurious records to the unwary. Pond vegetation is often enhanced now in Hertfordshire by the introduction of such things as greater spearwort and bogbean. This undermines our biological records, because if, say, bogbean were found in a new location, it would be assumed to be introduced, which might not be the case. Butcher's broom was seen at Whitwell in 1981, but no details were given. In October 1985 a single specimen was noted in the lane leading from The Bury. Butcher's broom is sometimes thrown out or planted in neighbouring woods. So, again, any new records near habitation must be regarded as introductions. Several plants are only mentioned once in the bulletins and are best regarded as occurring casually, if not introduced, although some may have germinated from old seed. Weasel's snout was found in a weedy garden tub at Welwyn North Station in August 1984 and thorn apple surprised everyone in Plashes Wood in the following year.

Certain flowers are always well recorded because of their beauty, distinctiveness, strangeness or scarcity. Some of these plants may occur or flower erratically so it is especially pleasing when they are found. Henbane is not seen that often in Hertfordshire but the BNA has several records. First sighting was in July 1956 in the Chess Valley then in 1957 it was seen in Woodhall Park. The Branch has also seen henbane more recently along the river Lea at Hertford Meads and in set-aside at Panshanger Park. Dyer's greenweed is a welcome record and there are quite a few sightings of this. In the 50s, Scratchwood and Northaw Great Wood were popular venues for BNA outings and the greenweed was often recorded from these two places. The Burleigh Meadow near Stevenage is another station and Croxley Common Moor produced great spreads of the plant on our outing in 1992. A near relative, petty whin has charmed Branch members over the years and this is also found at Burleigh Meadow. Our conservation days at Hertford Heath made us quite proprietorial about the few bushes of petty whin that we saw there. The first record seems to be June 1979, then again in 1983. There was bad news in 1986 when it was reported that "the usual bush of petty whin by the track at Hertford Heath has all but died. However, a new bush, full of flowers, has started up about ten yards away." By 1987, "The new plant is doing well and the old plant has revived a little." In June 1988, creeping willow was found but no petty whin. It is important that such plants should be regularly monitored.

Marsh arrowgrass is a plant of old wet meadows and therefore is quite vulnerable. This was seen on a flower-packed day at Oughtonhead in August 1957 (the last record) and was found in Panshanger in 1993. Common blinks, a plant of flushes and damp areas, is a trifle boring but is quite scarce in

Hertfordshire. The BNA found this in Northaw Great Wood in 1950 and 1955. Coralroot bittercress on the other hand is a handsome thing, which has been visited many times in Whippendell Woods and Harrocks Wood. In both these places the bittercress seems to have expanded enormously. In Harrocks Wood recent conservation work has enriched the woodland greatly and in Whippendell Woods coralroot bittercress is now quite frequent along one of the main rides, so much so that in 1997 two gormless ladies were seen with bunches of the flowers. Chorleywood Dell is another site for the flower. In one of the early bulletins, our Mr. Richard Ward, former Honorary President, is reported to have first seen coralroot bittercress in Whippendell Woods in 1937. Mistletoe is much easier to spot in winter when there are no leaves left on the host tree. The BNA records this plant curiosity from Knebworth Park, Widford, Gilston Park, Little Tring, Home Park Hatfield and the driveway to Moor Place. Adder's-tongue fern is quite unlike most other ferns and is always a good indicator of a rich habitat. In 1953 it was seen in a wood between Bayford and Essendon, then in 1978 it was discovered in Whippendell Wood. Later it was seen at Tring and Burns Green.

One of the BNA's best discoveries happened in 1979, when wood cudweed was uncovered in Harmer Green Wood. This was reported as "the first record in Hertfordshire for about 50 years." It has not been seen since. Hertfordshire was once a stronghold for cudweeds and these have disappeared except marsh cudweed *Gnaphalium uliginosum*, common cudweed *Filago vulgaris* (rare), and broad-leaved cudweed *F. pyramidata* (rare). The reasons for this poor showing are not fully understood; loss of habitat is partially to blame, but there may be an environmental effect. Mousetail, a rare and odd member of the buttercup family, is always a rewarding find. This was found by the author on a BNA ramble at North Mimms on the edge of a rape field. The plant likes damp gravelly soil. Previously mousetail had also been found at Little Hadham and since then it has shown up near Trenchern Hills. It is more readily found on some parts of the Essex coast.

Some plants are old favourites. Mountain bitter vetch is first recorded by the BNA in 1952 at Broxbourne Woods by the Roman Road, and in 1983 it was seen on the Bricket Wood Common walk. Mimms Woods produced another record in 1986. Little has been said about orchids, although recently, because of dry weather, there has been not much to report. Bee orchid is probably seen more now than in the past, but early purple orchids and even common spotted orchids are less common. One fine sight seems guaranteed, that is the large spread of early marsh, southern marsh and common spotted orchids and their tall hybrids on the fly ash, a power station by-product, at Cheshunt, with bee orchids appearing later in the nearby meadow remnant. Violet helleborine turns up in some unlikely places and it is good to have a day on the chalk hills, when white helleborine might be seen under the beeches with fly orchid. We have had several visits to the Chiltern gentian still surviving at the remains of the chalk pit at Howe Green. The plant has also been seen at

Oddy Hill and survives the motorcyclists who roar around the SSSI; maybe they do some good service in keeping the grass short. A splendid sight is the hundreds of pasque flowers at Church Hill, where spring sedge and wild candytuft may also be found.

The BNA has visited many exciting habitats in Hertfordshire and it is good to see long lists of notable flowers. In August 1979 a walk near Munchers Green uncovered violet helleborine, strawberry clover, stone parsley, pepper saxifrage, sneezewort, tormentil, spiked sedge, orpine and blunt-flowered rush. On my first walk with the BNA in July 1982, we met at Ashwell station and I was soon introduced to the delights of knapweed broomrape, basil-thyme, wild candytuft, prickly round-headed and prickly long-headed poppies. The next month the Knebworth area produced fine-leaved and tubular water dropworts, pseudocyperus sedge, sneezewort and marsh speedwell. There have been many days like this.

But it is not only the rarities that interest our members. Annual displays of bluebells under hornbeams, bright starry lesser celandines, meadows full of swaying buttercups and lady's smock or later scarlet with poppies, hedges burgeoning with blackthorn or fragrant with hawthorn blossom and riversides edged with the pure blue of forget-me-not or tall spikes of purple loosestrife all bring joy to the heart and gentle therapy to the work worn.

References:
Bentham, G. & Hooker, J.D. 1943 *Handbook of the British Flora.* L. Reeve & Co.
Dony, J.G. 1967 *Flora of Hertfordshire.* Hitchin Urban District Council.

Listening to the dawn chorus at Ashridge   Photo: Michael Demidecki

Lunch in Ashridge woods   Photo: Michael Demidecki

A wary Bittern　　　　Photo: Les Borg

Tree Sparrow　　　　Photo: Les Borg

Sparrowhawk　　　　Photo: Les Borg

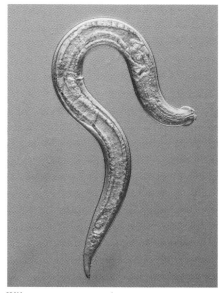

Wilsonema, *a nematode*
from a moss cushion　　　　Photo: Chris Doncaster

Hertford Heath

Photo: Trevor James

Badger

Photo: Michael Demidecki

The rust Puccinia punctiformis
on Creeping Thistle   Photo: Kerry Robinson

The rust Phragmidium fragariae
on Barren Strawberry   Photo: Kerry Robinson

Scarlet Elf Cup, Sarcoscypha austriaca
                    Photo: Kerry Robinson

Sulphur Polypore   Photo: Chris James

Pasque flowers

Photo: John Stevens

Green Winged Orchid

Photo: Trevor James

Frank Lancaster wading the Mimram, the first Long Trek, Sept.1978

Photo: Trevor James

Trapping moths with a home-built trap

Photo: Michael Clark

Small Elephant Hawk Moth

Photo: Kerry Robinson

*Long-winged
Conehead,
a Bush Cricket*
Photo: John Widgery

*Lesser Marsh
Grasshopper*
Photo: John Widgery

*Male long-winged
variety of Roesel's
Bush Cricket*
Photo: John Widgery

*Slender
Groundhopper*
Photo: John Widgery

Immature male Broad-bodied Chaser

Photo: John Stevens

The end of the day - Fallow Deer

Photo: Michael Clark

12. **A Walk in the Lea Valley**
June Crew and Graeme Smith

Southern
marsh orchid

This is an un-edited extract from the Bulletin *describing a walk in the Cheshunt area that took place on 1st July 1990 when eight members and one child attended.*

On Sunday 1st July when skies were overcast and the light was gloomy, the Hertfordshire and Epping Branches of the British Naturalists' Association and two members of the Cheshunt NHS met in the car park at the end of Windmill Lane, Cheshunt. Setting off north at a smartish pace along the towpath of the Lee navigation, everyone ground to a halt to don waterproofs. Young Edward James had to be helped, so while he caught up, Ann Boucher made a small detour to show Japanese knotweed, *Polygonum cuspidatum,* and giant knotweed, *P. sachaliense,* and a hybrid between the two to some alien spotters. The first orchid site (sight) on long ago dumped fly ash on the edge of the North Metropolitan pit was long past its flowering date, with just a few dozen flowering spikes of southern marsh and hybrids showing up amongst thousands of brown seed heads of the early marsh orchid. The rumoured nightingale did not show up, but the sun did, over the once lawn of an abandoned sailing club; now a haven for weed species and looking like promising reptile country. A dead grass snake had once been found there. Cinnabar caterpillars festooned ragwort and several skippers (appropriate for a sailing club) did just that over arbours of bramble. Figwort was found in velvety bloom at the end of the causeway by the decrepit jetty. By now the botanists had listed many dozens of plant species and were poking at at least a three star plant in the water filled gravel pit.

The next orchid site, not far past Cheshunt Lock and just a few yards from the river bank, was accessible only by scrambling over a fence and like Wordsworth we gazed and gazed, but at lupin-like mauve spikes of a myriad of southern marsh orchids. We waited for poetic inspiration and gaps in clouds to record on film a swathe as thick as WW's daffodils. Edward started recording the number by counting them with a stick, but fortunately didn't get past three!

At lunchtime we sat on recently laid crushed coke and watched a man mixing cement which he was applying to a partially constructed new bridge, an old right of way, over the river Lee navigation. (The bridge gives welcome access to the area noted on Sheet TL20/30 as 'El Tfmr Sta', a not uninteresting area, if in Essex. However, an access path has been driven across the Hertfordshire marshes towards the bridge and a quiet area will never be the same. Nevertheless the scope for circular or figure of eight walks here has been improved. 1991 has seen further 'improvements' in this area. The towpath has been upgraded, but pathside vegetation has been removed and bark laid down to stifle the 'weeds', although several clumps of vervain were a surprise. Timber seats and picnic benches have appeared all around the pits and there are now hides from which to watch what is left. There are mixed feelings about the orchid areas, where boardwalks have been installed to stop feet trampling the plants. The area was once a scruffy wilderness; it is fast becoming a public park.)

Still going north we reached Aqueduct Lock (over the old river Lea) and turned off east to walk the plank over a ditch. The old river Lea was a travesty of its former self, but supported greater reed mace, common reed and himalayan balsam. Having skirted another water-filled pit, we reached practically the only piece of original meadow missed by the gravel winners of 50 years previously. This vestige half acre of ancient water meadow that once extended along the whole of the Lee Valley is now a nature reserve with an information board calling it "the wild flower meadow". We counted a couple of dozen bee orchids. Edward was unimpressed and preferred to make a head count of the party using a borrowed walking stick.

Heading south in a now brisk wind and under leaden skies, we came across the deadly poisonous hemlock water-dropwort growing at the edge of another pit by a fisherman's swim. The Urals euphorbia (actually a hybrid) was growing in profusion in another small meadow. Cowslip plants were much in evidence. Taking the scenic route along a less well-trodden path on the edge of a steep roll into deep water and keeping the railway in sight on our right and a tight grip on Edward, we reached a more park-like part of the Lea Valley Park between Cheshunt Sailing Base and the railway, after which we reached Windmill Lane again.

A short detour to a much changed meadow south of Windmill Lane revealed tree lupins, melilot, a tall (alien?) sorrel, salad burnet and an emperor moth caterpillar.

We had walked about 3½ miles barely conscious of the small boy in our midst, though no doubt his Dad had not taken his eyes off him for more than a minute at a time (to count stamens and bristles and things).

13. **In Search of Butterfly Eggs**
Kerry Robinson

The first few months of the year are quiet in the butterfly world.
Yet there is life waiting to burst forth with the onset of sunny warmer days.
Eggs laid last summer lie hidden in secret places, generally on the caterpillar's
favourite food plant, awaiting the perfect timing of hatching
and the unfurling of the first new leaves.

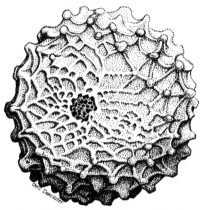

Egg of the chalkhill blue butterfly

My search for butterfly eggs begins in the first months of the year, with the hairstreaks. Four out of the five British hairstreaks overwinter in the egg stage and these are found most easily before the bushes have leaves. Oak buds are the home of the purple hairstreak. Wide rides with oak bushes or trees where branches on the sunny side are low enough to be reached are some of the best places to search. The eggs are laid individually on the stoutest oak buds, although more than one may be found on a single bud. They are greyish-white in colour with a raised network of ridges and a sunken middle, the characteristic shape for members of the *Lycaenidae* family. In some years they are particularly common and easy to find but in others they may be scarce, depending on the previous year's summer population.

Brown and black hairstreaks both lay their eggs on blackthorn but I find brown hairstreaks much the easier to see, mainly because the butterfly lays at between 4ft and 6ft from the ground, while the black hairstreak prefers the tops of the oldest bushes, which are often covered with green algae, obscuring the eggs, and are not so accessible either. Brown hairstreaks' eggs are found singly or in pairs on the upperside of the branch, often at the junction of a fork, and stand out well against the dark background. The eggs are spherical in shape, with a raised honeycomb pattern and are white in colour.

The black hairstreak tends to prefer the underside of the branch, making searching for the eggs that much more difficult. The eggs have a flattened appearance and are a greyish colour during the winter months, so they are not as prominent as the white eggs of the brown hairstreak. When first laid in June they are orange-brown, but this does not make them any easier to find.

Three of our most attractive and well-known butterflies, the small tortoiseshell, peacock and comma are amongst the first to appear, having hibernated for the winter as adults. They all lay their eggs on stinging nettles. The small tortoiseshell's eggs are very difficult to see when first laid as their colour perfectly matches that of the nettle leaves, although later they become tinged yellow. Both small tortoiseshell and peacock choose the tenderest shoots and lay large batches of over 100 eggs several layers deep. To distinguish between peacock eggs and those of the small tortoiseshell one has to count the number of ribs on them, the peacock having eight prominent ones while the small tortoiseshell has nine.

By comparison the comma lays its eggs singly on the upperside of the nettle leaf and usually towards the edge. They are green in colour with a glassy appearance, spherical and with ten or eleven longitudinal ribs. Our other common British hibernating butterfly is the brimstone which starts to lay in May. These are easy to find on the undersides of common buckthorn leaves. They are yellow and bottle shaped, with ten longitudinal keels and fine transverse lines between, so standing out prominently against the green. The orange-tip is on the wing from April, after overwintering as a pupa. It lays its eggs from mid-May on cuckoo flower and garlic mustard. The eggs are very distinct, being deep orange in colour and laid singly among the flower heads; they are thus very easy to find.

Another species that has become more common in the last few years is the holly blue, appearing regularly in the garden and our local woods. The second brood of eggs is laid in August among the flower buds of ivy and I find them much easier to find than those laid on holly which are so well camouflaged. The eggs are bluish-green in colour with a raised whitish netting and a sunken depression in the top. By moving the ivy buds gently apart the egg shows up quite well. Also if you see a small hole in the bud, the chances are that the egg has already hatched and the caterpillar has burrowed inside.

The Duke of Burgundy fritillary, the only British representative of the family *Nemeobiidae*, has eggs that are pale yellowish-green, smooth and glossy. With age they become pinkish-grey and just before hatching transparent, so if you look carefully you can see the tiny caterpillar inside. Eggs are laid from early June in small groups on the undersides of the leaves of primrose and cowslip.

By looking at the various eggs one will notice that in each family there is a characteristic general shape, with distinctive details, ornamentation and colour. A range of different shapes occurs from the primitive skippers, which have smooth-shelled eggs, to the spiny ones of the white admiral. The egg shell is made of chitin and in most species has a sticky end for fixing it in position on the leaf or branch. There are two exceptions to this, namely the marbled white and ringlet which both scatter their eggs at random.

When hatching the larva eats a round lid from the shell, just big enough for it to crawl out. Some species then eat the whole shell, especially if they are going into immediate hibernation, while others may eat only part. The silver-washed fritillary and the dark green fritillary both completely consume their egg shells on hatching. However, as yet I have been unable to find the eggs of any member of the fritillary family and there are many other rare or scarce butterflies, including the purple emperor for which I have searched long and hard without any luck. Perhaps one day I shall be in the right place at the right time.

14. Aberrant Varieties of the Chalkhill Blue Butterfly at Therfield Heath
Peter Alton

The Therfield Heath chalkhill blues were under threat. Collecting aberrant varieties had taken its toll but did not account for continuing decline. Conservation work has brought the chalkhill blue back from the brink.

Chris Doncaster

The chalkhill blue is one of the five blue *Lycaenid* butterflies that occur in the County and is aptly named both for its colour and for its favoured habitat of grassland on chalk or limestone. Horseshoe vetch is the caterpillar's principal food plant, but even when this is in adequate supply, other conditions must be right too. The caterpillar, as with most other 'blues', depends on a mutually beneficial relationship with ants and because ants can only thrive where the turf is short, close grazing by sheep or rabbits is a necessity. It is believed that the ants provide protection for the caterpillars against parasites and predators, in return for which they can 'milk' the caterpillars which, on stimulation, secrete a sugary nectar and also pheromones that calm the ants' aggressive tendencies. The ants sometimes provide further protection for the chalkhill blue over the winter months by burying the pupae until the adult butterflies are ready to emerge in June.

Therfield Heath, near Royston seemed to be an almost ideal habitat for the chalkhill blue until myxomatosis decimated the rabbit population in the 1950s, then the turf became over-grown and persistent insecticides began taking their toll too. Parasitic wasps and climatic changes probably also contributed to the butterfly's subsequent decline. However, from the turn of the century until the outbreak of the Second World War, Therfield Heath was a mecca for collectors, July and August being called the 'chalkhill blue season' when the butterflies were emerging in their thousands. Guest and boarding houses were soon filled at this time and there must have been an air of excited anticipation with so many collectors gathering together.

Although the chalkhill blue was then common it was its aberrant varieties that the collectors were after. The undersides of the wings of most of the blue family have a series of black dots and orange and white crescents, but in the aberrant forms these spots might be absent or joined into long streaks, looking quite striking on the pale grey or buff background.

To see the beautiful upper side of a butterfly with wings spread, the sun should be shining. How often and for how long do we wait for butterflies to open their wings when clouds keep crossing the sun! However the collectors of aberrant chalkhill blues needed no sunshine, since the prizes were visible while the insects rested with their wings closed. Searching was generally at emergence time early in the morning or when the butterflies were drowsy and resting before nightfall. So great was the number of aberrant chalkhill blues caught, killed and set that more than 200 different varieties were named.

Most aberrations, if not all, are under genetic control and are therefore inherited, but environmental factors such as climate can also play a part. However, any individual aberrations which would not recur in the next generation, as by accident or disease, would not qualify for a name.

The beautiful Adonis blue, a close cousin of the chalkhill, needs the same kind of habitat and was found on Therfield Heath until 1949, but not again and was declared extinct there in 1960. Aberrant forms occur in this species also, including so-called gynandromorphs, where because of a genetic mix-up during development sexual characters combine to a greater or lesser extent. In the Adonis it is the upper sides of the wings that are affected in this way, the clear blue of the male taking on more or less of the brown coloration of the female.

The chalkhill blue population on Therfield Heath, although still fairly strong, has sadly and dramatically declined over the past 40 or 50 years. While numbers do fluctuate from year to year, they are now on a slow upward trend due to conservation work and the introduction of grazing. Some entomologists think that the incidence of aberrations may reflect a weakening of the strain and L. Hugh Newman said that when, nearly a century ago, the chalkhill blue died out over the cliffs of Dover, aberrations had become increasingly common and he referred to the butterfly as becoming curiously 'shot-holed'. Has the Therfield Heath population suffered in the same way?

The vogue for intensively collecting dead specimens cannot now be blamed for the long decline and has thankfully been superseded to a large degree by interest in photographing live butterflies in their natural surroundings and also by increasing awareness of the importance of species and habitat conservation. Areas that are specially managed for the butterflies are helping recovery locally and small pockets of a few individuals do occur naturally along the Chiltern ridge in Hertfordshire. However other counties such as Lincolnshire have not been so lucky. More help for the Therfield Heath population may well be needed if we are to continue to find chalkhill blues there for any length of time in the future.

15. **Moth Trapping**
Katharine Hall

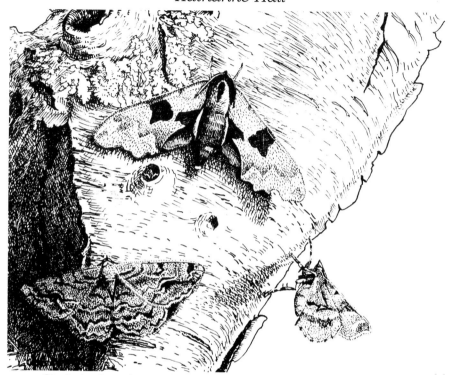

Clockwise from the top: lime hawk moth, purple thorn, mottled beauty

Moth trapping can be fun and can be instructive, but there are pitfalls.

I have been trapping moths for the past three or four years, first at Burymead Springs which is a small area of wetland, then in my own garden in Hitchin. The garden is about 10 metres by 5, but it is surrounded by similar gardens and there are parks not far away. I use a homemade version of a 'Heath' trap, which is a box about a foot cubed, with an ultraviolet light on top of a funnel to attract the moths. With this I have sometimes enticed upwards of 60 moths on a warm night in August. I am afraid I tend to ignore micromoths because there is no cheap and comprehensive guide to these.For large moths, I use Skinner's book (see appendix). Sometimes I use Chinery's book to point me in the right direction as it shows the moths in more lifelike positions (Skinner used museum specimens for plates). I always let the moths go after I have identified them as I have no desire to accumulate a collection to clutter up the house and looking after a museum wastes time I could better spend observing and recording.

Moth trapping is easy to combine with a job because the trap can be put out in the evening and brought in in the morning. Moths stay still when they are cold, as when they have been in a trap all night, so it is fairly easy to identify them before they warm up. Colin Plant, the moth recorder for Hertfordshire, tells me it is possible to put a trap in a cool cellar all day and to identify the moths at your leisure in the evening. Having no cellar, I once tried keeping the trap in the coolest part of the house, but when I opened it in the evening the moths all flew out and I was finding them flattened to walls and ceilings for days afterwards. However, I have successfully kept one or two in a box in the fridge all day, which is unfortunately not big enough to accommodate the whole trap.

I had about 80 different species last year despite bad weather and problems with the trap. The most spectacular were hawkmoths - elephant hawkmoth and privet hawkmoth; I only catch a few of these each year. But some of the commonest moths, the large and lesser yellow underwings, are very attractive at close range, when their brown upper wings fold forward to expose beautiful golden underwings. On the 2nd of September 1996, I had 21 lesser and 31 large yellow underwings in the trap at once.

The kinds of moths one catches depend on the time of year and the vegetation growing. Early on the heart and dart, which is a dull small brown moth, is common in catches, then later I get the underwings. But most catches have something attractive and I hope to improve the range by planting more wild flowers in the garden. Skinner gives a list of foodplants and many of these are quite easily grown, such as campion and bird's-foot trefoil. I already grow valerian, thyme, mallow, foxglove and lady's bedstraw, so I hope I am encouraging the moth population. I definitely get moths feeding on the local vegetation and one species commonly caught in my trap is the marbled beauty, which looks just like grey lichen. Its larva feeds on lichen, so it can hardly be a coincidence that my trap is next to a shed whose roof is covered with grey lichen.

Although there are moths flying all year (and I have caught the December moth inside a building in December to prove it) I catch few species before April and after October, so I do not trap in winter. Catches would be larger with a bigger trap. Some models with more powerful lights may catch 300 or more moths on a good night. However, they cost a great deal and also I am concerned about upsetting the natural balance if I were trapping regularly on that scale. If I want to expand my efforts I will trap on more nights and in different places. I will also extend my identification to include some of the micros, including those more easily identified by the mines their larvae make in leaves, than by trapping and examining the adults. I could also start looking for caterpillars, and try sugaring i.e. painting trees with a mixture of molasses and beer or spirits and then going round with a torch to look for those moths that prefer food to light as an attractant (the sensible ones!).

Moth trapping is very rewarding and unlike most branches of natural history the species come to you; you don't have to go chasing them. My main problem was getting a trap. At first I borrowed one, then someone made me one, but they can be bought (see below). Some traps can be run either from a car battery or from the house mains via a transformer. They are also easy to construct and instructions are readily available, but I'm not enough of an electrician to advise.

Recommended reading:
Skinner, B. 1984 *Colour Identification Guide to Moths of the British Isles.* Viking.
Chinery, M. 1986 *Guide to the Insects of Britain and Western Europe.* Collins.

Equipment:
Watkins & Doncaster, PO Box 5, Cranbrook, Kent TN18 5EZ,
Tel: 01580 753 133

Records to:
Colin Plant, 14 West Road, Bishops Stortford, Herts CM23 3QP

16. **Crickets, Grasshoppers and Groundhoppers**
John Widgery

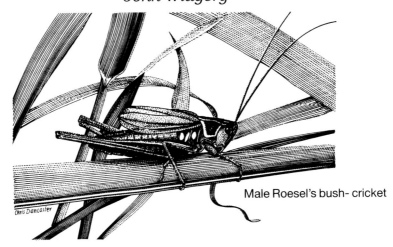

Male Roesel's bush- cricket

This article recommends the study of grasshoppers and crickets in Hertfordshire as a manageable subject with topical interest. The main identification features of each species are outlined in very brief terms.

Introduction

In Britain grasshoppers and crickets are a comparatively small group of rather large, brightly coloured insects, their sounds being characteristic of warm summer days, akin to the buzzing bee or the song of the skylark. It is surprising, therefore, that this accessible and easy to learn group is not better known and that it is studied by relatively few naturalists. However, in recent years their importance, not only in Britain and Europe but world-wide, has received much greater recognition since many species have been expanding their ranges quite dramatically. In fact, they are now regarded as being one of the best indicators of climate change. Hertfordshire is well placed to see part of this expansion taking place.

Species expanding their ranges in Hertfordshire

Crickets
Roesel's bush cricket, *Metrioptera roeselii*, was confined to the extreme south of the County a decade or so ago but, particularly through the 1990s, it has colonised the whole of Hertfordshire. It is a dark green insect about 22mm long when adult from July onwards and can be identified by the narrow yellow

band bordering the sides of the pronotum (the saddle-shaped structure which shields the area immediately behind the head) and by the yellow or pale 'port-hole' markings on the sides of the abdomen, just beneath and behind this area. Its nearly continuous buzzing song is a familiar sound from almost any long grass habitat along roadsides, footpaths or larger areas of unmanaged grassland. Remarkably, the normal form of this species has very short wings and is incapable of flight, but a long-winged form, which can fly, is produced in warmer and drier conditions and, significantly, this has become more common in recent years.

Another species involved in range expansion is the long-winged conehead, *Conocephalus discolor*. The arrival and spread across the County of this species has been truly spectacular. In its immature form it can easily be recognised by a very well defined blackish stripe running all the way down to the top of the otherwise green abdomen. Upon maturity, from about July, this slim, graceful, predominantly bright green cricket is about 30mm in length, with long straw-coloured body-length wings. The female has an ovipositor which is about 15mm long and is straight, not curved as in the short-winged conehead. Again, in warmer conditions, a form is produced with even longer wings which can extend up to about 10mm beyond the end of the abdomen and it is believed that it is this form which moves into new areas as it is capable of stronger flight. A couple of decades or so ago this was a rare insect in Britain, confined to coastal areas in the southernmost counties, but its recent steady range expansion has now gained impetus. It was first seen in Hertfordshire in the summer of 1994 when thirteen isolated individuals were spotted in widely spaced sites across the County. Three years later it was recorded in no less than170 one kilometre squares and several breeding colonies were located, even in the north of the County. Despite the fact that it is now widespread in the County, it is not easy to find by sight due to its habit of resting lengthways along a grass stem, where it is extremely well camouflaged, and moving round to the opposite side on approach, only flying as a last resort. It has a 'song' which is a prolonged, scratchy hissing sound, but this is almost inaudible to the human ear although a few of the younger generation can hear it faintly from up to about two metres away. However, it can be heard loudly and clearly from some distance with the aid of a bat detector which converts the ultrasonic sound waves into an audible signal. It is largely by this means that its spread has been monitored over the past three summers. Whilst by no means essential, the bat detector has now become an important aid for anyone intending to make a serious study of grasshoppers and crickets.

Grasshoppers

A further species to show an expansion of range in the County is the Lesser Marsh Grasshopper, *Chorthippus albomarginatus*. This is normally straw coloured, but green forms can occur, particularly on the chalk of north Hertfordshire. As with most of the grasshoppers (as opposed to crickets), the females are noticeably larger than the males. In this case, when mature from July onwards, the female is about 25mm long and the male about 20mm. They have two parallel lines running from behind the eyes along the top of the pronotum. This species was not recorded in the County until 1989, but since then has been found in numbers both in the north and the south. In Britain it used to be confined to damp grassland (hence its name) but in recent years it has been spreading into all types of grassland, thus echoing its habitat preference in continental Europe. Here again climatic factors are having an influence.

As I have mentioned in the introduction, the remarkable spread of many grasshoppers and crickets together with many other insect species, is not just a British phenomenon. It is happening throughout Europe and should the climate ameliorate (or even maintain its present mode) there are sure to be further exciting developments in the years ahead.

Other common Hertfordshire species

Crickets

The oak bush-cricket, *Meconema thalassinum,* is found commonly on a range of broad leaved trees and shrubs. It is a pale green, fully-winged insect, about 22mm long. In contrast to the species mentioned previously, which are all vegetarian, this insect is exclusively carnivorous, feeding on small aphids or aphid-sized insects. It is active at night and is often attracted indoors by artificial light. It can be found during the day by 'beating', i.e. gently tapping tree or shrub branches and catching what falls out into either a purpose designed beating tray or an up-turned umbrella; personally, I find the latter the more convenient. The oak bush-cricket can be found in its wingless immature form from about mid-May onwards and as an adult from mid-July. It does not have any audible call.

The dark bush-cricket, *Pholidoptera griseoaptera,* reaches adulthood about the same time as the foregoing species, when it has attained a body length of about 25mm. It is a very dark brown insect with no really distinct markings and is flightless, having very short wings of up to about 3mm in length. It can be found frequently in thickets of brambles and other low vegetation, and in herbage beneath hedgerows in the northern half of the County, but for some unknown reason it does not occur in the south. It is often easier to find in its immature stages when it commonly basks in sunshine on leaves, particularly nettles. In the younger stages it is easily recognised by a broad pale straw coloured stripe running down the top of its abdomen. Adults tend to hide in deep cover when they can be detected by their low-pitched *"rrrt - rrrt"* call which is the origin of the old English name for the species of bush cheep.

Another species which can be found commonly on broad leaved trees and shrubs or in low plants and sometimes long grass, is the speckled bush-cricket, *Leptophyes punctatissima.* In its adult stage, from about July, it is a

20mm long, rather plump, leaf green, flightless insect with only vestigial wings. At this time it becomes a rather secretive creature, not easy to see and is more likely to be found by 'beating' or by 'sweeping'. The latter involves sweeping a large pocket of cotton material, shaped like a fishing net, through low vegetation to see what one can catch. However, the best method of finding it at this stage is by use of a bat detector through which one can hear its normally inaudible sharp *"tic - tic"* call very easily. In its younger stages it can be found more readily because of its habit of basking on the leaves of nettles etc., similar to the foregoing species. Examination of these young insects with a 10x lens will reveal the intense dark speckles which give the species its name.

Grasshoppers

All the following species are of approximately similar size; the females, about 25mm and the males approximately 20mm in length. They all feed exclusively on grass. All reach adulthood in early June or July.

The commonest species in Hertfordshire is the field grasshopper, *Chorthippus brunneus*. It is fully winged and normally grey or brown in colour with two strongly indented lines running from behind the eyes down the length of the pronotum. It is found in a wide variety of habitats including long-abandoned industrial sites where sparse grass is growing and along thinly-grassed roadside verges. It makes a series of *"sst-sst-sst"* calls.

Almost as common is the meadow grasshopper, *Chorthippus parallelus*. This insect is nearly always green, although some brownish or even pinkish forms do occur, though rarely. The lines behind the head, running along the pronotum are usually not so well defined as in the previous species and they do not run parallel as the scientific name would suggest - rather they diverge very slightly in the rear half. The females have very short wings, only covering about a third of the abdomen, but those of the male are longer and cover about two-thirds. Neither sex flies but, as with some of the previous species, in warm summers occasional long-winged forms are produced which can fly. The song consists of rapidly repeated scraping sounds like *"zrezrezrezrezre"*, reminiscent of a baby's rattle.

Another widespread but more local insect is the common green grasshopper, *Omocestus viridulus,* which normally occurs in coarse grass, particularly old pasture and commons that have remained undisturbed for some years. It can also be found in grassy woodland clearings and along rides. It is of a leaf green colour with the lines along the top of the pronotum being gently incurved just above the centre. Its call is a very soft quiet warble lasting about 10 to 20 seconds.

Rare or local species in Hertfordshire

Crickets
The short-winged conehead, *Conocephalus dorsalis,* is superficially similar to the long-winged conehead, described earlier. The main differences are wings of usually less than half the body length (although very rarely a long-winged form occurs) and the curved ovipositor of the female. The immature insect is almost indistinguishable from the immature long-winged conehead i.e. it has a well defined black stripe down its back which contrasts starkly with the bright green body. It becomes adult at about the same time as the other species (July) and by this time is mainly green, the dark stripe having faded into a much paler reddish-brown which is not readily seen in the field. Its body length is about 25mm. Once again it is not an easy species to see, having the same habit as its 'cousin' in resting lengthways along a plant stem and moving to the opposite side when approached. Its song has similarities with the long-winged conehead's, being almost inaudible without the aid of a bat detector but easily detectable with one. It is more particular about habitat, being found in damper conditions where the grass is mixed with reeds, usually by rivers or ponds. In Hertfordshire, apart from an isolated record around a small pond in Potters Bar, it is confined to the Stort, Chess and Lea Valleys, the latter containing the strongest populations.

Grasshoppers
The mottled grasshopper, *Myrmeleotettix maculatus,* is the smallest of the species recorded in Hertfordshire. The body of the female is about 15mm long and the male 12mm. It is usually brightly marked and occurs in a variety of colours in a mottled or patchy pattern. The lines along the top of the pronotum are very strongly indented at the centre. It is typically an insect of heathland, a habitat which is very scarce in our County, and it requires very sunny situations where there is short turf and much bare ground. It has been found only on Nomansland Common and on Grim's Ditch at Potten End.

The stripe-winged grasshopper, *Stenobothrus lineatus,* is superficially similar to the common green grasshopper, being of similar size and colour, but the female has a white stripe along the base of the forewing and both sexes have a very distinctive white comma-shaped mark two-thirds of the way along each wing. It has been found only in a very small area of acid grassland in Panshanger Park.

Groundhoppers
This is a group of far more ancient insects in the grasshopper family but which are much smaller, not exceeding 12mm in length. The general colouration is brown or black, often matching the background colour of their habitat which makes them very difficult to find. They usually occur on bare

mossy ground either in woodland or around the edges of ponds, streams and rivers. Whilst the grasshoppers and crickets die in the autumn, groundhoppers hibernate during the winter, not becoming active again until April. There are two species in Hertfordshire which are both widespread but rather local. They are the common groundhopper, *Tetrix undulata,* which is a very bulky, humpbacked little insect and the slender groundhopper, *Tetrix subulata,* which is very much a slim line version without the humpback and with wings which noticeably exceed body length.

Appeal for records

Finally, I know that it is sometimes daunting for the inexperienced to try to identify these or any other species of insect. As a word of encouragement let me say that we have here a comparatively easy group, of which a fair level of knowledge and competence can be gained in quite a short time.

Please send any records you might obtain to me at the address given below quoting a six figure ordnance survey grid reference. If you want any help with identification I would be delighted to have a look at any photograph or specimen that you send. Live specimens are quite acceptable because grasshoppers, crickets and groundhoppers are very tough creatures and are quite able to survive journeys through the post unharmed, provided they are placed in a suitable container (35mm film containers are ideal) with a little grass.

Records to:
John Widgery, 21 Field View Road, Potters Bar, Hertfordshire EN6 2NA. Tel: 01707 642708.

Information on Bat Detectors:
From John Widgery at the above address.

Recommended reading:
Marshall, J.A. and Haes, E.C.M. 1988 *Grasshoppers and Allied Insects of Great Britain and Ireland* Harley Books.
Bellman, H. 1988 *A Field Guide to the Grasshoppers and Crickets of Britain and Northern Europe* Collins.

17. 'We did mean to go to Sea'
Chris Doncaster

One of our members, Betty Edwards, with her knack of finding projects to kindle enthusiasm in any naturalist had discovered an advertisement for Brian Dawson's "Nature Breaks." Initially these consisted of cruises from the Essex Marina, opposite Burnham on Crouch, along the Crouch and Roach estuaries to see the seal colonies at Foulness Point and the birds of marsh, shore and open sea. Our first cruise was in September 1996, but in some ways more exciting ones were to follow.

Hazel May is a 69ft, 50 ton diesel powered converted Dutch barge hand built of steel in 1923 for carrying farm produce. The present skipper, Gerry Lee. bought it in the 1960s. The hold was roofed over and converted into comfortable passenger accommodation and with Brian leading and managing bookings, cruises for up to twelve passengers, mainly naturalists, were started about 1991.

The oncoming autumn in 1996 had brought parties of avocets, big flocks of golden plovers, three curlew sandpipers, bar-tailed godwit and surprisingly a buzzard soaring high. We seemed to be too early for the rare grebes on the sea, but little terns were still with us and delighted with their buzz of wing beats as they hovered before diving. Strange distant 'wreathes of smoke' on the horizon turned out to be dense flocks of waders in flight over Foulness Point; the sand there seemed to be covered with birds. Eventually we were amongst the seals: two segregated groups, one of greys, the other of common seals. Heads bobbing up in the water could be identified by their nostrils when closed - parallel lines for greys, a 'V' for commons. A number of greys had bloody necks, probably from fighting and one skirmish in the sea seemed to confirm this. Breaks for tea and coffee and for our lunch were special socialising times and for contemplating such things as the difference between black-tailed and bar-tailed godwits on the basis of leg proportions.

Now, not only are there cruises for bird and seal watching, but Laurence Watts and John Skinner, marine biologists from Southend Museum, are systematically surveying the marine life of the estuaries through dredging and making plankton hauls from *Hazel May*. Participation in this study by visiting naturalists is now under way. Thus several of our members enjoyed two fascinating marine-life cruises in April and July 1997, each time seeing a different range of species brought on board by the dredge and plankton nets. For several of us, one of the beauties of these cruises was that we could bring selected specimens home and keep many of them alive for months in sea water aquaria and study them with stereo microscopes to reveal details of this unfamiliar world. While the aquaria are unsuitable for showing to interested groups because of having only one microscope for each, several individual visitors have gloated long and lovingly, saying "This is better than television, any day!" They might have been watching the armoured 'portcullis' of a sabellid worm slowly emerging from its tube of cemented sand grains, then opening into a delicately coloured horseshoe of stiff spines backed by a fuzz of fine vulnerable tentacles. The tentacles are used to gather both organic food particles and sand grains for adding more courses to the end of the tube.

Another member of the *Sabellidae* is the spectacular (by cool-sea standards) peacock worm with a fan of chestnut-banded tentacles, each more than an inch long and arranged to form a cone which may become a helical double or a triple one in well-grown individuals. A complicated system of ciliated filaments and grooves carry food particles and 'building materials' down to the mouth, grading them for size on the way. The food is consumed, but the mud particles are fixed onto the rim of the tube by cement from special glands near the mouth as the worm slowly rotates and presses the grains into position.

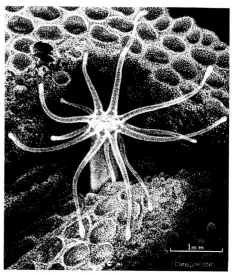

Very many of the sedentary marine invertebrates in widely differing groups have their own 'plankton net' in the form of a fan of ciliated tentacles for catching and extracting food from the sea currents. During the spring cruise we netted innumerable tiny crustaceans and worm and mollusc larvae, all of which were potential meals for the fan-bearers. The parent of one of these victims is particularly intriguing. This is the slipper limpet which came up from muddy patches in multiples of a dozen or so, all clinging atop of

The very local sea anemone,
Nematostella vectensis,
in skeletal remains of the Bryozoan,
Conopium seurati

each other in a stack. This limpet was given the scientific name of *Crepidula fornicata*, but I suspect at the time its morals were not well understood. It is now known that a stack of up to nineteen individuals is begun by a young one which at first becomes a 'bachelor' male; he feeds, grows and passing through a transitional phase, eventually changes sex. She (now) is then alighted on by one or more other small young individuals which, responding to secretions from her, now become males; they mate with her and eventually themselves change into females. And by repetition of this sequence the stack grows and grows, females at the bottom, would-be males at the top. Slipper limpets feed by sifting organic particles from the surrounding water. A female might lay 50-100 egg capsules into a gelatinous mass at each spawning. Each capsule contains 100-200 eggs and up to ten spawnings are possible annually. So from a possible 7,692 eggs from a single female in two weeks (work it out for yourself!) it was not surprising that some thousands of swimming larvae appeared in my aquarium a fortnight after the April dredge, and again at intervals, until by mid-June the females had presumably become exhausted in the artificial, mud-free conditions.

We have photographed and drawn some species that we have collected and are gradually compiling our list in the hope that, on verification, one or two might prove to be new additions to the official list. At any rate types quite new to me even now (October 97) continue to appear out of the 'gunge' encrusting one old oyster shell, not only because they lie hidden in submerged tubes or crevices, but because they are tiny and almost transparent. Thus I only recently realised that about ten of a species of tiny sea anemone, which is said to be extremely local (being confined to the North Sea and south coast) could be spotted once I got my eye in for the delicate buff pattern of its 'face' and its few long transparent tentacles. It is appropriately called *Nematostella*, the 'star of threads' (see drawing opposite). This has now achieved new record status on the Crouch/Roach survey.

Fish are not a good idea for a sea water aquarium because most are carnivorous and eat up the invertebrates. However, they can be appreciated on board ship as now and then they are brought up with a mass of old muddy oyster and other shells, star fish, crabs, sea-squirts and brown, foot-long strands of a gelatinous, colonial bryozoan (or 'moss animal'). On each of the marine-life cruises there were small glass tanks and a battery-operated aerator, so we could watch and photograph fish such as the strange bearded, bottom-feeding pogge, sea-scorpion (with poisonous spines), spratts and the occasional sole.

All the big stuff and lots of mud and empty shells encrusted with living invertebrates, came up with the dredge. This was a course string net supported by a heavy steel frame designed to be dragged slowly over the sea bed, scooping up every movable object it could accommodate, then heaved on board and its contents emptied into a deep plastic tray. The naturalist 'vultures' would then swoop down, rummage through the catch and crow with delight when a sunstar, the size of a man's hand and of a beautiful red-gold colour was uncovered. Eighteen-inch-long tubes of peacock worms were often caught and their lovely fans would soon emerge when put into the observation tanks. Sponges, big fronds of hydroids, anemones, shrimps, prawns, hermit crabs, shore crabs, spider crabs, swimming crabs and more all came up with the dredge, but what probably excited most were what the plankton net caught, especially on the July cruise. The sea was then warm enough for huge populations of comb jellies to develop. The commonest of these was the sea gooseberry, a clear orb of transparent jelly the size and shape of a gooseberry, with a delicate membrane bearing longitudinal rows of iridescent beating cilia. Reflecting a beam of white light the cilia split the light into its component rainbow colours and seen against a dark background the effect can be breathtaking. The sea gooseberry has two highly extensible side arms (hence its scientific name of *Pleurobrachia*). Unlike its near relatives, the hydroids, anemones and jellyfish. these arms have no stinging cells, but they stick to and entangle prey from microscopic sizes to those of fish larvae and draw the victims into the tubular mouth which opens at the 'southern pole'.

Plankton nets are elongated wide-mouthed cones of fine nylon mesh; but not so fine that summer flushes of diatoms clog them; fine enough, however, to catch the tiny copepod crustaceans and invertebrate larvae. They are towed for a few minutes at a stretch from the ship, now moving very slowly, and the catch is washed into jars of sea water and stored in an insulated cool box for the journey to the home aquarium.

Laurence and John were wonderful guides on the marine-life cruises, handling the dredge and plankton nets and pointing out distinguishing features of the creatures caught. They provided not only the observation tanks but also a stereo microscope for detailed study of the tinier creatures, such as hydroids. Laurence has a great reputation as a photographer of marine life, lecturing aboard *Hazel May* to audiences of 20 or more.

The sea is where life on Earth must surely have originated. There is infinitely more variety of life in it than on land and there is the perennial possibility of discovering new major groups. Indeed, as recently as 1995 *Symbion pandora*, a member of a phylum completely new to science, the *Cycliophora*, turned up on the mouthparts of a Norway lobster. It is a tiny nonparasitic hanger-on, altogether too unique to belong to any known phylum. The sea has a peculiar fascination for us all and to a naturalist it can be a veritable paradise.

Contact:

Brian Dawson *Nature Breaks*, 148 Handley Green, Laindon, Essex SS15 5XG. Tel: 01268 491540.

18. **From Beach to Microscope**
Chris Doncaster

The beauty of studying life under the microscope is that specimens can be brought in from far afield and one can spend as long as it takes observing them in comfort. One such study for me was the collection, extraction and filming of the micro-organisms that live actually between the sand grains on the sea shore. The film was commissioned for David Attenborough's "The Living Planet" TV series and, besides giving enormous pleasure, payment helped offset the cost of the equipment.

Almost nothing had been known about this micro world until the 1920s and detailed studies did not really begin until the 1960s, so there were still exciting possibilities of new discoveries. For me this was a completely new and fascinating field. Unsurprisingly nothing new to science introduced itself to me personally, but in 1983 R. M. Kristensen discovered members of a whole new phylum, the *Loricifera* (corset-bearers) in marine sands off the Brittany coast. Up to that time only two other new phyla had been discovered in the 20th century and one of these, the *Gnathostomulida*, was significantly also from marine sediments.

Living in such very small spaces between the sand grains in a constantly shifting environment, interstitial microfauna must themselves be very small. Some are squat and compact while others are long, worm-like and often flattened. How interstitial microfauna are induced to release their tenacious hold on sand particles, thus facilitating photography, is beyond the scope of the book, but it involves shaking up a sand sample in an anaesthetic solution, pouring the liquid and doped animals onto a fine sieve and picking off the catch by hand under the stereomicroscope, then mounting it in sea water between coverslips for viewing.

I collected my sand samples from Norfolk and these had a great diversity of microfauna, including representatives of ten phyla. The first thing of beauty the microscope showed me was the sand itself, where the fragments of quartz and shell were veritable jewels in reds and golds and diamond bright. The diatom-rich water film surrounding each grain was evidently a feast for several kinds of gastrotrich (= hairy tummy) (e.g. Nos. 8 & 9 in the drawing) which, by their ventral cilia, glided smoothly over the sand grains, or if disturbed could cling to them with an array of adhesive tubes. *Copepod crustacea*, too (No. 2) were abundant, tenacious and voracious vegetarians. However, nematodes are probably the most cosmopolitan and abundant of the interstitial microfauna with an estimated five million per square metre in those sediments that are rich in blue-green algae. Some of the interstitial nematodes that I found (see Nos. 6 & 7 in the illustration) had various structures that enabled them to move about like looper caterpillars, quite different from their more conventional terrestrial relatives. One comparative beauty, *Desmodora sanguinea,* was coloured bright carmine red – a very welcome change!

Larvae of many of the other invertebrates contribute to the lesser interstitial fauna: the baby sand mason worm, forever turning somersaults inside its transparent tube (No. 1 in the drawing); the bristling larvae of the spionid worm, *Polydora ciliata,* which bore their way into oyster shells, the adults lying hidden except for two waving thread-like palps; a veliger larva of a periwinkle which I first saw as a tiny shell gliding at speed over the sand grains, then, spreading its ciliated velum like a pair of ears, it took off in languorous flight through the water, light as a soap bubble with flickering peripheral cilia like flames and resembling some big-eared, disembodied smiling face (No. 5 in the illustration).

Just as several invertebrates use the same devices for tube building as for feeding, others combine feeding and locomotion. Thus No. 10, a member of another minor phylum, the *Kynorhynchia* (= locomotory snout), has an eversible snout armed with bristles inside its mouth. As the snout is turned outwards, the bristles may or may not connect with the ground to hitch *Echinoderes* (= spiny neck) along. On withdrawing the snout, any adhering organic material will be ingested. It can't afford to be fussy!

Illustration opposite:

A selection of animals that can be found between sand grains on the sea shore. Drawn from 16mm film sequences of live individuals. Three different scales of magnification - all sand grains about 0.5mm long.

1. Larva of polychaete sand mason worm (about 1.25mm long).
2. A copepod crustacean *Cylindropsyllis* species (about 0.75mm long).
3. Swimming veliger larva of periwinkle.
4. *Psammodrilus balanoglossoides*, an unusually small species of polychaete (about 1.3mm long).
5. A marine hydra *Halamohydra vermiformis* (very extensible).
6. *Desmoscolex* species and 7. *Epsilonema* species; both atypical nematode worms, special to marine environments.
8. *Dactylopodalia cornuta* and   9. *Chaetonotus* species - gastrorichs (= hairy tummy).
10. *Echinoderes* (= spiny neck) species, a kynorhynch (= locomotory snout).
11. An unidentified relative of *Nerilla*, an archiannelid (= primative annelid).
12. A water-bear, probably *Orzeliscus* species (about 0.1mm long).
13. Shell fragment of a foraminiferan (Protozoa).

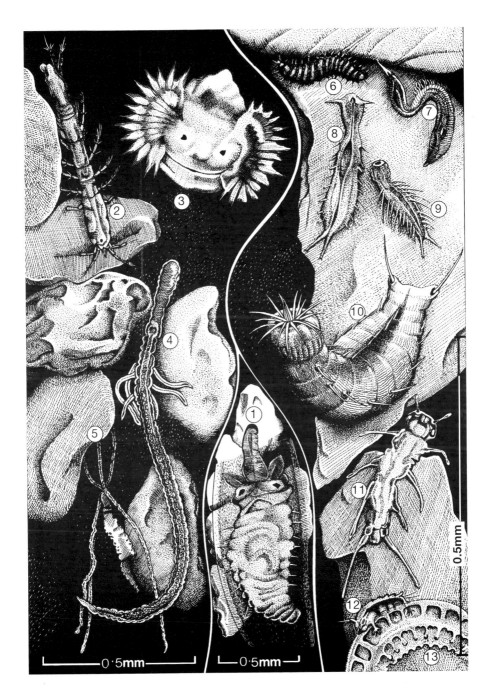

0·5mm

0·5mm

0.5mm

19. **Green Lacewings and Scorpion Flies**
Revd. Tom Gladwin.

This article encourages the study of lacewings and their allies
and promotes the use of English names of plants and animals.

A developing interest in insects commonly begins with the identification of the attractive adults of butterflies, dragonflies, and possibly larger moths. Conspicuous by virtue of their medium to large size, artistic patterning, beautiful colouration and sometimes dazzling iridescence, all have easily remembered English names. Descriptive names such as purple emperor, beautiful demoiselle, and peach blossom,

Chris Doncaster.

somehow make them special and add to their appeal. Additionally they are the subject of popular, modestly priced, readily available, and beautifully illustrated field guides. In the case of butterflies and dragonflies identification is made easier by the small number of species to be found in Hertfordshire and familiarity with those that are regular visitors to such places as our gardens. With a little experience most can easily be identified on sight and without any need to be disturbed or even caught.

Other insects, when we give time to see them for themselves, can be equally appealing. Who can have failed to notice the medium-sized green insects, with delicate wings of seemingly fine lace held tent-like over their bodies, which come indoors in autumn and winter? These are green lacewings of our most abundant species, *Chrysoperla carnea*. This, interestingly, is one of only two species which hibernate, during which time some individuals are seen to turn various shades of reddish-brown. It is also the only species so far observed to generate a 'song', which it produces by vibrating its body against a branch during courtship.

Regrettably our lacewings and scorpion flies, which I shall come to later, have yet to be officially graced with deserving English names. This, however, should not be allowed to deter the observer. For me the award of an English name somehow honours a species' worth and celebrates its life as a dignified activity. In contrast, scientific or Latin names, whilst necessary for certain purposes, seem to reduce an animal to a mere object for scientific inquiry. Perhaps this is why I value and remember English names more readily than scientific ones. It is the peacock butterfly which appeals to my spirit and receives my welcome every spring, not the same insect known as *Inachis io*. Likewise, what greater excitement there is in announcing that one has heard the first cuckoo, than coldly referring to a large grey bird otherwise known as *Cuculus canorus*? The English names for such as these are an integral part of our cultural history and heritage, and we standardise - as for example is being attempted in the case of birds - abandon or fail to add to them at our peril. Surely, therefore, we have a duty to ensure that such names remain in common usage and are perpetuated through future generations of country lovers. Perhaps it will not now surprise the reader to find that I have come to know some of our commoner lacewings by English names that have comfortably and quite naturally become part of my language over many years. Thus I gain greater benefit by knowing the familiar *Chrysoperla carnea* as house lacewings. Perhaps this might also add to our culture. I hope so.

It was on a BNA ramble in Panshanger Park on 18th May 1957, that I first discovered green lacewings and scorpion flies for myself. A lovely sunny day, it was to produce one of those moments so treasured that I still savour it with a clear memory over forty years later. We had stopped and were listening to a nightingale, which were still common in the district, when I was attracted to a small patch of stinging nettles. On the fresh green back-cloth of nettle leaves were a variety of colourful insects; a blood red cardinal beetle, black and yellow wasp beetle, two partly iridescent yellow-green nettle weevils, and two other insects which I later discovered to be a scorpion fly, *Panorpa*

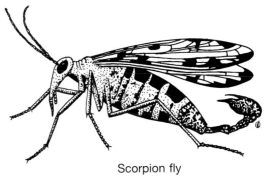

Scorpion fly

communis, and green lacewing, *Chrysopa perla*. Thus began my interest in these fascinating insects.

Just three species of scorpion flies and a snow flea (*Mecoptera*) and 66 species of lacewings (*Neuroptera*) have been identified in Britain. The British lacewings divide into six families including 12 species of very small insects covered in white powder and appropriately known as wax-flies; 30 of brown lacewings; 3 aquatic sponge-flies; an ant lion commonly found on the heaths around Minsmere and Dunwich in Suffolk; the amphibious giant lacewing; and 19 forms collectively known as green lacewings, of which only 17 are green and two are brown.

As evident from the illustration, adult lacewings are easily recognisable. At rest their wings, which never lie flat or overlap, are folded tent-like over their bodies. Caddis-flies, the only other insects with which they might be confused, also hold their wings in this way. However, unlike lacewings, these have fine hairs all over their wings which generally have fewer veins (venation). They also have longer antennae. green lacewings are active at dawn and dusk (crepuscular) or during the night (nocturnal) although they very quickly take to flight if disturbed during the day. Feeding voraciously on aphids, they are welcome visitors in the garden.

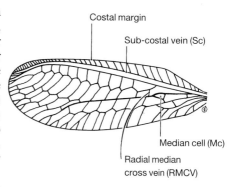

Basic venaton of green lacewing

The best places to search for green lacewings in Hertfordshire are tall grasslands, hedge banks and verges - especially along scrubby woodland edges, deciduous woodlands, and, of course, gardens. One species associated with pine trees, *Chrysopa dorsalis*, in which the sub-costal vein (Sc- see illustration) is black, may occur in the County but I have yet to find it. With a little experience, and in some cases the assistance of a hand lens, the twelve forms (11 green and 1 brown!) I have found in Hertfordshire are quite easily identified and can be simply described as follows.

The one brown species, which I call the red-headed lacewing, is *Nothochrysa capitata*. This is a dark reddish-brown insect with a distinctively redder head and wing span of about 30mm. It may not be common in the County as I have found it on only four occasions, all in coniferous plantations.

The British house lacewings are now known to comprise two species, *Chrysoperla carnea* and *C. lucasina*, both of which hibernate. The abundant house lacewings are best distinguished by examining the pattern of veins in the wings (wing venation). Knowledge of wing venation is essential to the serious study of lacewings so this is a good species from which to become familiar with this important feature. Green lacewings have a small cell in the forewings known as the median cell (Mc in the diagram). In both species of house lacewings the apex of this cell never reaches the first of the cross veins (RMCV in the diagram) which connect the radial and median veins. *Chrysoperla lucasina*, unlike *C. carnea*, remains green i.e. does not turn carneous (flesh-coloured) or brown in winter.

Nineta flava, the oak lacewing, is quite common in deciduous woodlands. It is a large yellow-green insect with a wing span of up to 50mm. It is easily identified from the conspicuously concave leading edge (costal margin - see diagram) of its forewing. *Nineta vittata*, another large species found in deciduous woodland, has recently become commoner than the oak lacewing. In this species the costal margin is only ever very slightly concave. As a check, in *N. flava* the length and width of the scape (basal segment of the antenna) are about equal whereas in *N. vittata* they are visibly twice as long as wide. (A third species of this genus, *N. inpunctata,* has only been found once in Britain.)

In two species, *Chrysopa perla* and *C. commata,* the second segments of the antennae are black. *C. perla,* found abundantly in tall herbage and hedgerows, is blue-green with many black cross veins and a lot of dark markings between the antennae and on the head generally. In the bluish-green *C. commata* the joints along the sides of the thorax and first two segments of the abdomen are black. This species appears to be rare in Hertfordshire where I have found it on only two occasions, once in a light trap and once in long grass, on both occasions in Panshanger Park.

Three species, the very common and widespread *Chrysopa pallens* (garden lacewing), *Dichochrysa prasina and D. ventralis,* have a conspicuous black spot between the antennae. In *D. ventralis* the underside of the abdomen is also black. I have found it only occasionally and then mostly in wet woodlands. The more widespread *D. prasina* is distinguished by having a black spot at the base of each wing. *D. flavifrons,* which I have found in woodlands around Bramfield, also has dark but less distinguishable spots at the base of each wing.

The remaining two species are *Cunctochrysa albolineata,* which has a pale longitudinal stripe on the upper surface (dorsum) of the thorax, and *Chrysopidia ciliata* which does not. *Cunctochrysa albolineata* is a very pale-green insect which I have frequently found in deciduous woodlands. The green *Chrysopidia ciliata* is another deciduous woodland species which appears to be less widely distributed in the County.

Scorpion flies are so named because the swollen tip (genital capsule) of the male abdomen, and the way it is held over the body gives them a scorpion-like appearance. In contrast the females have a normal straight pointed abdomen. They are the only British insects with a beak-like facial extension. There are three British species of which two are both common and widespread in Hertfordshire. They are weak flying insects with a wing span of about 30mm. The adults are most abundant from late May to early August with reducing numbers being observed into the first half of September. They are found on brambles and tall herbage along hedgerows and woodland edges and in floristically rich grassland.

The two species found commonly in the County are *Panorpa communis* and *P. germanica.* The males are easily identified; *P. communis* has conventionally shaped curved pointed callipers on the underside (ventral surface) of the genital capsule, whilst those in *P. germanica* widen at the tips to give a clubbed appearance. Identification of females is more difficult.

In the males of *Panorpa cognata,* the third species recorded in the County, the arms of the callipers are straight and divergent. This species, known only in Hertfordshire from Therfield Heath, may be restricted to calcareous habitats.

Whilst this account describes some of the characteristic features of the species more commonly found in Hertfordshire there is always a risk of wrong identification and the use of keys is always recommended (see below).

I hope that this summary account might encourage others to study fascinating and less well known groups of insects such as lacewings and scorpion flies. They have certainly given me a lot of pleasure. I am very grateful to Colin Plant, the author of the recommended key, for his kind and constructive comments on the draft of this contribution.

Recommended identification guide:

Plant, C. W. 1997. *A key to the adults of British Lacewings and their allies (Neuroptera, Megaloptera, Raphidioptera, and Mecoptera.*

20. **The Long Treks**
Frank Lancaster

I recall the Annual Meeting in 1978 when there was a discussion about widening branch activities to focus on a long-term project. With somewhat gay abandon I suggested an annual weekend 'trek' during the month of September, traversing Hertfordshire from east to west or from north to south. I organised four such events.

To the surprise of many, this episode in BNA history spanned a period of four years. More surprising still, the few who ventured forth were to discover that there still remained hidden by-ways within a twenty-five mile radius of Marble Arch.

The criteria were simple, namely to travel light, to sleep under the stars using a bivouac bag on the Friday and Saturday nights, to partake of a large cooked breakfast cooked over an open wood fire - to be supplemented during the day by iron rations of one's choice.

We called our weekend walks treks, but I would suggest that these were poor substitutes for the real thing. The Aborigines have been trekking for some 40,000 years and until one has been privileged to observe them in the outback, one has little conception of the undertaking. Their gait is the epitome of minimum physical exertion in the searing heat. Their arms remain loosely at their sides. In comparison, the European resembles the tick-tack man at Epsom on Derby Day. To the best of my knowledge, the Aborigines do not suffer from blisters!

An extract from the *Bulletin* for the 1979 Long Trek records a sorry tale. "Boots are made for walking and feet need to be cushioned by comfortable socks, and boots need to be fully broken in. More than one member had patches covering blisters and chaffed skin and the leader realised that Ashridge would not be reached that night. The pace was re-geared and the group veered towards Studham. The day had been grade A walking (as per Y.H.A. handbook) and having been abroad and on the move for the best part of 15 hours, the leaf mould mattress felt luxurious and the band of trekkers were asleep within minutes."

A more notable feature of the Aborigines is the absence of unnecessary luggage. On the first trek in 1978, the *Bulletin* recalls that some members were extravagant in their preparations. "Despite the well publicised desirability for absence of extraneous baggage, one member of the party, who shall remain nameless, had two independent loads; a small rucksack and a bedroll/pillow etc. harnessed up with ropes, string and elastic bands. The locals in the nearby pub could be forgiven for thinking they had seen the outline of a camel"

The following are shortened accounts from the *Bulletin* of our treks about Hertfordshire.

September 8-10th 1978:
The Trek across the Top of Hertfordshire

"A group of five gathered at a member's home at Ashwell on the Friday evening. Events during the following forty-three hours disproved any suggestion alluding to an army-style survival course, since a total of only twenty-four miles was walked. Allowing for the two night stops and three pub visits, the pace averaged 1.5 miles per hour! This was possibly due to our packs of 25 lbs and two members admitting to blisters on the Sunday.

"Apart from two hours of light drizzle on the Friday evening, the weather during that first trek was superb. Our route headed south-west and was to pass through some of the most remote and beautiful parts of Hertfordshire. We walked directly into a headwind which freshened, so that by Saturday afternoon it was strong and accompanied by delightful sunshine.

"At 21.15 hours we were ferried to Barley, near the Cambridgeshire border and set forth in the dark. Without the moon there was little to see, but the verges either side of the track were heavy with the noise of crickets. This orchestrated cacophony was to be disrupted by the slow approach of a vehicle hidden from view by the folds in the hills, but every few minutes a beam of light swathed the hillside and one sensed that sinister happenings were abroad. The two safaris were to meet. The foot-sloggers were overtaken by a Landrover, with two marksmen standing in the back with rifles at the ready. These were unlawful deer poachers, intent to kill and at a distance we heard them calling up fallow deer using a tape recorder.

"One of our Group had heard that poaching had been reported in this area and he recommended that we kept our distance since they could well resort to violence. During the next two hours we were aware of their activities but no shots were heard. It was at 23.15 hours that we finally located an old chalk pit, the venue for rest and within minutes sleeping bags and groundsheets were unfurled and heavy rain clouds scudding across the sky brought the day to a close." It would be difficult to draw a more dramatic opening to this period in the Branch's history.

"Next morning, the alarm was sounded by a flurry of jackdaws. The light of day revealed unexplained mechanical junk scattered in the quarry, which had a 90% ground cover of stinging nettles, plus common hound's-tongue, longleaf and pink campion." Victualling is of the essence in trekking where the cooking is over a wood fire with mashings of tea brewed in a dixie. Breakfast is without doubt the best meal of the day and comprised eggs, sausages, bacon, fried bread and tomatoes.

"With many miles to walk, we climbed out of the chalk pit at 09.00 hours and set off on the first of many green lanes which thread their way across the north of the County. These were little used and were a good refuge for local wildlife, including the chest high stinging nettles, never to be forgotten by the leader clad in shorts! The most memorable sights of that morning were the disturbance a large tawny owl and a stand of giant hogweed upwards of twelve feet high. Early autumn movements of lapwings were noted, including a flock of about forty near Sandon. We also noted two spotted flycatchers and goldfinches. Roe Wood yielded one muntjac deer and six turtle doves.

"Our approach into Wallington was uphill and with brilliant sunshine tanning our brows and in the knowledge that Greene King Abbot Ale was to be had in the village, one of the group was sent ahead to locate the pub with instructions to have five pints lined up to slake our thirsts. Meanwhile we listed the flowers growing on the roadside verges and records show chicory, wild carrot, blue fleabane, clustered bellflower and greater knapweed.

"It is probably appropriate at this juncture to introduce Adrian. Life is full of surprises; not all members walk in the shadow of David Attenborough. Adrian, a church organist was about to embark on a music degree at Durham University. As he was in limbo, he was invited to join us. He claimed no specialist knowledge in natural history, so it was suggested in general terms that he brought along a reference book of his own choosing. His 'bible' was to become an integral part of the first weekend trek – The Good Beer Guide – as the saying goes, follow that.

"We had chosen well in selecting September, which is the month of harvest and in these parts perhaps 80% of the country is given over to cereal crops. The scene was deeply rural, the predominant colour resembling rich butter, quilted in deep green by woodlands, spinneys and copses one of which was noted to be of importance for glow-worms. By late afternoon we were approaching our biggest obstacle, crossing the A1(M) and at the same time avoiding the fringes of Stevenage and Letchworth. Some of the footpaths did not exist on the ground at Graveley (they had been ploughed), but with some deft map reading the group was led round the back of Graveley Church, alongside a crop of field beans and through a small but almost impenetrable wood to drop down next to the A1(M) within 15 yards of an underpass.

"Darkness had fallen by the time we entered a large wood and by feeling around with our feet we each selected a bed space and lay down at 21.15 hours. Our bedroom was vast and before sleep overtook us, we heard the movement of deer close by and in the far distance a searing noise which grew in volume and passed overheard quivering millions of leaves as a warm funnel of air forced its way through the tree canopy. The principal guardian during the night was a tawny owl which gave us the full benefit of its repertoire, followed at dawn by a nuthatch and a robin.

"Close to our camp site was an open space of a quarter acre rich in flora including lady's mantle, thyme-leaved speedwell, yellow pimpernel and common centaury. It was while we were sitting in this oasis that we were watched by a pair of marsh tits flying amongst tall marsh thistles. The backcloth to this setting was probably the largest larch tree in the County, delicately bathed in sunshine. In such surroundings we could be excused for our slow departure at 10.15 hours. Emerging from Hitch Wood we were confronted by the same bough-bending wind and had a distant view of the lazy wingbeat of a tawny owl flying into an ash tree and calling it a day. Woodlands became more prominent compared with the previous day and we were able to supplement our rations with blackberries and elderberries.

"Keeping well to the north of Whitwell we surprised a large fallow deer in open country and its light fawn colouring set against the darker hue of a stubble field was idyllic as it defied gravity in the eye of the beholder by bounding out of view – a beautiful episode. (A complete contrast to the previous day when we studied the dark form of a sika deer caged in a grotty pen at the back of the pub in Wallington).

"Midday found us at Bendish, confronted by our first river crossing, the river Mimram. The map confirmed that we were near its source and observation showed a very active spring which discharged into a large pond supporting dragonflies. To cross the ford we were obliged to remove all footwear. Whilst gratefully downing the first pint at the pub, we decided to finish the trek at the Hertfordshire/Bedfordshire border at Chiltern Green. Whilst waiting there for transport, an assessment of the first Long Trek revealed that 12.5% of our walking - 3 miles - had been on metalled lanes and it was somewhat startling to recount the number of road deaths encountered. A rat, mouse, chaffinch, moorhen, blotch and shrew meant that there had been two fatalities per road mile. How many more must be added to cover the road system of the British Isles for one calendar year? The following is a brief but pertinent extract from *Journey through Britain* by the late John Hillaby who covered 1,100 miles on his trip:

'On the roads, even the little lanes between villages, the number of wild animals found dead, run down by cars, seemed out of all proportion to the weight of traffic encountered. Why, I wondered, had three hares died so close to each other? Were they fighting, playing or chasing a female? And was it an instinct for the soft and familiar that enabled a badger with a broken back to drag itself to a bed of stitchwort before it died?' "

September 14th-16th 1979:
A Ver Valley Loop

"It is not until every effort has been made by the backpacker to bypass all but the smallest of hamlets in a trek covering a distance of thirty-six miles that a true appreciation of Hertfordshire can be obtained. 'Small is beautiful' becomes meaningful, describing so much which previously has gone by un-noticed or un-discovered, especially when measured against those other counties with perhaps more spectacular landscapes.

"As in the previous year, the trek took place in the middle of September and, again, the weather was superb. Six trekkers started out from St Albans, feeling a little conspicuous as they walked through the lamp lit streets and out into the darker night.

"Little thought was given to the elements of frost and ice as we came to rest in water meadows north of the town at about 23.30 hours but the unusually crisp air accounted for anoraks being worn inside sleeping bags! Looking out of our 'bivvy bags' at the clear star-studded sky we knew that we were in for a cold, cold night and the only conversation at fifteen minutes to midnight was that of coots in the nearby reedbed. So when the night turned to dawn at 05.50 hours, the leader extracted himself stiffly from his bivvy bag which had collected an encrustation of frost and ice. The tufted water meadow was also white with frost and a thick band of mist clinging to its margins betrayed the line of the river. At this hour, nature was already awake and a solitary heron moved upstream on silent and leisurely wingbeats, the coots continued to argue (do they ever sleep?) and a pair of wrens remonstrated at the snapping of dead wood as the leader gleaned fuel for a pre-breakfast brew-up.

"Amidst this quiet activity a red sun rose and gave added colour to an already beautiful morning. With the flames and the fragrant woodsmoke of a new-born fire for company, it was for me the most tranquil episode of the trek. I remember a white layer of mist and a red sunrise which momentarily quivered as 21 mallard flew out of and back into the misty curtain – a setting for the brush of an artist.

"Tea was dutifully provided to others still abed and viewing their cold surroundings in a different light! It was only now that we heard about one trekker's experience of a visit at about 3.00 am by a whiskery creature of the riverbank, possibly a (now rare) water vole, which had explored both the ground and the bivvy bag by her head!

"Camp was struck at 08.15 hours and we moved off northwards towards Kensworth Lynch, the true source of the river Ver. This early start allowed us to watch the effects of the sun transforming the frost to a heavy dew and to flush the only wader of the weekend - a snipe feeding in the cattle ford. Hugging the river, even in a dry season, can be a muddy experience. A quick clean up and an hour later we threaded our way through the old and the new of Redbourn, a village of many contrasts. Our path crossed first the little known river Red which flows quietly into the Ver from Redbourn Common and then the secretive little branch line from Hemel Hempstead to Harpenden (now closed and known as the Nicky Line).

"The picturesque ford in one of the many quiet corners of Redbourn (those who have only seen it from the A5 should stay awhile) was five inches deep; a very encouraging observation as, 200 yards upstream, the river is dead due to water extraction for the industrial area of Luton. After this, we had many opportunities to view the dried up bed of the river, through meadows, ploughed fields and a golf course which no longer has a natural hazard, but which instead shelters the edible dormouse, *Glis glis*, known to thrive in Ashridge.

"We successfully navigated the underpass of the M1 and called a halt in the corner of a cornfield stacked with straw bales. The forty minute rest was necessary to dry our bedding and to give attention to blisters. We sank down to absorb the warmth of the September sun and the relaxation was bliss until a rogue wind blew across the field, sweeping our drying survival bags high into the air. We were caught completely off guard; sleeping bags followed suit and bivvy bags disappeared over the tops of hedges. Mine even went over pylons and viewed from the ground it took on the shape of a paper bag. Fortunately, it lost height quickly and was retrieved after a sprint to a neighbouring field full of Friesian cows which had become very excited. All of this had been watched by a greater spotted woodpecker which kept laughing to itself in a nearby tree.

"Crossing the A5 at Red Cow Farm we climbed out of the Ver valley, kicking off traces of black ash, the then all too familiar debris of stubble burning, an agricultural practice now illegal. It was interesting to note on our Long Trek the previous year that very few farmers in the north of the County adopted this scorched earth policy. We spent the night in a sheltered wood near Studham and when we awoke at 06.45 hours we were to discover that we shared the wood with a rookery. The birds were probably among a flock we saw yesterday in the vicinity of Pepsal Green. The leader decided that it would be impossible to adhere to the original plan so the group turned back towards St Albans, keeping the M1 a few miles away to the east. We passed on footpaths through many woods unknown to BNA and were made very aware of deer - both fallow and muntjac - which crashed away through the undergrowth. Wood violets and the leaves of primroses were also prominent, while a big feature of the weekend was the very large number of wood pigeons seen.

"It is great fun to travel cross-country for miles, leaving one footpath for another, at the same time avoiding habitation. Eventually St Albans' Abbey came into view and we quietly made our way towards Gorhambury, dropping down to Shafford Bridge and so joining up a thirty mile loop. Not long after, we were reclining in armchairs drinking tea from cups with saucers. Elliot was two inches shorter and the leader's bathroom scales showed a weight loss of 4lbs."

September 5th-7th 1980:
The Lost Trek

"The third BNA Long Trek, was cancelled at short notice due to the leader spending three days in the loo. The opportunity was taken to read Tolstoy's *War and Peace* and a doubtful benefit gained in the time was the loss of 14lbs in weight – not a pretty sight."

September 3rd-5th 1982:
Therfield to Cuffley

The final trek undertaken during this era of BNA's history, commenced in north Hertfordshire close to the Cambridgeshire border at Therfield Heath and finished not far short of the border with Middlesex at Cuffley. During the two days we passed through Kelshall, Cottered, Benington, Watton-at-Stone, Bramfield Forest, Panshanger and Little Berkhamsted.

In retrospect, of all the happenings on the treks, the most cherished memory I have spanned sixty seconds as we trekked in moonlight on 3rd September. "The small select group hit the trail at 20.50 hours on the Friday evening. September is the month of the harvest moon and as we headed for higher ground a full moon rose above a distant wood to reflect a mackerel sky. The fluting call of the peewit on the wing is beautiful, none more so than when heard at night and seen wheeling in the halo of a full moon. What made this small incident even more memorable was that our nostrils were sweet with the newly-cut corn.

"One of our objectives during this trek was to open up ancient green lanes, the first of which was undertaken in the dark. Moving uphill we waded through stinging nettles (the leader in shorts) concentrating on the hidden and irregular course of a ditch. Much noise and pushing was taking place on the other side of the fence as we were under the eye of a herd of excited cows. We also wished that we had been equipped with infra-red binoculars to enable us to be on equal terms with a fox which was following our progress and barked repeatedly for twenty minutes as we proceeded to our first night's stop.

"At 22.20 hours we settled down on a bed of dog's mercury. Four hours later I became aware of a hopping movement and with the aid of a torch, I came eyeball to eyeball with a stoat. The chimes of Sandon Church peeled across the countryside during the night; some we heard, some we did not. Not so the tawny owls which from various quarters of the wood kept up a crescendo of noise; there being at least six.

"During breakfast at 06.00 hours the following morning, the constant calling of great and lesser spotted woodpeckers replaced that of the owls and there were sightings of goldcrest, two treecreepers and a spotted flycatcher. A brief call from a third species of woodpecker was lazily recorded as a green woodpecker by the leader, but another more awake member registered that this was mistaken. Binoculars were quickly grabbed and we set off into a large clump of dead elms in search of a wryneck. It called three times in ten minutes, but evaded all our efforts to prove positively its identity. September is the normal migratory month for this uncommon visitor to Hertfordshire.

"We continued to enjoy the warmth of September and found our way to Cottered on as many green lanes as possible. A brief stop was made at The Bell, Cottered and we took a dry lunch at Munchers Green - a deserted mediaeval village site. We enjoyed an acrobatic display by a flock of 350 peewits.

"After a 30 minute siesta we proceeded in the direction of Benington; here we witnessed the latest form of flying, a microlight hang glider plus engine - a godforsaken noise. It had frightened a small herd of fallow deer and a fawn which glided silently across a field of stubble in front of us. At this point the old village yokel of Benington introduced himself to us - without disrespect it would have been difficult to have improved on a scarecrow! He was happy having collected a bag of clover for his rabbit and said he managed on £23 a week with none spent on drink as he was teetotal.

"Whilst pubs are not an obsession, they are very much appreciated on these occasions, but we arrived at Watton-at-Stone an hour before opening time. Several options were discussed - waiting or walking to a pub at Bramfield or Stapleford. Whether the old village yokel was responsible is open to debate, but a temperance decision was taken and we set off for Bramfield Forest, hoping to replenish our water bottles en route. Some would say this was a boob and in a sense it was! A promising house came into view and we were amply rewarded. As we walked up the drive, a young lady climbed out of a van and to all intents and purposes, out of her sundress as well. Quite unexpectedly we were each given a large one – pots of lemon squash and water.

"Our night stop was reached at about 18.45 hours and without ceremony we curled up in our sleeping bags within an hour. It was now Angus's turn to experience the night life; at around midnight a couple were heard nearby transmitting by radio, calling off numbers and, from time to time, bursting into song. Each to his own! Later Angus was to get a corkscrew neck trying to pinpoint a fox which was circling our site, on its departure leaving a strong scent.

"The following morning after a leisurely breakfast, two other Branch members joined us. As we were about to set off towards our final destination, I was given another lesson in avian alarm calls. The party was hemmed in by trees and a 'woodpecker' shot across at treetop height. It was one of the County's increasing populace of sparrowhawks. Later in the morning we heard a similar call, but made no positive sighting. We had a good view later of a little owl which was disturbed from a haystack. With a County survey of barn owls in mind, we inspected several derelict buildings but all drew blank, most being too draughty. Later still, we enjoyed a fascinating five minutes standing under an oak tree at Letty Green observing one of two pairs of free-flying budgerigars – the male a brilliant yellow and its mate a shimmering green.

"Our arrival at Little Berkhamsted coincided with opening time and the next hour was spent topping up and emptying glasses, a relaxing interlude. It was not long before the Great Wood at Cuffley came into view at three miles distance; our advance quickened by the sound of a thunderstorm and we completed the trek at 15.45 hours. Carefully made plans meant that a camper van and welcoming cups of tea greeted our arrival and while we gratefully imbibed, the rain lashed down outside. Having completed 32 miles, our final trek came to an end."

So, these are the accounts of three immensely rewarding BNA events undertaken by a small group of members of wide-ranging ages. With the approach of the millennium, perhaps the Branch will resurrect the Long Trek, which can be enjoyed by all those with eyes to see - in a word, empathy.

Long-tailed tits

21. **Looking at Ladybirds and other Insects**
Trevor James

Over the years our Association's members might not have been so attracted to beetles as to some other groups, but every now and then beetles have impinged on our general consciousness in quite spectacular ways.

On 4th September 1977, a natural history meeting at Knebworth took the British Naturalists' Association party through arable fields at Burleigh Farm and we found ourselves walking carefully to avoid treading on the myriad seven-spot ladybirds littering the ground. One member stopped to take a closer look and made a few sample counts - there were at least 60 per square metre, and the path from the edge of the wood to an orchard near the farm buildings was at least 200 metres long. These insects were pretty uniformly spread along the path and out into the arable

Sixteen spot *Halyzia* ladybird resting on hogweed

as well for an unknown distance either side (although they were not elsewhere on the walk in such abundance). Even the track of the footpath alone, therefore, must have had upwards of 12,000 ladybirds! This of course is a well-known phenomenon with these insects - their numbers expanding rapidly in hot summers with plenty of aphids to feed on earlier in the year. The aphids in turn had benefited from a combination of a good summer the year before and reasonable winter conditions allowing them to thrive. By the time September came round, though, the ladybirds had run out of food and tended to swarm to find a new source. This was evidently a swarm that had landed. That this effect could be replicated hundreds, if not thousands of times across Hertfordshire at the same time just gives an idea of the vast numbers involved.

This simple observation was also one of the earlier detailed records made by me of an insect group which was later to form a major study. The beetle recorder for Hertfordshire was then Bryan Sage, also Hertfordshire Branch BNA chairman, although his active work on beetles had tended to take second fiddle at the time to birds and dragonflies. Shortly afterwards Bryan left Hertfordshire and I eventually undertook the task of acting as County Recorder for the *Coleoptera* (for the Hertfordshire Natural History Society and later for BNA) in his stead. In the 1950s and early 1960s, quite a few meetings of the BNA were enlivened by Bryan's detailed examination of a rotten tree or under large stones by a hedgebank. These observations served gradually to build up knowledge of various groups of beetles, including the ladybirds.

Now we are at a stage when we have a fair understanding of the occurrence of the better known beetles in Hertfordshire. Of these, the *Coccinellidae* (the ladybird family) is a particularly well-recorded group, if only because quite a few people record them. However, it includes a number of insects which might not immediately be recognised as ladybirds. If these are included there are no less than 34 species confirmed from the County, of which 21 would generally be easily recognised by the common name of ladybird. Apart from the ubiquitous seven-spot, there are three other widespread usually red species with black spots - the common two-spot ladybird, the somewhat less frequent ten-spot and the usually somewhat local eleven-spot. The ten-spot lives mainly on trees, while the eleven-spot is usually an insect of dry sandy or gravelly ground, like gravel pits, sometimes appearing in numbers in hot summers.

Of course there are a whole range of others; the cream-spot, found on bushes and trees; the bright yellow and black twenty-two-spot which specialises in feeding on grey mildew on plants in late summer, and the chequer-board black and yellow fourteen-spot, which usually likes rough herbage in such places as woodland rides. Some are special to certain plants, mainly because their insect food specialises on them. The eyed ladybird is a specialist on pines, while the so-called larch ladybird, often hiding inconspicuously on larches, is also found on other conifers. Down by water we quite often find the nineteen-spot ladybird, alias the water ladybird, which seems to specialise on insects living in reeds and reed-mace etc.; while on what remains of our heathland, we could still find, with luck, the heather ladybird, although this can easily be confused with the widespread kidney-spot ladybird, a species common sometimes on the bark of certain trees and shrubs, such as willows. Both these are black, with one red spot on each wing-case and are of a distinctive, very rounded shape.

The advent of more easily accessible books on the subject has led to an increase in observations. The beautiful plates by Sophie Allington (a former Hertfordshire resident) in the book on ladybirds in the Richmond Publishing Co.'s *Naturalists' Handbooks* series have especially encouraged people. However, there have been some odd, un-confirmed records which tend to be generated by such publications and it is worthwhile being a little wary of a plethora of records of the striped and eighteen-spot ladybirds, for example, without supporting evidence for their identification. The oddest of the lot, perhaps, is a record which has been reported of the scarce seven-spot ladybird. This looks very similar to the common seven-spot, but has two extra white marks by the legs underneath. Its main claim to fame, though, is that it appears to be entirely commensal with wood ants, *Formica rufa* - the ones that build large heaped nests. The problem is that there is no confirmed record of the common wood ant in Hertfordshire either, although it has been reported from Broxbourne Woods in the past, and does exist just over the County boundary in former Middlesex.

A few meetings of the BNA over the years have been devoted specially to various insect groups and the *Coleoptera* have had some attention amongst these, especially in relation to special study areas. Recording beetles systematically, however, takes an inordinate amount of effort, not only in collecting specimens for subsequent identification (many not being readily recognisable without microscope work), but also through the unreliability of actually finding species on the day. Some special study days at Panshanger or Hertford Heath over the years, for example, have been only moderately successful, while other days, with a chance occurrence of ideal flying conditions, will produce unexpected results. One such day was a visit by the Hertfordshire Branch of BNA to Broxbourne Woods on 21st June 1992. This was not scheduled as an insect study meeting, but it turned out to be one of those days when everything was on the wing. The clearings in Broxbourne Wood, resplendent with flowers, were also littered with colourful and scarce leaf beetles (family *Chrysomelidae*) such as *Byctiscus populi* and *Chrysomela populi*, the former bronze-green and the latter bright red. It was a heap of cut oak logs which eventually turned up the greatest surprise. During a coffee break no less than three nationally scarce species were found flying around, including a beautiful blue jewel beetle (family *Buprestidae*) called *Agrilus sulcicollis*, which was the first time the species had been seen in Britain.

Perhaps second only to the ladybirds in conspicuousness is the family of longhorn beetles (*Cerambycidae)* named from their long antennae. Most species are quite large insects and often visit flowerheads of plants like hogweed. Their larvae mainly develop over several years in timber and so it is not surprising that their appearance as adult insects can be unpredictable. Just occasionally it can be spectacular. One day - 2nd June 1996 - was specially favourable at Panshanger Park when a BNA special study found six of the seven recorded species of longhorn beetle ever seen in the area, including the quite scarce and exotic-looking *Molorchus minor*, which develops in pine wood. The appearance of several of these on an old dumped log by the road was the first record in Hertfordshire for many years. In fact, Hertfordshire's beetle species associated with old timber and rotten trees, including many of these longhorns, have been a special focus of recording effort at a number of places, because the County tends to have been ignored by those involved in the documenting of nationally important localities for old timber species. In turn,

Britain tends to have some important relics of these habitats because of the public love of old trees. Records of scarce longhorn beetles made during BNA visits have therefore made their contribution to the national picture of what is a threatened group of wildlife.

References:

K. W. Harde *A field guide in colour to beetles*, edited by P. M. Hammond. Octopus Books, 1984

N. H. Joy *A practical handbook of British beetles.* Witherby, 1932 (reprinted, 1998, by E. W. Classey)

M. Majerus & P. Kearns *Ladybirds.* Richmond Publishing Co., 1989.

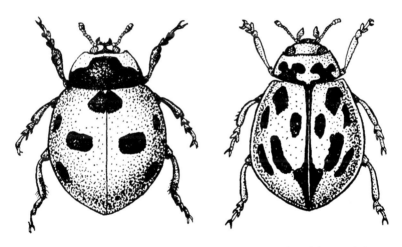

Coccinella 7-punctata   *Propylea 14-punctata*

22. Horse-stingers and Devil's Darning Needles
Revd. Tom Gladwin

Emperor dragonfly at Amwell Quarry Reserve

Born out of ancient folklore these uncomplimentary names for
our harmless dragonflies were still in common use during my boyhood.
So colourful are these insects that they have inevitably
attracted and inspired many great naturalist writers.

Richard Jefferies, whose great love of nature and countryside and unique senses of wonder and observation are manifest in his essays, describes them in *The Pageant of Summer* (Longmans Magazine. June, 1883): " On the wings of the dragonfly as he hovers an instant before he darts there is a prismatic gleam. These wing textures are even more delicate than the minute filaments on a swallow's quill, more delicate than the pollen of a flower. They are formed of matter indeed, but how exquisitely it is resolved into the means and organs of life!"

To observe this, and to watch the great transformations of nature that result in such beauty, is described by Jefferies as "the great pleasure of summer." It was such moving experiences that led him to conclude that "to be beautiful and to be calm, without mental fear, is the ideal of nature."

Dragonflies are indeed beautiful insects. For them life starts as an egg dropped into water, deposited on mud In some species the eggs hatch within a few weeks. In others, hostile winter conditions are survived by delaying hatching until the following spring. The rather ugly, slow moving, aquatic larvae take one to four years to develop before emerging as adults. As they grow, the larvae repeatedly shed (moult) their cuticle (outer skin). Eventually the near-adult insects climb out of the water, usually up a vertical surface such as the stem or leaf of a plant, and shed their final larval skins (exuviae). Warmed by the sun they expand their wings and abdomens. Thirty minutes to two hours later their full brilliance is revealed as they take their first flights. So adult life begins. An informative and very readable account of the fascinating lives of these attractive insects is provided in the appropriately titled *Dragonflies* (Miller, P.L. 1995).

Adult dragonflies are easily identified, especially those to be seen in Hertfordshire. Clear descriptions of all 50 species of dragonfly recorded in Britain and Ireland are to be found in Steve Brook's (1997) outstanding new field guide which has been beautifully illustrated by Richard Lewington.

The British dragonflies divide into two groups or sub-orders. The strong-flying larger dragonflies, the horse-stingers of earlier country folk, belong to the *Anisoptera*. This name refers to the differences in the shapes of the fore and broader-based hind wings. In contrast the smaller, weaker-flying, slender damselflies, *Zygoptera*, or devil's darning needles, have slender, narrow-based, similar shaped wings. Another difference is the way they respectively hold their wings when resting. When perched, the larger dragonflies hold their wings in an open position i.e. extended from the body, whilst damselflies fold them back over their abdomens. This ability, to fold their wings over their bodies, enables some damselflies to descend underwater and lay their eggs (oviposit) whilst submerged.

Dragonflies are flourishing in Hertfordshire. The disappearance of many farm ponds in the last 50 years, the pollution of some watercourses and the recent trend for the upper sections of some rivers to dry in summer, have been more than compensated for by the increase in reservoirs and, more especially, flooded gravel pits and garden ponds. As a result the populations of all but one of the County's 17 resident species, the white-legged damselfly now restricted to the lower Lea Valley, are stable or in most cases, increasing. Hertfordshire dragonfly populations are mostly very healthy indeed.

Just 28 species have been observed in the County. Of these six species which have always been rare here; the beautiful demoiselle, scarce emerald damselfly, variable damselfly, scarce blue-tailed damselfly, common hawker and downy emerald have not been seen in the County for many years.

Some of the larger dragonflies, especially those known as darters (*Sympetrums*), are great migrants. Three species, the yellow-winged darter, red-veined darter, and vagrant darter, periodically appear in the County as migrants from continental Europe. In 1995 there was an exceptional immigration of yellow-winged darters, which were soon observed ovipositing at several sites in the County. However, careful searches in 1996 failed to produce conclusive evidence of successful breeding. Two of the much rarer vagrant darters were also seen in 1995 and three red-veined darters in 1996.

The single black darter which was seen in 1995 may also have been an immigrant. However, this species, a lover of acid ponds, used to breed in the County, as did the hairy dragonfly. The latter, until recently a scarce insect, has been increasing both its numbers and range in Britain and in recent years has been seen again in Hertfordshire. This is an early flier and any large adult dragonfly seen in May or early June is almost certain to be this species. There is good reason to be optimistic that this attractive insect, perhaps assisted by warmer summers, will soon be breeding again in our County.

Hertfordshire's dragonfly-rich open water habitats i.e. ponds, lakes, flooded gravel pits and reservoirs, are mostly located on the impervious acid clays and along the gravel bearing sections of river valleys, which are concentrated in the southern half of the County. It is in this area, therefore, that the greatest aggregations of species are found. Reference has already been made to the white-legged damselfly, but what about the other 16 breeding species?

Metallic-bodied and strikingly beautiful banded demoiselles are common along the slow flowing lower stretches of the rivers Colne and Lea. This species has a long flight period and adults can be seen from mid-May to early September. The red-eyed damselfly, an increasing species which requires large-leaved floating plants such as pondweed and water lilies, also occurs along suitable parts of these rivers. However this latter species, which is still only found in the southern third of the County, is commonest on larger ponds, lakes and gravel pits with relatively large areas of floating vegetation. Four other species are also restricted to the south of the County. Acid ponds on the London clay, especially in woodlands, are currently the best place to search for the large red damselfly. This species, which has a short flight season lasting from late May to early July, is slowly colonising some gravel pits in the upper Colne Valley. The rare four-spotted chaser also breeds in a few of the acid ponds. Why this species has not successfully colonised flooded gravel pits, as for example in Bedfordshire, is still something of a mystery. Although similarly mostly associated with acid woodland ponds, emerald damselflies and ruddy darters are additionally present at a small number of other shallow well-vegetated ponds and waterways. In some years the population of the latter species is augmented with large numbers of continental immigrants. Fast flying, restless, black-tailed skimmers prefer larger lakes and gravel pits with bare or sparsely vegetated margins and are therefore most numerous around new or relatively immature gravel pits.

The remaining nine species occur in suitable habitats throughout the County. The ubiquitous, very common, relatively pollution tolerant and aptly named blue-tailed damselfly is the most widely distributed species of all. Adult females, although generally similar in colour to the males, display an interesting variety of colour forms ranging from green to violet. However, the most abundant and densely populating species, which has an identically long flight season lasting from mid-May to early September, is the common blue damselfly. The similar but much less numerous azure damselfly is rarely found away from small well vegetated ponds. All three species variously breed in garden ponds throughout the County.

The remaining six species also occur in all parts of the County. The pale blue males of the medium sized broad-bodied chaser appear similar to those of the black-tailed skimmer, but are easily distinguished by the dark basal wing patches that are present in both sexes. Broad-bodied chasers are an early summer species with a flight period starting in late May and occasionally extending to the end of July. In recent years, particularly in the northeast quadrant of the County, they have been increasingly observed at garden ponds. The largest and possibly most agile of all our dragonflies, the magnificent emperor dragonfly, has also increased and become widespread in Hertfordshire in recent years. Also a visitor to large garden ponds, even in urban areas, its flight season lasts from early June through August. Brown hawkers, a large species with their characteristic amber coloured wings, first emerge in mid-June and may even been seen into early October. The southern hawker, migrant hawker and common darter are all abundant late summer and autumn species. Their flight seasons which in normal years start in mid to late July, extend well into October and in mild autumns, in the case of the last two species, even into November. Large congregations of immature migrant hawkers are often seen feeding in woodlands. Both southern hawkers, another species often seen along woodland rides, and common darters breed in a wide range of freshwater habitats including small garden ponds.

It is not surprising that observing such beautiful, conspicuous and easily identified insects continues to give great pleasure. Horse-stingers or devil's darning needles - they are not to be avoided!

Recommended reading:

Brooks, S. (1997). *Field Guide to the Dragonflies and Damselflies of Great Britain and Europe*. British Wildlife Publishing. Hook. ISBN 0 9531399 0 5. £18-95p Softback.

Miller, P.L. (2nd edition. 1995). *Dragonflies*. Richmond Publishing. Slough. ISBN 0 85546 300 7.

23. **A Fading Murmur**
Rosemary and Barry Peck

Carder bumblebee and peach flowers

*The sound of bumblebees, so evocative of lazy summer afternoons,
is fast disappearing from our gardens and countryside.*

Bumblebees, also called humble bees, have been around since the late Cretaceous period, nearly 100 million years ago. They co-evolved with the flowering plants, but like so many other species today, their numbers are in decline, threatened by pesticide use and loss of nesting sites and forage plants due to the destruction of the natural habitat. Worldwide there are some three hundred species of bumblebee, most of them living in the temperate regions of Europe, Asia and North America.

Nineteen species of bumblebee and six species of cuckoo (parasitic) bumblebee have been recorded in this country. Two species have not been found for many years and are probably now extinct. Of the remainder, many are localised and in decline. In the 1920s many of the British bumblebee species were found in Hertfordshire, including *Bombus cullumanus* which is now considered extinct in Britain. Today there are only six or seven common species countrywide and all of these can be found in Hertfordshire.

Most bee species are solitary, but honey bees, bumblebees and the tropical stingless bees are social insects which live in a colony consisting of the parent queen, the infertile female workers and males. This pattern is common to most social insects. Honey bee colonies are perennial and a hive in summer

102

can contain more than 50,000 individuals. At her peak a queen can lay up to 3,000 eggs per day - more than her body weight. Bumblebee colonies only last for a year and the number of individuals rarely exceeds two or three hundred. Young queens mate and then overwinter underground to come out in the spring to start their colony. On British Naturalist Association rambles in early springtime we have often seen the young *Bombus terrestris* queens investigating old mouse or vole nests, one of their favoured nesting sites. Other species build their nests just beneath the surface or above ground, amongst vegetation, in sheds, compost heaps and bird boxes. Initially the eggs produce workers, who tend the nest, defend it and forage for food. Usually many workers are produced before the males and young queens develop. These leave the nest to mate; the old queen and the colony dying out by the end of October.

Unlike most winged insects, bumblebees can fly in quite cold weather, which explains why they are amongst the first to appear in spring and why they fly even when the weather is overcast or wet. Bumblebees warm up by shivering their thoracic muscles and research has shown that they also use a biochemical reaction for warmth. This allows them to forage in the cooler mornings and late afternoons. Honeybees tend to forage in the warmest part of the day whereas bumblebees will not visit flowers then to avoid being over-heated.

Pollination by bumblebees and honey bees is vital both for natural systems and agriculture. Fruit trees especially require pollination by bees. Bumblebees have various tongue lengths and the longer-tongued species are very efficient pollinators of flowers with long corolla tubes such as field bean and red clover. Unfortunately some of the short-tongued species 'cheat' and rob these flowers of nectar by biting through the corolla without carrying out pollination.

Recently honey bee populations have been decimated by varroa mite infestations and perhaps bumblebees will become increasingly important as pollinators. Some are already being used commercially, especially for the pollination of tomato plants, strawberries and other greenhouse crops.

Bumblebees belong to the order *Hymenoptera* which also includes wasps and ants. They are members of the family *Apidae* (social bees) and the genus *Bombus* which means 'booming'. They have two pairs of wings, unlike flies with only one pair. Like other insects the body of the bumblebee comprises three parts; head, thorax and abdomen. Wings and legs are attached to the thorax. Bumblebee queens and workers have so called 'pollen baskets' on their rear legs, which are used for carrying pollen to the nest.

The queen is the largest individual in the colony, the workers, at the beginning of the season, being considerably smaller, but as the colony prospers they become larger. Males are also smaller than the queen. *Psythirus* species (cuckoo bumblebees) do not have pollen baskets on their rear legs. Two or three species of cuckoo bumblebees may be seen in Hertfordshire but they are difficult to distinguish.

If you are interested and wish to learn more, I would recommend *Bumblebees* in the *Richmond Naturalist Handbooks* series, which gives keys to help you identify the various species.

Bibliography:

Sladen, F. W. L. 1912, republished 1989. *The Humble-bee, its Life History and how to Domesticate it.*

Free & Butler 1959 *Bumblebees* New Naturalist series.

Alford 1975 *Bumblebees.* 1978 *The Life of the Bumblebee.*

Heinrich 1979 *Bumblebee Economics.*

Prys-Jones & Corbet 1987 *Bumblebees* Richmond Naturalist Handbooks.

Matheson etc. 1996 *Bumblebees for Pleasure and Profit* IBRA.

24. **Wildlife Photography on a Shoestring**
Chris Doncaster

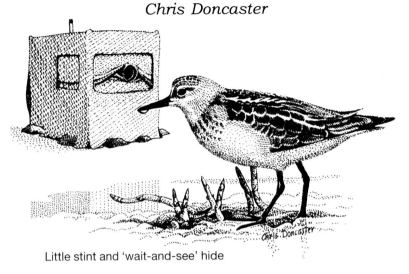

Little stint and 'wait-and-see' hide

I remember trying to describe to an armchair naturalist friend some thrilling natural history experience, only to be greeted blandly with "How-exciting-did-you-photograph-it?" Well, a peregrine deftly playing a powerful up-draught deflected by a cliff face high in Snowdonia would have been difficult to photograph to say the least, even with all our mod. cons. of featherweight automatic cameras and wonderful lenses that will even focus themselves. But my friend had almost the right idea that with high-tech modern equipment and films there is not very much that can not be done.

However, innovation is far from dead and if time, trouble and experience have been saved by modern technology, enterprise and virtuosity in accurately and often beautifully recording natural phenomena and occurrences have indeed blossomed. Is there a rare vagrant bird that has evaded the super telephoto of some enthusiast or other? I doubt it; and superb, full-colour portraits of such rarities regularly appear in the bird watching magazines.

But are we forgetting the creative artistry demonstrated in the older black and white prints of birds, mammals, plants and a whole range of invertebrates? Let it be remembered that the foundations of modern photography were the ingenuity, skill and experience of the early exponents and there is great beauty still in the rich warm tones of their meticulous home processed photographs. Think of John Markham's British mammals or D.P. Wilson's wonderful back-lit portraits of echinoderm larvae, not to mention the many bird portraits where the whole background and the foreground too is needle sharp. This was achieved through the use of a camera with a swing-back for slanting the plane of focus; impossible with any single-lens reflex body.

The old wooden field cameras were very basic in operation and were the most widely used by early wildlife photographers, despite the need first to focus onto a ground glass screen and then to change the screen for a plate or film holder. Exposure setting was by guess or from an independent light meter. Lenses and often shutters were interchangeable and by today's standards prices were very cheap. However, setting up time was enormous. Single-lens reflexes were sometimes used to shorten this time, but nevertheless, reflexes with long focus lenses were usually essential for away-from-the-nest bird photography from a hide – 'wait-and-see' as it was dubbed.

In 1952 I bought what I then regarded as a miniature camera; an English Agiflex single-lens reflex that produced 2¼ inch square negatives (like the aristocratic modern Hasselblad or Bronica) and I bought a 12 inch focal length telephoto lens for it. All were dirt cheap by present day standards. Eager to try my hand at wait-and-see, I visited Pagham Harbour. There were some rusty iron pipes sticking out of the mud and I set about draping them with copious fronds of wrack as a makeshift hide. I squatted inside and optimistically waited for waders to come for their portraits. None did, but a large square man strode across the mud to me and said, "You won't get any bird photographs like that you know. Anyway this is my hide framework you're covering with rotting seaweed." I meekly pacified him, admitting my folly and got an invitation to tea and to see what a wait-and-see bird photographer's equipment should be like.

Well! This is hardly an exaggeration; there was an immensely chunky fixed-length tripod of rough-sawn wood which supported an equally splinter-bristling baseboard about 4 feet long. The board had a wartime 36 inch RAF reconnaissance lens strapped to the front, with its rear end plugged into a row of dried milk tins that could slide telescope-wise inside one another in lieu of the usual camera bellows. The tins connected up with a quarter plate reflex camera whose own rack and pinion focusing caused the camera body to slide to and fro over the baseboard and provided fine focussing. The camera alone weighed 6lb and the lens at least 15lb. Finally, out came the photographs. There seemed to be dozens, all home-processed, of good-sized sharp images of curlew, dunlin, godwits, redshank, lapwings, grey plover and others I can't remember now. His print quality could have been better, but nevertheless it had great potential.

Through John Reynolds, my new found mentor, I bought a very second-hand 30 inch camera obscura lens and a First World War periscope. The lens weighs 10lb; I still have it. In 1954 we (my wife, John and I) set off for the Dutch island of Terschelling. I had made a square-section extension box to hold my big lens at one end and bellows, rack and pinion focussing and Agiflex at the other. The front was hinged to allow the contraption to tilt forwards from a baseboard and slotted stays provided support and variable slant. I made a plywood carrying box with a flat top as a table, rucksack straps at the back and four adjustable legs. John thought it was disgustingly elaborate. A 5½ foot hide had been specially made. The carrying box stood inside at the front, its table top enabling the camera baseboard to be slid over it and yet remain rock steady in any one place. I sat at the very back with the periscope going through a hole in the roof for seeing where the birds were, out in front.

John was a good naturalist and teacher, a biology master by profession. In a shallow pool behind the sea wall a little stint was working a small muddy island, on the first day of our visit. There we erected the hide, left it overnight and the next day the stint was back in its favourite feeding area and we got some presentable photographs. More followed during that holiday and there were subsequent visits to other European countries, notably Denmark and also to Cley before the days of public hides, but with specially permitted access to the pools. In 1959 a lovely juvenile red-necked phalarope was so intently feeding on the seething populations of ostracods in a small brackish pool that, without a hide, I could get close enough to photograph it with a mere 18 inch lens. I still used my carrying box-cum-table as my camera support, so much more stable than a tripod. In the 1960s the era of lightweight cameras, colour films and superbly sharp, powerful telephoto lenses really took off, enabling twitchers to bag almost everything that came.

My passion for bird photography had begun about 1934 at school: first Abbotsholm on the river Dove, then Leighton Park in Reading. Leighton Park regarded hobbies as an essential part of a sound education. Armed with a quarter-plate reflex camera and flash bulbs, my friend and I scoured the school park for roosting birds, photographed what we could and eventually got out a paper for *British Birds* magazine on roosting habits. During school Easter holidays on Skokholm Island we got flash pictures of Manx shearwaters and albeit terrible daylight ones of puffins and of the first Lapland bunting recorded for Wales.

Flash photography then involved flash bulbs about the size of a 100W bulb. They were filled either with magnesium foil or wire and were expensive, bulky and could be used only once. Magnesium flash powder was available, but unsuitable for synchronisation with the camera shutter. After the war, electronic flash was developed for general use and in the early 1950s I bought a DIY kit fairly cheaply. Flash units were then potentially lethal, having a 2,500V charge and enormously heavy because of the huge capacitors they needed. Mine, together with a booster unit to double its power and two lamps, must have weighed nearly 20lb. Not only have modern units of relatively infinitesimal weight been developed, but the flash can be adapted for microscope illumination, as well as for general inadequately lit subjects and fill-in lighting.

There are plenty of publications that give instructions on all branches of the art of nature photography. Personal contacts with others in one's particular field are vital and in the mid 1950s I joined the Zoological Photographic Club where portfolios of members' photographs were circulated and comments made about each print. Constructive criticism and genuine appreciation from friends and experts are so important for developing skills. The ZPC helped me greatly in my efforts at bird photography.

In the 1960s I began to fall for the fascinations of ciné, both as a hobby and to use as a research tool in my work at Rothamsted Experimental Station and from then on still photography took a back seat. At RES ciné was used to help understand such life processes as feeding, egg laying and hatching, defecation and locomotion of microscopic nematodes. The films could be viewed repeatedly for analysis and research papers were then written, and there was a spin-off in the form of university teaching films and sequences for television programmes. My hobby filming yielded a half-hour Survival Anglia film on grey seals under the title *Children of the Storm.*

It is the norm for naturalists to love to record their special subjects photographically. The BNA runs an annual photographic competition for its members, and a wide range of wildlife subjects is covered. A pooling of skills and facilities is one of the joys of belonging to a society, where giving is just as stimulating as the taking. The BNA has a pretty good record in this respect. Hobbies can indeed be valuable in both recreation and work and with them how can you be bored in retirement? Stay creatively happy. Have fun!

25. **Life under the Microscope**
Christine Rieser & Chris Doncaster

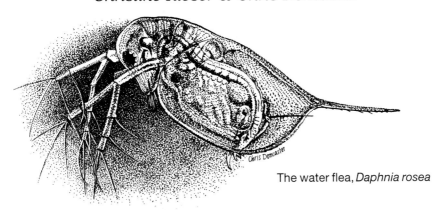

The water flea, *Daphnia rosea*

Not only in the 'pathless woods' but in the water meadows too there is a pleasure as we go down to the river on a clear sunny morning.

Fishing nets and sorting trays, sieves and funnels are taken, as well as bottles and jars, hand lenses and maybe a low power field microscope. There water is strained and mud by the reeds is dredged to sample freshwater life. A plankton net is tethered under the bridge and the shallows are waded and stones turned to catch scuttling insect larvae, to find algae and microscopic creatures clinging to the pebbles and, perhaps, a freshwater sponge growing on old submerged brickwork. Back on the bank the catch is turned onto white trays to be examined and sorted. Then come shouts of delight at success in finding and recognising creatures that stir our memories of previous sorties or are species rarely recorded in the County.

The catch must soon be returned to the river before the heat of the sun and the loss of oxygen turn them into poor gasping bodies. A few unidentified specimens are put aside in jars and samples of the water are taken in tubes and whisked away for further study. Back home, microscopes are set up with lamps aligned and focused and examination of the specimens proceeds. The binocular stereoscopic microscope is very easy to use for people with no previous experience and gives wonderful 3D pictures of specimens at magnifications of about x20 or even up to x60. Top lighting is usual and daylight or an ordinary 40W bulb are adequate at low magnifications. A big advantage of this type of microscope is that there is no reversal of image such as happens in a compound microscope. So where left is left and right is right there is no difficulty in picking up small swimming specimens in a pipette or dissecting off stem leaves of a moss for further examination under a higher powered microscope when necessary.

The bigger insect larvae, water beetles and small fish from the river catch can be examined at leisure and movements of animals such as hydra stretching out its long tentacles to catch food or tadpoles developing within the egg are fascinating to watch. This method of examination is also important for identifying insects held in a Petri dish and animals of leaf-litter and soil such as spiders, mites, harvestmen, pseudoscorpions, woodlice, centipedes, millipedes, springtails etc, and for examining the contents of owl and bat pellets too.

Through the stereo microscope, moss and liverwort specimens reveal their true beauty. After wetting up dry moss, the leaves, which are mainly one cell thick, quickly uncurl and swell so that light shines through their translucent cells or is reflected from papillose surfaces and the intricacy of structure is displayed. Very often the species may now be determined from such distinguishing features as the form of the leaf edge, the presence or absence of cell ridges on the leaves or the form of the hair point at the leaf apex. A vivid picture can be presented, for example, by the bright red teeth of the capsule of *Shistidium apocarpum* partially hidden in the dark green surrounding foliage. Indeed moss capsules are spectacular when ripe, the capsule teeth opening and closing under our very eyes as the humidity of our breath affects them. Many of these features can of course be seen in the field with a x20 lens, but for the inexperienced, a stereo microscope gives a fascinating picture and is one of the main tools of experts and professionals.

However, compound microscopes can give higher magnifications, but with a reversed image. They are usually fitted with a choice of objective lenses and together with, say, a x10 eyepiece can give overall magnifications of x100 and x400 which are adequate for most specimens. Whatever the size of the budget, for a beginner to become adequately equipped and genned up on the use of the compound microscope, he or she does need to have quite comprehensive instruction, more than could possibly be provided in a short article such as this. It is not necessary to spend huge sums on a serviceable microscope and second-hand equipment can be entirely satisfactory, if you can find it, providing all mechanical parts are at least potentially sound and that the lenses are undamaged and of good quality. It is the refinements that can dramatically raise costs and which ones you go for depend very much on what you want to use the microscope for. The Kodak guide (see appendix) will be valuable here. If you wish to photograph or film live, moving organisms, the Zeiss publication is very helpful. This tells you how to make up simple or more complex observation chambers for maintaining a range of organisms for study at up to the highest magnifications of the light microscope.

We would recommend joining a microscopical society. The Queckett Microscopical Club is the doyen of all such organisations. Otherwise you could join a more general society, such as the BNA, where you might get guidance on sources of second-hand equipment, techniques etc.

Unlike the stereoscopic microscope, the compound microscope is designed for viewing translucent specimens illuminated from below. There are ways of increasing the translucence of the more opaque ones and great detail can be revealed by careful preparation and by correctly setting up the microscope and the lamp. For full and clear advice on how to get the best from your microscope, both for visual work and for photography, we recommend obtaining a copy of the Kodak publication mentioned at the end of this article. Especially for small aquatic specimens, quite serviceable results can be obtained without any fuss if the specimen is mounted in a drop of water on a glass slide with a thin cover glass on top. The cover should be lowered onto the drop carefully so as to exclude any air bubbles which could ruin the image. To allow tiny live organisms some freedom of movement the cover glass should be supported by touches of Vaseline at the edges before it is lowered into position. Such mounts are suitable for tiny aquatic animals such as rotifers with their crowns of cilia beating in sequence, giving the impression of rotating wheels and which serve both to propel the free-swimming ones and to waft food particles into their gullets, or water fleas darting about by flicks of their antennae which they use like oars; or nematode worms like slow-motion or high-speed miniature snakes (according to species); or ciliated protozoa flashing in and out of view. Adding a little wallpaper paste to thicken the water can slow down many of the fast movers.

Measuring tiny organisms under the microscope is often essential for identifying them. This is done by the use of an arbitrary scale in the microscope eyepiece which is calibrated against an actual scale of, say, 1mm divided into hundredths that is placed on the stage below the microscope objective. A chart is then made of what the divisions in the eyepiece scale represent, using each of the objectives in turn.

Without necessarily getting addicted to one particular group enormous pleasure can be gained by merely observing microscopic plants and animals and the way they function. Indeed without the use of the microscope the teeming life that surrounds us is hidden merely because of the inadequacy of the human eye.

Recommended reading:
Photography through the microscope. Kodak Publication P-2
Microtechnique for the observation of living micro-organisms by Hans-Henning Heunert. Zeiss information.

Recommended contact:
Queckett Microscopical Club.